SNOWLINE

The 'snowline' is the smuggling route for base morphine'
from India to Marseilles. The drug is transported by
hippies, organized by Indian and Italian crime syndicates. But recently the snowline has been cut, blocked off
in Turkey by stringent new laws, and a new route is
being opened up. It is the job of Idwal Rees, the veteran
British agent, to locate this route; his Pathan servant,
Safaraz, is also on hand to get him in and out of trouble.
Beginning explosively in Calcutta, the action develops
into a pursuit across India to Bombay, and reaches its
climax in the Seychelles Islands. The story is an enthral-
ling adventure: exciting, often very funny, and with
vividly rendered settings—from the squalor and horrors
of Calcutta to the fascination and beauty of the Seychelles.

SNOWLINE

*

BERKELY MATHER

THE
COMPANION BOOK CLUB
LONDON AND SYDNEY

© 1973 Berkely Mather

This edition, published in 1974 by
The Hamlyn Publishing Group Ltd,
is issued by arrangement with
William Collins Sons & Co., Ltd

*Made and printed in Great Britain
for the Companion Book Club
by Odhams (Watford) Ltd.*
600871797
8.74/279

Foreword

ALTHOUGH I TRAVELLED AGAIN in India and Pakistan last year, and then went on to the Seychelles and, as a result, am convinced that certain hippie elements are being used by well-organized syndicates to smuggle basic drugs in large quantities from the Far East to Marseilles, I stress that this book is a work of fiction, and no character appearing herein is meant to depict a living person.

My thanks are due to Andrew Crawshaw, who accompanied me on this journey and whose medical training and keen powers of observation were of immense help in gathering background material.

Brede, Near Rye,   B. M.
Sussex
AUGUST 1972

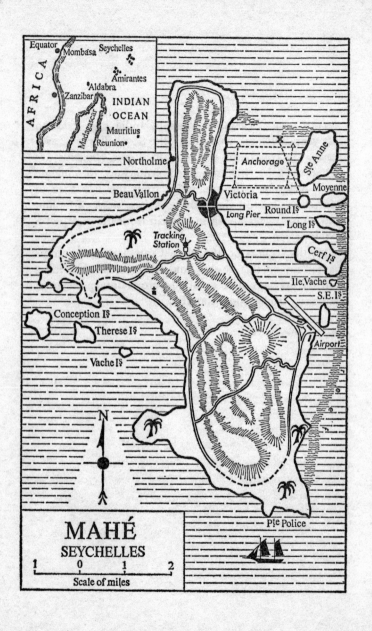

Equator
Mombasa Seychelles

AFRICA

Amirantes
Aldabra
Zanzibar

INDIAN
OCEAN

Madagascar

Mauritius
Reunion

Northolme

Anchorage

Ste Anne

Beau Vallon

Victoria

Moyenne

Long Pier

Round Is

Long Is

Tracking
Station

Cerf Is

Ile Vache

S.E. Is

Conception Is

Airport

Therese Is

Vache Is

N

Pte Police

MAHÉ
SEYCHELLES

1   0   1   2

Scale of miles

Chapter One

MOST VISITORS TO CALCUTTA dodge that bit of what was once called Chowringhee but is now Jawaharlal Nehru Road. If you're staying at the Grand Hotel, of course, you can't avoid it, because The Thing is right outside the entrance. I'm about as case-hardened as a lifetime out East can make one, but even I find The Thing hard to take. He's blind, and something has happened to his vocal chords so he can only make mewing noises, and he has no legs and only one arm, pipestem thin with a misshapen hand on the end of it. He lies on the littered sidewalk for some eighteen hours a day, and because the cracked paving stones get charcoal-grill hot around midday he can't stay put in one position for long, so he rolls his truncated body from side to side, bringing his single hand, which is now one huge callous, down flat on each turn with the noise of a pistol shot. His handlers bring him along each dawn on a little cart and dump him down, strong-arming any other beggars who might have designs on his pitch, then go on to place other properties in strategic spots round the city. This particular syndicate handles a dozen really advanced lepers, some small blind girls and an assortment of Bangladesh war orphans. They come round again and collect them all up, together with the day's take, about midnight. It's a business like any other, and it's been going on for centuries, so it's no use girding against it. All one can do is to mollify one's social conscience with a couple of rupees in his begging bowl and hurry past with averted eyes. One certainly doesn't sit on the sidewalk and giggle at the poor bastard. Not usually.

But that's what this one was doing.

I would have put her at no more than eighteen to twenty, dressed in an ankle-length flowered skirt, a stained T-shirt, beat-up-pulled-down felt hat with 'Make Love Not War' picked out on it in white beads and, under a layer of dirt, she was pretty, and her straggling blonde hair was undoubtedly European and not peroxided Eurasian. She was smoking a thin untidy cigarette, and I caught the unmistakable stink of bhang, the local, murderously strong pot, as I passed her. I felt rather than saw a quick movement behind me as I went through the swing doors of the hotel, and turning, I saw her hand shoot out and grab the two coins I had dropped into the beggar's bowl. I went back and said softly, 'English?'

'Of course,' she answered, smiling up at me. 'And free for a couple of hours until my boy-friend gets back. You staying here?'

'Yes, but you're not,' I told her. I grabbed her wrist and twisted it and recovered the two coins. 'If I catch you rolling poor devils like that again, sister, I'm going to hand you over to a large Bengali cop of my acquaintance who'll give you a very rough ride indeed. Git!'

'Which is probably more than you could do, uncle,' she jeered, then took off quickly as the Sikh hall porter loomed up the other side of the glass door. I dropped the coins back into the bowl and went on in.

The Sikh said, 'Thank you, sahib. That one is persistent.'

'Then get the police, for God's sake,' I snapped. 'Or put your foot behind her yourself.'

'I am an old-fashioned menial,' he said primly. 'Who am I to be disrespectful to the white overlords and their ladies?' And I went my way grinning sourly. Most of a Sikh's face is beard, but you can always tell when they are laughing at you. White overlords? They say the last one died in geriatric loneliness in the mouldering ruins of the Bengal Club twenty-five years ago.

There were more hippies inside, a dozen of them squatting on the dusty marble floor near the elevator which didn't run, and I could hear others in the palm lounge—more of them

8

than the house dick, another Sikh, could cope with. He tried to catch my eye but I hurried past. No, there were no over-lords nowadays, but hotel servants will always try and enlist the help of a white when dealing with others of the same colour. It was something our great-grandfathers implanted in them for their own protection. 'Clobber a white man,' they were told, 'and the gods will wither your arm and curse your seed.' We learnt it from the Brahmins who do the same thing with their own lower castes. To thump a Brahmin means reincarnation as a worm in the bowels of a dog.

A brunette, willowy and graceful in a dark sari, with the tilak caste mark of a Marwari on her brow, sank into the posture of supplication before me, hennæd palms upward and outstretched. I stepped round her and she murmured, 'Bread, man, bread,' and then, as I ignored her, she shot a mouthful of filth after me in a Birmingham accent.

There were two more in the corridor outside my room—male, though one of them might have raised doubts in a geneticist. These were American, dressed in the Bengali dhoti and khamis, and with white-bleached shoulder-length hair and beards. The bigger one said, 'We bring you great news, brother,' and the other lisped, 'Jesuth thaves,' and struck a chord on his guitar. They paid for the lot. I grabbed them both by the hair and dragged them along to the stairs and booted their arses down them. Language they never learned in a Sunset Strip mission floated up at me from below.

It had been getting like this since 1970, but they were more dilute at first because they used to fan out at the Afghan border after the overland hitch by native truck through Iraq and Iran, some making for Nepal and the phony yoga mills, others for Delhi, where European and American consulates would give them handouts just to get them out of town. Others went direct to Bombay where prices for the hash they all carried were highest. During the Bangladesh war, how-ever, things had tightened somewhat. Nepal closed its frontier

9

first, then Kashmir, then Delhi, seat of the Indian Government, was taken over by the army and became a sensitive area where bums were no longer welcome, so they now all converged on Calcutta, the sewer of south-east India, already staggering under its insupportable burden of two million homeless destitutes with, even allowing for exaggeration, at least the same number of war refugees. But these were the mute victims of circumstance. The hippies were here from choice, like lice feeding on a dying carcass.

I poured myself a stiff drink and kicked off my shoes and made for the bathroom, and ran straight into this fellow coming out of it. He had his hand in his pocket and you don't take chances in those circumstances, so I let him have the whisky in the eyes and then belted him—and got a severe shock when he went over backwards and kicked upwards with both feet together, *à la savate*. They caught me on the breastbone and I sat flat on my backside.

He said, mildly, 'I'm terribly sorry. Your man let me in. I was just using your lavatory—' and then Safaraz came in through the service entrance with ice and soda. I recognized him then. He was one of the minor functionaries from the British High Commissioner's office in Harrington Street. I had thought that he handled Press conferences for United Nations do-gooders. Maybe he did, but that kick in the pump had been delivered by an expert.

Safaraz said quickly in Urdu, 'I let him in because I thought he might be bringing work for the sahib. Allah knows we need employment.'

I looked at the chap quickly, but quite obviously he hadn't understood a word. That's the sad thing about the new officials. They only do two-year tours of duty, so none of them has time to learn any of the languages. Then I remembered his name—Hallaby. I said, '*You're* sorry?' and rubbed my aching chest. 'I think you've busted a couple of slats. Where did you learn that one, Mr Hallaby?'

He said something about being a youth leader at a church club in London, and started to apologize again, but I brushed it aside and offered him a drink. He shook his head so I repoured my own and waved him to a chair. As Safaraz had said, sure, I could do with a job. I'd declined the last two that the Gaffer had offered me, for reasons that I won't go into here, and other propositions had been rather thin on the ground, largely because of the war and the consequent running down of commerce. Poor bloody India was in one hell of a state. Yes—I needed a job.

'We've had a communication from the London police,' Hallaby said without preamble. 'They're asking for our co-operation.'

'In what?'

'Hippies.'

'What the hell have hippies in India to do with the Yard?' I asked.

'That's what we wondered, too. Something to do with dope smuggling, we think.'

'Oh, yes—hippies carry junk all right. But how do I come into it?'

'There are two officers coming out to conduct certain inquiries. They want a local man as well—somebody not connected with the police here—but who can cope with the language and all that sort of thing.'

'They could get an English speaking babu—with a degree from the Calcutta University—for about one tenth of what I'd be costing them.'

'We pointed that out when they asked for you——'

'*They* asked?'

'Oh, yes—they asked for you by name. Apparently they want rather more than just an interpreter.'

'I'll bet they do. I wonder how *my* name came up though. I don't normally touch straight police work.'

'Oh, they know all about you.'

'I'll bet that, too. But who did they hear it from?'

'Sorry—I wouldn't be knowing. The point is, do you take it up or not?'

'Don't be silly. I'd want to know what the job was exactly —not just intelligent surmises—and, naturally, what the terms would be.'

'Would it help if I told you that they said you could name your own terms? Within reason, of course,' he added hastily.

I smiled gently. 'It wouldn't do you the least bit of good,' I said. 'That way I'd know that the job was a lousy one—and also that it didn't come from the police. They don't have that sort of carte blanche.' I got up. 'Well, if you won't have a drink I'll wish you good afternoon, Mr Hallaby. Sorry.' I didn't mean it, of course. I was just running the price up in advance by playing hard to get.

But he didn't stir. 'I'm authorized to say that the High Commissioner would be personally obliged if you'd help,' he said.

'Damn nice of him. Does that mean I'm persona non grata if I don't?'

'Good heavens no—but you must admit that the—er— personal goodwill of our senior official is—er——'

'Personal goodwill my arse. Listen, I sign his visitors' book whenever I come to Calcutta, as a polite bloke should, and if there's a drink party going while I'm here, and if the list is not full of more socially desirable types, I get invited. That's as much as the H.C. ever does for me—and I'm certainly not likely to ask him for anything more. If it comes to that, I don't think the current one even knows me.'

But he still didn't get up. 'Mr Rees,' he said, 'this is important. Really important. Even if I can't take an acceptance back, at least don't send me off with a flat refusal. My job——'

'Depends upon it and you're supporting an aged mother, a wife and eleven kids, all starving. That's what babus say when they're applying for a raise, Mr Hallaby. It doesn't cut a hell of a lot of ice with anybody who has been out here for more than a couple of months.'

'I was born here, you spawn of a camel louse,' he said, which sounded a little odd coming from a London church youth leader—particularly as it was delivered in faultless Urdu. I blinked at him, and he went on in English. 'Or rather in what is now Pakistan. My father commanded the Second-Ninth Frontier Cavalry. I've been home to school since, of course, then I did a short hitch in the Army.'

'Who are you serving with now?' I asked.

'Sorry—I thought I'd told you. The High Commissioner.'

'Bollocks. You know what I mean.'

'If you mean what I think you mean, you know very well that I wouldn't tell you.'

'Quite right. Well trained agent, Mr Hallaby. What were you doing in my bathroom?'

'Pissing—certainly not looking for secret documents. You haven't anything worth looking for. You haven't worked since the Palinovsky affair.'

I blinked again, and felt it wasn't entirely lost on him.

'So you don't want to take a refusal back?' I said.

'I'd rather not.'

'All right then—no promises, but tell me what's behind all this and I'll think about it. Who sent you?'

'The High Commissioner.'

I got up once more, and this time I crossed to the door and opened it—and meant it. 'Hop it, Hallaby,' I said. 'You play it just a *leetle* bit too close to the chest. The answer's a straight no. If whoever wants me does so badly enough, he'll reopen the bidding—but you can tell him, meantime, not to send *you* along.'

He grinned ruefully as he passed me. 'I've made rather a bugger's muddle of this, haven't I? I really am most awfully sorry, but my controller was emphatic. He said if I blew the principal in this matter he'd have my guts for bloody garters.'

'In those actual words?'

'More or less. Why?'

'Because I thought we might both have been working for the same fellow some time in the past. It certainly sounds like someone I know.'

He shook his head. 'I'm afraid that's a bit too esoteric for me. The answer is still no?'

'Still no—but tell whoever it was that I said thanks for thinking of me. Incidentally—do hippies actually come into it? And are there Yard cops coming out?'

'Oh, yes—that part of it is true enough.'

'Pity—I'd probably enjoy it. I don't like hippies. They've generally been harmless enough in the past, but the type we're getting out here now are peculiarly offensive.'

'You can say that again. And the dope angle is correct, too. They are being organized we think. They carry five ounces at a time—cannabis to start with, heroin when they've proved themselves. Four is cargo going the whole way to Istanbul— one their own—smoke it, pop it or sell it—please themselves.'

'If all this is known why do they need the Yard out here? They can't *do* anything about it.'

'There's another angle to it,' he said quietly, nodded and went.

Safaraz was tidying up the room when I turned back into it, and looking glum. He doesn't understand English but he had obviously gathered from the general atmosphere that there was no deal. He said, 'So we do not work?'

'Your pay will be there at the end of the month—as it is always,' I said.

'You try to shame me. Did I say anything about pay?'

'No, but you're looking like a bunia cheated on a bill.'

'Then I am sorry. It was not money I thought of—but the hope that we would be leaving this accursed city for a time. This is a place for rats. You and I are men, sahib. Ee-ai! What would I not give for a sight and a smell of the mountains.'

14

I went through to the bathroom, stripped off my sticky clothes and showered. I was feeling troubled and restless. I had been too long without work, yet here I was turning it down. The money angle wasn't particularly important—I could go many months, even a year or two, without undue worry. Of course I knew what was bugging me. Wainwright. There was a case of an agent who had always done a good if not brilliant job, but who hadn't had the breaks—and the slob we had both worked for, the Gaffer, the most cordially detested but quite the most able figure in present day Intelligence work, had held it against him—had ridden him into the ground, destroyed his confidence and even his self-respect —until finally his judgment went, too, and he literally threw his life away getting me out of a tight corner that I'd have got out of anyhow had he not come hoofing in.

That was one aspect of it. The other was, of course, Claire, who loathed the very idea of this type of work, and who had given me the gate because of my involvement in it. All right, so I'd quit—but what good had it done? It certainly wouldn't bring Wainwright back—and Claire wouldn't even answer my letters. And, when the whole thing was put into proper perspective, there was no other job I could do. I'd been raised in it—trained for it since I was a child—and here I was sulking, fighting not only my bread and butter, but also my principles, such as they were. I believed in what we were fighting for, and I don't apologize for the pompousness of that either. I *did* believe—and I did feel for these people—the poor, the hungry, the bewildered and dispossessed. I don't think that we do a hell of a lot for them, but at least our side doesn't exploit them as They do. We sneer at our own do-gooders, but they do feed them and run their refugee camps—and doctors and nurses do come out and work themselves into exhaustion and even death for them. Wasn't Claire one of them, with her hospital up in the hills? I hadn't seen any from Moscow or Peking though. Commissars and little red books were all that emanated from that side of the Curtain. And now someone wanted me to chase hippies. As if it mattered. The hippies were, after all, only doing what I was doing. Opting out. I didn't like them—but I had no vocation for making their lives miserable. Drug trafficking? Admittedly that was horrible, but they weren't *all* engaged in it. Let the cops deal with them. I wanted no part of it. That scruffy little tramp who swiped the two rupees from a blind beggar's bowl. So what? It wouldn't have benefited the beggar anyhow. His handlers would have got that, and he'd have had his bowl of rice just the same. Who was I to play judge, jury and God Himself?

There didn't seem to be an answer to that, and I had no appetite for dinner, so I just poured another one, bigger than the last. I was drinking too much—both for my liver and also my bank balance. It cost two hundred rupees—fourteen pounds—about thirty dollars a bottle, on the black market. There's prohibition in India, varying in the severity of its enforcement from province to province. You've got to register yourself as an addict in Bombay, and form up at the same office as the junkies for your monthly certificate for two bottles of whisky—but at least you get it at controlled price—about fifty rupees. In Calcutta nobody bothers about certificates and people drink quite openly in bars, but all liquor is either bootleg—smuggled—or moonshine, distilled from anything and everything, from coconut palm sap to crushed jaquirity berries which cause blindness and paralysis.

Safaraz walked through with my clean laundry. He noticed the extra drink, and probably the colour of it, and sniffed disapprovingly. Moslems are forbidden alcohol by their religion, but he was a Freethinker normally, though he could be as rigid as a Presbyterian pastor when it suited him. It suited him now, and he not only sniffed, but clucked his tongue. That was too much.

I got up and crossed to my bureau, unlocked my cashbox

and made a quick check. There was about five hundred rupees there. I took it out, turned and slapped it down on the table.

'Five months' pay,' I told him. 'You go tonight. Tomorrow I shall send another seven hundred to the post office in your village. I thank you for the service you have given me—ever since I took you out of the military prison fifteen years ago.'

'Thank you, sahib,' he said impassively. 'It has been an honour to serve you.'

He picked up the money and went. What the hell had come over me? I wondered. There had been no need for that. Well—it was done now. My mind was finally made up. England it would be even though I'd always been frightened of the place. I had been born and brought up out here—in Shanghai to be exact, and I'd lived in China and India ever since—until I thought like them—acted and *re*acted like them. I was Oriental in everything but name, colour and features —and as unpredictable. Here I'd just fired a man who had given me nothing but faithful, selfless service—with as much compunction as a vicious child will pull the wings off a moth —just for the sheer, thoughtless hell of it.

'What an utterly charming bastard you are, Rees,' I muttered to myself, and poured another.

The telephone rang then. It was Hallaby again.

'Have you dined yet, Mr Rees?' he asked.

'Yes—I'm just getting to the bottom of the second bottle,' I told him. 'Why?'

'Could I come round and see you? Something really important has cropped up.'

'No,' I told him, and hung up.

I had another, and another then—and finally there was a knock at the door, and I opened it and the Gaffer walked in.

'What the bloody hell's the matter?' he asked. 'You're behaving like the head girl at Madam Eileen's. Why?'

'Because I knew you were behind this thing,' I said wearily. 'Go away, Gaffney. The answer's no.'

Chapter Two

FOUR IRISH DEMOLITION WORKERS, three wearing lumberjack's boots and one with a pneumatic drill, were inside my skull trying to blast their way out. I opened my eyes, then closed them again quickly, swung my feet off the bed and stood up, shakily. Something wriggled and moaned faintly underfoot. I looked down and found that I was standing on the Gaffer's face. I was glad I was still wearing my shoes. I stumbled across to the bathroom and got under the shower. A voice, a thousand miles away, said, 'If the sahib would take his clothes off he would greatly benefit from the cold water.' I stepped out cursing weakly, and a long iced beer found its way into my hand.

'I thought I'd fired you,' I said when I was able.

'Yes, sahib,' Safaraz answered. 'No breakfast, but I have told the bawachi to send up black coffee and mango fool—without sugar. The same for the Gaffer sahib.'

'What the hell is he doing here?' I asked.

'At the moment holding his head and praying. Last night when I was packing my bag in the servants' quarters and sorrowing greatly, the Parsee manager came and begged my help. You and the Gaffer sahib were making much noise up here.'

'Doing what?'

'Fighting, sahib.'

'*Fighting?* What bewakuf is this? The Gaffer is an old man.' I looked at him as intently as my out of focus eyes would permit, but a Pathan's face gives nothing away when he doesn't want it to.

'Old and evil,' Safaraz agreed. 'Perhaps it was the devil that he enlisted to his aid.'

'Go and see if he is all right—then get rid of him,' I said.

'He *is* all right, sahib. I didn't hit him very hard.'

'*You* didn't hit him? You said he and *I* were fighting?'

'You were, sahib—but you were getting the worst of it. The Gaffer sahib is a very beautiful but very dirty fighter. I stepped up behind him and struck him on the head with a whisky bottle—one of three *empty* ones which were lying on the floor, beside another that was broken and a remaining one that is, thanks to Allah the Compassionate, still half full. Ee-ai! At two hundred rupees a bottle many hungry ones could have been fed——'

'Get out you bastard,' I said, 'and hurry with that black coffee.'

He went, grinning happily. I had got the worst of that one, too, it would seem.

It was beginning to come back now. The Gaffer and I had argued and argued, and I'd got a lot of the bile off my chest at him, refilling the resultant vacuum with whisky. He had drunk a hell of a lot also, which was unusual for him, because he had a duodenal ulcer. I hoped it was giving him as much grief as my head was giving me. I couldn't quite remember who took a swing at who first. I did recall giving him an elbow smash on the bridge of his nose—and getting a knee in the groin in return, and I was beginning to realize that it wasn't just my head that was aching. God, what a spectacle. I wondered what the average British taxpayer, who paid the Gaffer's salary and my contract fee, would have thought of it. It would have been the equivalent of a Guards colonel brawling with a lance-corporal—always assuming that the Guards recruited bums like us.

I finished my shower, gingerly avoiding the raw patches, dressed and went back to my room. He had picked himself up and was slurping black coffee noisily. On the whole he seemed in better shape than I, but then he was such a repulsive looking old bastard at any time that it was difficult to judge. He was fat, sway-bellied, oystery-eyed and the possessor of the filthiest set of yellow teeth I have ever seen in a human head. And he was sixty-odd, which meant that he could give me rather better than twenty years, but against that he was the toughest man I have ever known—of any nationality, in any part of the world.

He looked up at me and sneered, 'You'll pick your bloody mark next time, won't you, Mister Bloody Rees?'

'Finish your coffee and get out,' I told him.

'Sure—but there are a couple of things you ought to hear first.'

'There's nothing I want to hear from you, Gaffney.'

'All right then—hear it from the High Commissioner.'

'Him either.'

'So it will have to be the Immigration Authorities.'

'What the hell are you talking about?'

'Your passport, you bloody fool.'

'What about it?'

'Oh, my God—you *were* pissed, weren't you? It was what you were ill-advised enough to take a poke at me over last night. I told you your passport was not in order.'

'Don't try and con me, Gaffney. There's nothing wrong with my passport.'

'Except that it's a temporary one—issued in Hong Kong.'

'In place of one that was stolen from my apartment. I have another—a full British one—on its way from London.'

'You want to bet?'

I felt myself going hot and then cold. It was coming back to me quite clearly now. Yes—the old swine had threatened me. He said he could—and would—stop the British one, and ensure that the three month thing I had from Hong Kong would not be renewed.

He was looking up into my face, grinning nastily.

'Remember now, eh? No passport, Mr Idwal Rees—not from London, Hong Kong or anywhere else. In a bit of a bloody fix now, ain't you?'

'No fix at all,' I said with an assurance I was not feeling. 'I've already held a British passport——'

'So have a hell of a lot of wogs from East Africa. They're not getting through London Airport with 'em though.'

'I *am* British——'

'Your old man was—a Welshman from the Rhondda or somewhere, wasn't he? But *you* were born in Shanghai—of a White Russian mother.'

"I'm still British.'

'You're going to have one sod of a job proving it. You're not registered at Somerset House for a start—so that means you won't be able to get a copy of your birth certificate. The only place there may be an entry about you will be in the Baptismal Register of the English church in what was the International Concession, Shanghai—and that's a bloody ping-pong palace now.'

'I got my original passport without any difficulty at all——'

'On a statutory declaration, your British Army record, three unimpeachable sponsors—and *my* recommendation. Could you muster any of those now?'

And he was right. Try getting a British passport, outside Britain, if somebody doesn't want you to have one. I felt black rage rising again and nearly choking me. My hand went out for the whisky bottle on the table—thumb down. I saw him tense.

'I wouldn't if I were you,' he said. 'You're out on a limb, Rees— Be man enough to accept it. Either we settle this here and now, sensibly, or you're going to be picked up as an illegal immigrant—a stateless person within the meaning of the act. The Calcutta police will put you on a plane for Hong Kong. Hong Kong will say sorry—plenty no savvee—passport out of date. Do you want to spend the rest of your life flying from one airport to another? There's a hell of a lot of poor buggers who are, you know.'

And once again he was right. A word from him in the

proper quarter, and the barriers would be up against me—everywhere except, perhaps, in certain defined areas the other side of the Curtain—Iron and or Bamboo. That I'd never do —cross over, I mean. Not from choice, anyhow.

'Of course you could always try America,' he went on. 'You *have* worked for CIA, haven't you? And the Yanks are usually grateful and will stretch a point now and then—unless, of course, some nasty person puts the dirts in on you with them. Can't you hear it—" Rees? Um—doubtful, I'm afraid. No— wouldn't care to give him full security clearance. Bit too pally with the Comrades lately. Of course, his old man was a convinced Marxist, you know. Sorry." Come on—I don't have to spell it out for you, do I? You've seen the old Hebe McShabbers being worked on others, haven't you? Done a bit of it yourself, if it comes to that.'

Yes, I could hear it.

'What do you want?' I asked.

'Stop being rhetorical, Rees, for Christ's sake. You know damn well what I want. I want you to quit acting the twot and come back to work.'

'What sort of agent would I be—working under duress?'

'The very best sort in my experience. I don't want starry-eyed patriots brimming over with loyalty. Give me the bloke who is shit-scared of the boss, or what the boss would do to him if he got out of line. That way you get service. You know something? That's all I ever had against you in the past. Too damn independent. Too ready to tell me to stuff the job if you weren't getting it all your own way. I don't like that.'

'Then you'll have to go on disliking it, because that's what I'm telling you now,' I said. 'Stuff it, you bastard.'

'Okay, if that's the way you really want it. I'm not asking you again—now or ever. But what I said about the passport stands, Rees. You're going to have some grief over that.' He got up and walked towards the door. And then a miracle happened and I suddenly remembered something *I* had on *him*—something that just about floored him when I sprung it, and he came back, grinning sheepishly, and said he didn't mean it. Like hell.

What happened was that I just capitulated—and I make no apology. That's the penalty for being born in the wrong place at the wrong time. You just don't have the right papers—and without the right papers you can't live the way you choose, nor where you choose. It's as simple and as humiliating as that.

I said, 'All right—you win.'

He came back, and he wasn't grinning, sheepishly or otherwise. He just grunted, 'That's better. Same terms, usual expenses. You'll work with Hallaby.'

'Who and what is he?' I asked.

'Wainwright's successor. He did well at the school and he's handled a couple of minor jobs out here quite competently. Nominally he'll be your boss, simply because he's on the regular roll and you aren't. Actually I'd like a rubber heel on him at the end of it.' Nice work. A job I didn't want, and I was expected to play Judas on it as well, by reporting on my supposed superior.

'You'll be working with the police—the Yard people, I mean. They're here with the full knowledge and permission of the Indian Government, but that's not going to endear them to certain officials out here. Your job will be to butter the local police along and secure their goodwill and wholehearted co-operation—blah, blah, blah. Got the picture?'

'No. How come we're working with the police?'

'Hippies and junk.'

'So Hallaby said, but I still don't get it.'

'We think somebody is organizing them.'

'He said that too, but what for?'

'Carriers, couriers—low grade droppers and mobile letter-boxes. That's the bulk of them. The more intelligent have to take bigger risks. The hard junk addicts are completely in their hands, or so we think. All are paid in pot or horse—in fact the

23

entire Intelligence networks are financed by dope. But you know this already.'

'Who are the Yard people? Special Branch?'

'No—Narcotics. If they were Special Branch the Indians would know immediately that there was a political angle to it, and we'd be politely warned off.'

'So we're just after dope?'

'Oh, come off it, Rees. What would I be doing mucking about with dope? *They*—the Scotland Yard people—are after dope, or rather the handlers, suppliers and carriers of it. On the surface you and Hallaby will be helping them in this aspect of it. Actually, of course, your main preoccupation will be the political one.'

'Will the Yard people know this?'

'They will have received certain broad hints—but at the same time we don't want to give them the impression that we're merely using them as a front.'

'Where will we be working? Just here in Calcutta?'

'Wherever the job takes you.'

I pounced on this—not that I gave a damn, but merely to annoy him. He hated being interrupted during a briefing.

'That's just the point,' I said. 'Assuming they are following something up here, and I get a buzz somewhere else, or Hallaby does, who wins?'

'In circumstances like that you will take the lead without letting them know it.'

'They're going to follow me—just like that?'

He snarled, 'How the hell do I know whether they'll follow you—just like that? It's up to you to train them, isn't it? Look, Rees—I quite understand you having a cob on because I twisted your arm a bit, but don't take it to silly bugger lengths just to get even with me. You're going to need all the info I can give you—which isn't much anyhow, God knows.'

'That's why I'm asking questions.'

'It isn't. Here, take this, for Cri'sake.' He fished into an

24

inside pocket and hauled out a thin roll of notes. I hesitated as he held them out to me, and saw his eyes harden, so I took them, and a little of the tenseness went out of things. A little. It was the usual symbol. I was on the payroll now, and thereby under his orders. It was the equivalent of an eighteenth century ploughboy taking the King's shilling from a recruiting sergeant. I hated his living guts even more now that I was officially on the book again, but he knew, and I knew, that I wouldn't renege on him now. It wasn't anything to do with honour or loyalty; it was purely self-interest. You don't rat on your controller in this business. Not if you want to live to a ripe old age. Double agents? They're different—a breed apart—cleverer, greedier and undoubtedly braver than I—and they *don't* live to a ripe old age—not usually.

'That's better,' he said. 'Okay—I'll give you the whole ploy as I see it. You know Bessim, don't you?'

I nodded. He was a maqadam in the Istanbul Administrative Police, which would be about the same as a Detective Chief Superintendent on one of our Crime Squads. He was a loyal Turk, which is tautology, because I never met a Turk who wasn't loyal—but he saw nothing wrong in passing on a tip to our people if our interests didn't conflict with theirs.

'Their Narcotic Squad knocked off a load of British hippies in a beat-up mini-van, returning to England from a transcendental meditation binge somewhere out here. Usual crowd of scruffs, only this mob was carrying more than the usual bundle of junk—base morphine, bound for the heroin factories in Marseilles. They had pot too, but that was for their own consumption. The cargo was purely commercial—say a million dollarsworth after processing. Now that sort of bagful carries a hell of a big penalty if you're caught. Death for their own people—fifteen to thirty years for a foreigner. The prosecutor made a deal with them—a guarantee of twelve years apiece in return for copping out on a guilty plea—and an equal guarantee of thirty if they didn't. They were wise enough to accept. Our starry-eyed bleeding-hearts and permissives at home set up a squawk, but they collected their dozen each all right—all except one. The others made a tight ring round him. He was as innocent as a new-born lamb. He had absolutely no knowledge of the cargo. He had just hitched a ride with them. He didn't even smoke pot, they said. Clean as a whistle. Now Bessim knew that this was balls. It was this feller who had supplied the dirt to the prosecutor in the first place, in return for a promise of special consideration. You can't turn State's Evidence in Turkey—not officially, I mean. You make your own arrangements ad hoc. He had just stool-pigeoned in cold blood. Nothing to raise eyebrows about that. It's been done before. But the thing that puzzled Bessim was that the others knew it. Yet they leaned over backwards to let him out of the net.'

'Bagman?' I asked.

'Able to whistle up funds for their defence, you mean? If that was the case he shortchanged them, because they only got a run-of-the-mill dock-brief hack—and that was merely for a plea in mitigation of sentence. No—they just held the door open for him, and he was on his way, rejoicing.'

'Must have liked him. Blue-eyed boy.'

'Probably—most of the bastards are gay—but that wouldn't account for their protective instincts. Queers are spiteful. There was a reason for it, of course—and Bessim had a theory. This fellow was obviously carrying something else—something damned important, which he'd had time to jettison before being nicked, and which he intended picking up later if he was lucky. Well, Bessim passed the tip on to his contact in our Embassy, and eventually it trickled through to me—and it just so happened that it fitted in with a theory of *mine*, so I had the client gazeboed—when he landed at Dover—and he sang like a bloody linnet.'

I've often wondered what would happen if the truth about gazeboing ever leaked out to the great British public. It was done only by the Gaffer's department. It was far too hairy for any respectable Intelligence agency to have anything to do with. A couple of the old devil's legmen, both ex-detectives and with all the indelible earmarks of Scotland Yard upon them, picked the client up very quietly at night on a fake warrant. He was whisked off to a certain country house with a blanket over his head—which is normal procedure in a criminal arrest nowadays. When the blanket was removed he found himself in the charge-room of a police station—correct in every detail—official notices on the walls—desk sergeant— couple of yawning uniformed bobbies just coming off duty— a drunken driver being blood-tested—the lot. He was offered the inevitable mug of lukewarm tea—searched—watch, belt, tie and shoe-laces removed, and he was shoved into a cell— and just left. There was a large jug of drinking water there, and a toilet bucket in one corner. He could sit and look ahead of him, twitch, walk up and down, yell, bang his head against the wall—or do whatever else he felt inclined to. But nobody came near him for at least three days. The high, barred window was shuttered, the blinding overhead light was left on and, most effective of all, not a sound penetrated from outside. Eventually a policeman sauntered along and looked in through the judas hole in the door, expressed mild surprise at finding the place occupied—left the minimum of food there, and sauntered off again for another few days. Then a rather vague detective would interview him in a name other than his own, and he would be told that he was to be charged with the murder of his uncle—or his wife—or with the embezzlement of fifty thousand pounds from his employer. Obviously the whole thing was a case of mistaken identity—but it was no good the client insisting on this. The detective just got vaguer and vaguer. Twenty-four hours later he would be interviewed again, and a half apology would be tendered—Sorry, the papers got mixed up—of course he wasn't Amos Nancarrow late of Bodmin, and he certainly hadn't murdered his uncle or whatever. He was Arthur Lotherington of Bedford—and what did he know about the attempted rape of his landlady's daughter at number seventy-three Harper Terrace, Eltham? Care to make a statement? By this time the client was usually psychiatrist meat, babbling the truth about who he really was, and what he had been doing—*insisting* on telling all, complete with the most minute details, names, dates, places—the lot. You couldn't stop him if you tried. Anything to prove his real identity and to hell with the consequences. Fiendishly ingenious and very cruel—and invented by the Gaffer—who was fiendishly ingenious and very cruel. Other countries, having nicked a client purely for information, had either to trump something up to charge him with or, the other side of the Curtain and in certain of the less Arcadian of the Latin Americas, quietly rub him out to shut his mouth afterwards. The Gaffer's way was perfectly free from awkward consequences. Nobody was ever known to go squawking to a real police station—and if they had they would have been laughed at. Nonsense—the British police just wouldn't dare to behave like that, and the client would probably find himself under observation in a nut-house.

'He was one Les Horton of Luton,' the Gaffer went on. 'Dropout from the local Art School. Bummed around Piccadilly for a time, then joined the Indian ant run. He looked a composite of all the long-haired, bearded, dirty yobboes you ever saw—head-band, love-beads—the lot—but he evidently had a mite more intelligence than the average, and someone out here recognized it and he was recruited as a Captain of Six. Heard the term before?'

I shook my head, and he went on, 'Sounds pretty corny—like something out of the Wolf Cubs—but it's the old cell structure under another name, that's all. Okay—so we would like to get in on the ground floor—penetrate a Six, and pyramid upwards to see who the top boys are. Got it?'

My fingers were counting in my pants pocket the notes that he had given me. They were hundreds—and there were ten of them. I knew what I was going to do with two hundred anyhow. God, what a job—what a lousy, dull, boring job. Bearleading a couple of ponderous Yard dicks around the dirtiest city in the world, and writing a confidential on a squirt I didn't like. Well, I'd get some sour satisfaction out of that part of it anyhow.

'I've got it,' I said dully. 'But thank God I don't have to love it.'

Chapter Three

THERE IS no half-way mark about airports. You either love them or loathe them—with one exception, Dum Dum, which is Calcutta's sole concession to the jet age. I've never met anybody who didn't inwardly heave at the mere mention of that one. It is just a dusty plain in the dry weather, that won't support even Indian goats, which aren't the most sybaritic of animals, God knows. In the monsoon it becomes a foul, malarial swamp. A hundred years ago the British Indian government built an ammunition factory there, because at a penny an acre it was the cheapest land they could find, and an early superintendent beguiled the fever-haunted nights away by inventing the first hollow-nosed soft lead rifle bullet which, instead of making neat entry and exit holes will tear off a limb or completely disembowel, according to what part of the body it hits. The Geneva Convention has banned them for many years in 'civilized' warfare, but the Tribesmen up in the hills still use them. It is just the sort of place that *would* nurture sweet little brainwaves like that. The ammunition factory now houses traffic control, all other functions, functionaries and the travelling public itself being accommodated in Nissen and Quanset huts hastily erected in World War II and never improved upon since.

Hallaby and I stood at the barrier watching a dispirited trickle of reluctant voyagers wending its way towards Customs and Immigration. You could actually see the heat shimmering up from the cracked concrete dispersal areas, and even the crowd of freelance baggage coolies, beggars, touts and black-market currency dealers who haunt the place and make a nightmare of the arrival of foreign aircraft were listless and subdued. There were only two Europeans on this one, standing out like a couple of fantail pigeons in a flock of crows. They came out of the door on to the stairway and I saw them both stagger at the contrast of the outside temperature and the air-conditioned interior of the plane, and before they had reached the barrier they had shed jackets and loosened ties.

Hallaby chuckled thinly and said, 'Good. *They* won't be staying long if they can help it. They'll hop it like the Gaffer.'

'Heat doesn't worry that old bastard,' I said. 'He slid off yesterday because he is unknown by sight to the London police, and he wants to keep it that way.'

We pushed our way through to the Arrivals area and saw the two Englishmen having the usual thin time of it with the babus who quadruple-man every job in the place—two to look at passports, one for disembarkation cards and one who shakes his head sadly and says, 'Great difficulty. Please wait. Will see what to do.' Then comes Customs, where the Great Difficulties really pile up and after that Health, Immigration and a going-over by Currency Control. The whole thing usually takes an hour or more and there's not a thing anybody can do to speed it up. These two were looking savage when they came out. They gave us a quick, all-encompassing cop's scrutiny when Hallaby greeted them and introduced himself.

'Bayliss—Detective Chief Superintendent,' growled the older of the two, and then jerked his head at the other, 'Thorlby—Detective-Inspector.' He glanced at me questioningly.

'Idwal Rees,' Hallaby said. 'He's assigned to help——'

'Local Force?' asked the other.

'There are no foreigners in the Indian Police,' Hallaby began, 'but——'

'Then who's he helping? And who assigned him?'

'He'll be helping *you*. The High Commissioner assigned him.'

'Thanks,' Bayliss said dryly. 'My compliments to the High Commissioner but *I'd* rather specify such assistance as I require.'

'Which suits me fine,' I butted in. 'Add my compliments

to those of the Chief Superintendent. I'll find my own way back to town.' I walked quickly towards the passenger exit and heard Hallaby running behind me.

'Oh Christ—no more of it, Rees,' he begged. 'I thought we'd got everything sorted out.'

'We had—but apparently that top dick doesn't approve. Who the hell does he think he is? I'm not going to be upstaged by some monkey who probably came up from pounding a beat through Traffic Branch to polishing his arse in Administration——' They caught up with us just as I got this far and Bayliss was actually grinning.

'Okay,' he said. 'I only wanted to know the form.'

It served me right, of course, but it was no comfort to know that I'd fallen for the oldest cop's trick in the business. If you want to know something fast, needle somebody, rudely and preferably without apparent reason.

'I was never in Administration,' he said amiably. 'You had to be the Commissioner's son-in-law to get there. Traffic—sure. Started on motorbikes and went clean through to squad cars.' He was still needling, but I was on my guard now. 'Pleased to meet you, Mr Rees,' he went on, putting his hand out. 'Come on, Thorlby, where's your bloody manners?'

Thorlby nodded but didn't offer to shake.

I sat next to the driver going back to town in the High Commissioner's Daimler, and studied them covertly in the rear vision mirror. Bayliss was a big man. Size is the bugbear of so many Yard detectives who all come through the uniformed branch, which likes them burly. It sticks to them always in plain clothes and makes them easy to pick out. He had little twinkling eyes in a puckish face, and when he grinned it made him look almost coy, but it wasn't deceiving me. I know a tough and mean gent when I see one. Thorlby was different—perhaps ten to fifteen years junior in both age and service, recruited when they'd lowered the height requirements and upped the intelligence tests. He was about thirty-five—commissioned in the Army during National Service, I would have said at a guess, followed by six months' uniformed duty in the Metropolitan Police before going through the CID College. Bright boy. The oldsters like Bayliss usually hated their guts.

They were looking out on the Dante's Inferno that is East Calcutta and the effect was more marked on the older man.

'Jesus Christ, I'd heard things were bad here—but not as bloody awful as this,' he breathed. 'Are those poor sods lying on the sidewalks alive or dead?'

'Some of each,' I told him. 'The police vans go round at night and sort them out. If they're still breathing they leave them until next night.'

'No follow-ups? Inquests? Investigations?'

'They'd have a job on their hands. I don't know the figures —I don't think anybody does with certainty—but I've heard that they are up to the thousand-a-night mark at present.'

'I don't believe it.'

'Please yourself—but remember that there are three million war refugees from Bangladesh in West Bengal now, more than half of whom are inside the city limits. Those figures *have* been verified—at the checkpoints. Most of them were already starving when they got here, and now there's cholera, typhus and dysentery among them.'

'Doesn't United Nations do anything about it?'

'Sure—and World Council of Churches—Oxfam—Save the Children Fund—Red Cross—the lot. That's half the trouble. There are so many of them that they're falling over each other and fighting over relief supplies of food and medicine that are jamming the docks and that airport we've just left.'

'Doesn't anyone *care*?'

'Of course they do. There's enough goodwill here to put things right overnight. It's the administration of it that is falling short. It's not the fault of any one person or group. It's just that the problem is too big—that of normal famine conditions, worsened by cyclones and a tidal wave in the Bay of Bengal last year that drowned thousands and ruined the rice crop. Cap that lot with a short but very dirty little war between the East Bengalis and the West Pakistanis and you've got quite a situation.'

He shut up then and just looked through the window, tight-lipped.

It was Thorlby who was puzzling me. He didn't seem stupid, insensitive or particularly tough, but it was making no impression on him at all. Hallaby was sitting between them, and I caught his eye in the mirror. He shrugged slightly in the manner of a man who hadn't any of the answers, then, as Thorlby yawned, closed his eyes and settled himself back in the seat more comfortably, Hallaby's lips formed a dirty word. I agreed with him. Indifference jars me worse than outright cruelty.

I'd booked rooms for them at the Grand at Hallaby's request. I'd questioned the advisability of this but he'd said that they'd attract less attention there than if they were put up in official accommodation, so I didn't argue further. But it seemed that I'd been borne out in my contention the very moment we climbed out of the car and fought our way through the crowd of beggars that closed in solidly on us. There were, as usual, three or four hippies among them and I heard over the clamour one of them yell, 'Jesus, man, the fuzz! That's Bigpig Thorlby.'

I didn't think the others had heard, but I'd underestimated their hearing, because Bayliss said as we were going up the stairs, 'Know that love-child?' and Thorlby answered without particular interest, 'Threlfall, James, horseman, got done at Croydon CC for B and E in February. A swinging deuce.'

Bayliss twinkled at Hallaby and me and said, 'Real little computer, ain't he? He means that Mister Threlfall is a heroin addict convicted of breaking and entering enclosed premises, for which he received a suspended sentence of two years at Croydon Crown Court. Hm—You're not supposed to leave

34

the country while under a suspended sentence. I wonder what he's using for a passport?'

'The bastard had three to my knowledge,' Thorlby said, 'but I could never find them on him.' I found myself envying Mr Threlfall a little.

'He might be a starter,' said Bayliss thoughtfully. 'How easy is it to come by in this town?'

'What?' asked Hallaby.

'Horse—heroin.'

'Cheaper than tobacco if you know where to go. Why?'

'Just a little wishful-thinking daydream,' Bayliss said. 'Nice cosy room somewhere—preferably soundproof. Push him in and leave him to simmer. If it's all that cheap he's on massive doses. He'd be singing like a bloody reed warbler by his next Glaxo time. Not allowed in England,' he finished wistfully.

'Here either,' Hallaby told him. 'Not officially, anyhow. The High Commissioner——'

'On whom be peace,' murmured Bayliss, crossing himself. 'Don't worry, laddie, we're here to *uphold* the law, not bend it.'

He winked at me and I found myself disliking him very much indeed. He had the same line of gallows humour as the Gaffer at his most vicious.

We left them in their adjoining rooms and went along to mine for a drink.

'What do you think?' asked Hallaby as I gave him a beer.

'I'd rather not. Bayliss is a horror, but at least he has some sort of feelings—or seemed to have as we were driving through the bustees. The other one's a zombie though. See those eyes? like blue enamel—hard as a brick but no depth. What security classification has this job got?'

'Top Secret on the Intelligence level, "Police—Confidential" on theirs.'

'Well, it's busted wide open now. Every hippy in town will know by nightfall that there's a couple of Yard birds in their midst. And we've been seen with them. It has taken me six years to build a foolproof front in this place.'

'It doesn't help,' he agreed gloomily. 'But don't take it out on me, Rees. I don't like the damned job any more than you.'

We finished our beer and went down for lunch, which at the Grand is always a self-help curry buffet, unless you like cold mutton and wilted lettuce. The curry is invariably good though. Hallaby went back to Harrington Street then and I went up to my room. The policemen were going to have a post-flight rest, then they would phone Hallaby and, presumably, call me in when they had doped out some sort of programme. I stripped off and had a siesta but when Safaraz woke me with a cup of tea late in the afternoon, I still hadn't been summoned.

I hung around for the rest of the evening. There is absolutely nothing to do in the way of night life in Calcutta these days, even if you go for that sort of thing, which I don't. There's a floor show of sorts at the Grand itself, and usually one of the four cinemas in the immediate vicinity shows a dubbed British or American film of uncertain age but there is nowhere to drive to, and to go out on foot in western clothes after dark is asking for trouble, so after dinner, which, following the magnificent lunchtime curry was an anti-climax, I went back to my room and tried to read. What the hell was the Gaffer playing at, I wondered for the hundredth time? What did this pair of heavy-footed incompetents think they were going to achieve out here, anyway? Just how far up the Departmental totem pole was Hallaby? Wainwright's successor, the Gaffer had said. That could mean anything so far as I was concerned. On any given job we worked on together, Wainwright was nominally senior, because he was a regular agent, whereas I was a casual. In actual practice I was given to understand that I was in charge though, which was one of the things that used to needle Wainwright. It looked at first as if this was to be the case with Hallaby also, although not by my choice. But it wasn't working out. Not so far. The coppers hadn't called me, nor had Hallaby. Fine. That suited me down to the ground, I told myself. Just let me sit on my can here, and draw my pay at the end of it, when the Yard men had given up and flown home—because that's what they'd do in the end, for the simple reason that you've got to know the East, either by birth and upbringing or by very, *very* long and observant residence, before you can operate in that disreputable sphere into which Intelligence—political or police—falls. Yes, that's what I was telling myself, but not very convincingly. I'm not particularly good at sitting on my can. It's not that I'm a hyper-thyroid type. It's just plain curiosity. I like to know what's going on.

My hand kept going out to the telephone. I was supposed to be their adviser, wasn't I? No harm in calling them to see if they wanted me. Like hell. I would appear to be making myself indispensable. Our man on the spot. The expert. No, I wasn't risking a snub. Hallaby? He was different—or was he?

When I could stand it no longer I called the night number he had given me, and listened to it ringing for two full minutes before giving it up.

Then, there being positively nothing else to do, I had a few scotches. Perhaps just one too many—but at least I slept.

Safaraz was shaking me gently. I sat up and saw somebody behind him, blinked my eyes into focus, and recognized one Shyamprasad Mukherjee, Superintendent, Criminal Investigation Department, Calcutta City Police. It seemed I was to be haunted by dicks—local as well as imported. This was one I liked though—or thought I did until I looked at my watch and saw it was just on three a.m. Safaraz said, in a Frontier patois which he was convinced no Southern Indian could understand, 'I told this taker of bribes and scourge of the poor that the sahib slept, but he pushed his way in. Have I the sahib's permission to throw him out again?'

'Yes—if you wish to eat Hindu rice in Alipore Jail for the next year or so,' I told him.

'Rice? He'll be lucky,' said Mukherjee in the same tongue.

'We feed Pathan bastards on pig guts. I'm sorry to disturb you at this hour, Mr Rees, but it's rather important,' he added in English, and grinned as Safaraz slunk out looking sheepish. Well, at least it was to be friendly, I thought as I got up and put on a robe.

'Delighted to see you at any time, Superintendent-ji,' I said. 'A little whisky to keep out the morning cold?'

'No thank you, Mr Rees.' He shook his head and tapped his breast-bone. 'Slight stomach upset.'

Serious, I thought, as my wits gathered themselves. He usually called me Idwal, and I'd never before known him to refuse a drink at any hour of the day or night. I stayed my hand as it reached out for the bottle. I was probably going to need those wits.

'Oh, sorry about that,' I said. 'What can I do for you?'

'Hippies, you call them, no?' he said with apparent irrelevance.

'Hippies? You mean the hairy European and American bums hanging about outside?'

'That is right, Mr Rees.'

'Oh sure—but don't ask me to explain the term to you. It originated in America——'

'I am knowing that. In San Francisco—nineteen-sixty-two isn't it?' His English was every bit as good as mine normally, but he was deliberately using babu's chi-chi—a typical Indian policeman's trick in interrogation. That way they could pretend not to understand your answers immediately, so they had to get you to repeat them more than once in the hope that they could confuse you into contradicting yourself. There's a counter to it, if you're qualified to use it—you switch to their language. But that meant tipping your hand and showing that you knew what they were trying. I played it dumb and English.

'That's right. But what about them, Superintendent-ji?'

'Troublesome.'

'I couldn't agree more.'

38

'Smoking charas, bhang, khif—using heroin, isn't it?'

'It is.'

'Begging in streets?'

I nodded solemnly. He hesitated and looked down at his feet and his voice sank to a portentous whisper. 'Some ladies engaging in *prostitution*?' he said. There is nobody more old-maidenly prudish than an educated Hindu discussing sex.

'I wouldn't be at all surprised,' I whispered, equally portentously.

'That is what the police officers from Scotland Yard have come here about?' he asked next.

'Ah, I see you know about it,' I said, since there would have been no point in denying knowledge of it. 'Yes—hippies.'

'Why?' he shot at me.

'Well—er—not a very nice thing, is it?' I asked. 'Not a good picture of our race, Superintendent-ji.'

'But what can they do *here*? Our laws are the same as yours, Mr Rees—your people brought them to us—Code Britannica, isn't it? Just being a hippy isn't a crime. What to do? No powers of arrest anyhow. So why are the police officers coming here?'

'Ah, you'll have to ask *them* that.'

'I'm asking *you*.'

'I'm sorry, I don't know anything other than that they arrived yesterday.'

'What would you say if I called you a liar, Mr Rees?'

'I'd end the interview and ask you to go, Superintendent-ji —and I'd be very sorry. We've been friends a long time.'

'I'm *not* calling you a liar.'

'I'm very glad to hear it.'

'But I *am* asking for your co-operation.'

'Which I am offering to the full.'

'But you are not telling me why your bloody coppers are coming on to my patch, eh?' He grinned and I chuckled at this beautiful mélange of stilted babu idiom and police slang.

'Sorry,' I said. 'I can only suggest that you go and ask them.'

'And you are thinking that they are telling me?'

'They can certainly tell you more than I can.'

He sucked in air and puffed out his cheeks, obviously considering his next question deeply. Then he switched languages on me.

'Each of us knows the other wears mukhtalif pagri, is that not so, Idwal sahib?'

It's hard to translate 'mukhtalif pagri.' Literally it means 'different turbans'. I suppose the nearest one could get to it would be to say one has two jobs, but it implies that one of them is secret. Sailing under false colours if you like. Your ostensible job covers your real one. And he was damn right. Twice. *I* was supposed to be a market investigator in Calcutta —and *he* was a police superintendent, but I knew, and he knew I knew, that he worked for Central Intelligence, New Delhi, as well.

'It has so been said,' I intoned.

'You're goddam right it has.' He was back into English now, with American nuances. 'Come on, Idwal, quit stalling. What are those two jacks really on? You know I can help you —in many ways—*and* have.' Which was true enough.

'Surely they've been cleared with you, haven't they?' I asked him.

'Not with *me*. I think it stopped about three levels over my head. Work it out for yourself.'

'Chief Superintendent, Assistant Commissioner, Commissioner,' I counted and whistled. 'Well, *he'll* tell you anything you ought to know, won't he?'

He grinned again, somewhat sourly this time. 'It was the bloody Commissioner who told me to drag my arse out of bed at two in the morning and get my goddam nose to the ground —and not to go back to bed until I had something to tell him. Something that bore a vague resemblance to the truth. The truth from you buggers! Rama, Krishna and bloody Ganesh!'

'Well, if *he* doesn't know it, how the hell do you expect me to? Yes, yes, yes—I wear mukhtalif pagri and all that—but I'm only a very unimportant little legman, Shyam, and only casually employed at that.'

'I *am* calling you a liar now,' he said, and robbed it of offence by adding, 'And I'll have that scotch you were waving under my nose a while back.'

'Spoken like a Hindu gentleman,' I said, and poured two stiff ones.

'A Parsee gentleman,' he corrected. He knocked his drink back in one and held his glass out again. The Parsees, with the Gurkhas, are supposed to be the soundest drinkers in the whole sub-continent. I gave him another.

'Thanks, Idwal,' he said. 'All right—off the record from now on—word of that same Hindu gent.'

'*Sure,*' I said solemnly.

'Personal curiosity only. Where does Hallaby fit into it?'

'Hallaby? Oh, that bloke at the High Commissioner's office. Can't help you I'm afraid. Why don't you ask him yourself?'

'Several reasons. One, diplomatic immunity. Two, he's been too well trained at that spy school of yours to be able to tell the truth any more than you could—and three, the night squad lifted him off the Maidan an hour ago—as dead as an English kipper.'

Chapter Four

WHEN WAINWRIGHT was rubbed out I took it very badly. It was not because we had been particularly friendly—in fact we had always cordially disliked each other—but there just has to be some sort of bond between people working together in this line of business. More than a bond. It has to be the complete trust which comes of interdependence. In commerce and industry you trust your capital to your partner's integrity. In spying you have to trust your neck. You can prevaricate and cover up, twist and lie like a trooper to anybody in the world you want to—even to your debriefing controller if you're good enough at it—but never to the man you're actually working with. That is the cardinal law, unwritten and unspoken but unbroken, our first, and often our only protection. You may have known him for years or only been teamed up with him the day before, but once you have accepted each other, that's it. So if he is knocked off suddenly, you are apt to feel a little bereft. And also a little angry.

I turned away and pretended to pour myself another drink. 'Who did it?' I asked.

'That's what I want to know,' Mukherjee said. 'Level with me and I'll set him up for you. Hanging takes place at Alipore Jail every second Thursday. I'll even get you a ticket.'

'How the hell can I level with you?' I asked. 'You probably know more about him than I do. I met him for the first time the day before yesterday.'

'But you were on this together—you, Hallaby and these Scotland Yard people.'

'All right, so you know that. But I can't tell you any more. The job hasn't started yet. I'd only been retained for it.'

'Who by?'

'Oh, come on, Shyam! You know better than to ask that.'

'We're on the same side of the fence—your people and mine.'

'Which makes me very, very happy, but we still don't indulge in girlish confidences. Not about who our respective ponces are, anyway.'

'Quite right,' he said and rose. 'No Gaffers, no pack drill. I can't help you then.'

'You can give me the details—the ordinary police details I mean.'

'Little enough of them. Our night squad was collecting dead along the edge of the Maidan. They're always naked because the others strip them of their few rags when they don't need them any longer. Anyhow, the havildar in charge noticed that this one was bleeding so he stopped the truck outside Park Street station and had a closer look—then called the sub-Inspector who happened to know Hallaby by sight.'

'Cause of death?'

'Shot through the head. Pistol—close quarters.'

I thought I had covered the start I gave at this, but he wasn't missing anything. Wainwright had been shot through the head also.

'Why the surprise, Idwal?' he asked softly.

'Just a thought that occurred to me, that's all. Has the High Commissioner been told yet?'

'Not yet. We were hoping to find out something about it first. We'll cover the delay by saying we couldn't establish his identity for a time. I take it I can rely on you to keep it dark for the moment?'

'Absolutely,' I told him.

He walked to the door, paused and turned.

'Idwal,' he begged. 'Try and get clearance from your people on this one, and let's work on it together. It's vital that we get it sorted out—vital to me personally. This is a diplomatic killing and we're having a lousy Press internationally, what with the war and the election assassinations and now this

43

famine. Life won't be worth living round Headquarters until I nick somebody and make it stick.'

'I'll do my best,' I promised, and he nodded and went.

I sat and chewed my fist over this for more than an hour. Shot. That meant a measure of intent. If he'd been stabbed, clubbed or strangled it would have pointed to a dacoity, that is ordinary robbery with violence in which killing, if it occurred, would be unpremeditated. It happens every day— but it very seldom involves Europeans or Americans, for the simple reason that they are numerically few in India, and those few take abundant care not to go to places where this sort of thing is likely to happen—certainly not after dark. In any case, the ordinary Indian goondah, which is their name for hoodlum or mugger, would hesitate under normal circumstances to attack a white man—not from any awe or affection he holds us in, but purely because of the resultant commotion the police stir up. India is peculiarly sensitive in respect of her image abroad, and the death of a foreigner as the result of a crime would attract adverse publicity, therefore on the very rare occasions that it does happen, the police are apt to throw out a dragnet and pull all possible suspects in and just twist the screws on them until somebody talks—and the culprit, or more often somebody they think might look like a possible culprit, is sorted out and dealt with. I'm not saying that the Indian Police frame innocent people lightly—but they are certainly realists. Dacoits and goondahs all belong to the Scheduled Criminal Castes in India. They are literally born into crime and can be identified by the cognoscenti from their dress, caste marks and sign language—so you can hardly blame the police for a certain prejudice in their disfavour.

No, I didn't think this was an ordinary criminal case. Not an Indian one, anyhow. The hippies? After all, this is who we were supposed to be embarked against. No—that would be completely out of pattern. The hippies were the shiftless and the idle, the drifters, bums and parasites if you like, but they were seldom violent—even the confirmed junkies among them. Sure, the latter would steal, but usually only to sustain a habit, as they put it in their own jargon—to obtain enough money to buy their daily fix of heroin or quarter ounce of bhang—and that cost little enough out here. No—the hippies wouldn't kill—certainly not with a gun. The people who were organizing them, if the Gaffer's theory was correct? Maybe—but why pick on Hallaby? He wasn't identified with the hippy-bashers, any more than I was—not yet. That fellow who had recognized Thorlby? What was his name? Threlfall? As Bayliss had said, 'He might do for a starter.' I'd keep him on ice anyhow, in case all else failed.

And now what about Bayliss and Thorlby? Did I go and tell them of this latest development? As far as they were concerned I had no official standing. I was just a local who knew the territory and who had been assigned to help them—a mere underling of Hallaby's. Who gave me my orders now, I wondered? I certainly was not prepared to accept them from these two policemen. Still—I'd better go and tell them. Maybe that would get them off my back. Maybe it might even spell the end of the operation. I wouldn't have earned anything but my retainer, but that didn't matter. The Gaffer couldn't in justice monkey about with my passport, since what had happened to Hallaby wasn't my fault.

It was getting light and across Chowringhee—sorry, I can't think of that broad and shabby thoroughfare by its new name any more than a New Yorker can call Sixth Avenue the Avenue of the Americas—the homeless were stirring from the parched and trampled grass and beginning their daily hopeless circulation through the city, thousands of them shoulder to emaciated shoulder, swarming across the tram tracks that run down the side of the Maidan, making in the first instance for the market refuse heaps and the soup kitchen that Mother Therese, the Salvation Army and the Quakers run each morning in Free School Street. I leaned on my window sill and watched them—a trickle that became a flood, bringing the thin traffic of beat-up trucks and ancient cars to a standstill, swarming over and under them, yet carefully splitting to avoid two sacred cows that had decided to rest in the middle of the road. Someone in the crowd must have looked up and seen me, because a backwater from the tide started to eddy round the wall beneath me, and hands were being raised and the cry that was the theme song of Calcutta started as a whimper and swelled to a high-pitched wail—'Ham bhuka hain—ham maut jaega' (We hunger—we die). I pulled my head in and closed the window because I knew that even the hope of a coin thrown down to them would result in a mad struggle that would undoubtedly leave many of them crushed underfoot. Deaths occurred that way every day round the soup kitchens, deaths that had to be accepted unless the kitchens were closed, because nobody has yet thought of a way to control upwards of a million starving people within sight of food, short of machine-gunning them.

I shaved, bathed and dressed, then called the desk and asked for Bayliss's room, but got no answer from it—so I tried Thorlby's with no success there either. I assumed that they had got up early and gone for a walk round town and I was silently wishing them the joy of it when there was a knock at the door.

I opened, and Bayliss came in. He was looking angry. I said, 'I was just trying to call your room.'

'Is Thorlby here?'

'No.'

'Then where is he? He's not in his room.'

'How should I know?'

'His bed hasn't been slept in. What's Hallaby's number?'

'He hasn't got one I'm afraid. He was murdered last night,' I told him, and if I'd been doing it for effect I couldn't have got a more positive reaction. His eyes popped and his jaw dropped, then he remembered that he was a senior policeman, and as such deemed to be unflappable, and got a grip on himself.

'Who by?' he asked.

'Person or persons unknown,' I told him in his own cop's language.

'But Christ! Thorlby was with him last night. Weren't *you*?'

'No. I haven't seen Thorlby since we left you both in your rooms yesterday, nor Hallaby since he left here after lunch. I, myself, haven't been out of the hotel.'

I saw rank disbelief in his face. 'That's not what I understood,' he said.

'I can't help what you understood. I'm telling you what *is*.' I made no attempt to keep the dislike out of my voice, and it had the effect of cooling him down a little.

'I wasn't feeling too good last night,' he said. 'Planes always upset me, so I turned in early. Thorlby stuck his head in the door and said you and Hallaby were down in the lounge and had something to tell us. He went down on his own and I dropped off to sleep.'

'Well, either Thorlby or you were mistaken. I certainly was not there,' I told him.

'Suppose you give me some details?'

'I know very little. A Detective-Superintendent of the Calcutta police called on me a couple of hours ago and told me that Hallaby had been picked up off the Maidan, shot through the head.'

'Nothing about Thorlby?'

'Not a word.'

'Then we'd better get round to their Headquarters and start things moving, hadn't we?' He went to the door.

'Might I offer a word of advice?' I asked him.

He turned and looked at me as suspiciously as a bull elephant sniffing the wind.

'If you've got anything to *tell* me I'd certainly like to hear it,' he rumbled.

47

'The local police are keeping this sub rosa until they are a bit farther along in their investigations,' I told him. 'I feel that it would be better at this stage just to pass the word to the man in charge of the case that Thorlby was with Hallaby, rather than go straight in off the street and have to talk to a lot of people not immediately concerned.'

Surprisingly, he agreed, albeit doubtfully, 'Maybe you're right,' he said. 'But I have a letter of introduction to the Head of their CID which I'm supposed to present in person. I'm going to look bloody silly saying that one of us got himself on to the Missing Persons blotter the first night here.'

'Let's leave it until mid-morning,' I suggested. 'Either Thorlby will have turned up by then, or we might have got some news of him.'

'Like that he'd got himself rubbed out too?' he growled. 'Jesus! What sort of damn fool am I going to look to my bosses back there when I report this?'

'It's hardly your fault,' I said.

'I know bloody well it's not. But it certainly *looks* funny, doesn't it? Have you any idea of what's behind it? Hallaby's murder, I mean?'

'Nothing that I'd bother you with at the moment.'

'I'm used to being bothered. Come on, what's it all about? You're the expert, aren't you? Just a simple robbery?'

'Could be, but I doubt it. The local villains generally leave foreigners alone. Too much trouble afterwards if one is attacked.'

'Think he might have been done in a joy house?'

'Hardly. He's not the type who uses them.'

'What—queer?'

'Not that I know of, but established Europeans out here don't usually go to those places.'

'What's an "established European"?'

'A European of a certain standing—as distinct from, say, visiting sailors and people like that.'

48

'Blimey! Class consciousness raising its ugly head, even in the banging business. How Poonah-Poonah can you get? "Visiting sailors and people like that."' He gave a gravelly chuckle.

'All right—visiting policemen, if you prefer it. Do you think that Thorlby might have gone out on the prowl on his own initiative?'

'To a brothel? Not with me rubber-heeling on him, he wouldn't. He's got his eye too firmly glued to the promotion roster. Anyhow, as a copper he'd want it for free—and he hasn't been here long enough to get things organized yet.' He'd got over the initial shock and was back on the humour tack, but it was plain to see that he was still a very worried man.

He mooned around the room and I felt myself creeping with impatience. I wanted him to get out so that I could call Mukherjee and give him this latest bit of news.

'Why don't you go down and have some breakfast?' I suggested. 'I'll get in touch with you the moment anything breaks.' But he only muttered something about it being too hot to eat and carried on mooning, so in the end I called Safaraz in and told him in Urdu to go round to Headquarters in Lall Bazar and tell Mukherjee that one of the 'police sahibs' had been with 'dead one' the night before and was now missing, and that I couldn't call him myself at the moment because the 'other police sahib' was with me, so avoiding names that Bayliss might pick up.

Safaraz nodded and went.

'What was that all about?' Bayliss asked suspiciously, 'And who's the big nigger?'

'Just some instructions about my laundry,' I told him. 'That was my servant. He's a Pathan and understands the odd word or two of English. I'd be careful how I referred to him if I were you. His feelings are easily hurt, and when that happens he's just as likely as not to cut somebody's throat.'

49

'You're scaring the pants off me,' he said. 'All right then, so when do we notify the fellow in charge of Hallaby's case?'

'That's been attended to,' I told him, and he wheeled on me accusingly.

'I know bloody well it's been attended to,' he snapped, and the phony humour had gone now. 'What sort of goat do you take me for? Listen, Rees, it's time you and I had an understanding.'

'Fine,' I said. 'You start. What are your beefs?'

'My beefs are that you know a damn sight more about this than you're disclosing to me—and I want to know why? That'll do for starts.'

'I was engaged by Hallaby—not you. Hallaby isn't here any more, but that doesn't mean that I automatically come under your orders.'

He bit back some dirty words and took a deep breath.

'So you're not going to help?'

'I didn't say that at all,' I said. 'I'll help all I can, but it will have to be in my way. I'm not saying that my way is any better than yours—but at least I know the local form. If that's not acceptable, just say the word and I'll drop out now.'

He pursed his lips and cocked an eye at me, thinking hard, then apparently decided to be the laconically funny man again.

'I'm like the housemaid backed up against the kitchen stove by the butler,' he said. 'Listen to reason or get a burnt arse. Okay, Rees—your way—but for Christ's sake tell me who we're working for now that Hallaby's no longer amongst us.'

'Hallaby was a High Commissioner's man,' I said, 'but I never had direct contact with his office.'

'That's something you can clear up for me. Who and what is this High Commissioner everybody talks about?'

'*The* High Commissioner is in New Delhi—the people here and in the other provinces are his representatives. He's Britain's man-on-the-spot——'

'You mean our Ambassador?'

'He's rather more than that—Ambassador, Consul General, Chief Trade Representative—the lot. He takes his orders straight from Whitehall, and has the ear of everybody from the Prime Minister down.'

'Including the Metropolitan Commissioner of Police and the Home Secretary, my joint bosses, I take it?'

'Undoubtedly.'

'Powerful bloke. Okay, so I watch my lip round there. Does he have any say with the local police?'

'Officially none whatsoever, but they'd give a very polite hearing to any request of his, which would, of course, never be made direct by him.'

'Ought I to go and see him myself?'

'That's entirely up to you.'

'I'm asking your advice.'

'I'd be inclined to leave it for the moment. This is the position as I understood it from Hallaby—officially the High Commissioner doesn't know you're in the country—actually, of course, he does, and will render you all possible assistance. The higher echelons of the police here had been given the tip and were apparently agreeable to your working on the case—but the lower ranks don't know, and if you got into any sort of a clamp you'd be on your own. Hallaby, as you know, was your contact. Whether or not the HC will appoint somebody else in his place remains to be seen.'

'You, obviously,' he said.

I shook my head. 'I have no standing, official or otherwise. I can advise but I can't direct.'

He winked and tapped the side of his nose. 'Bugger the protocol,' he said. 'Hallaby told me a few things about you. Quite a lad, aren't you?'

'I'm afraid I don't follow you.' I did. He was beginning to realize his aloneness. Little boy lost in a big strange country and liable to put his hoof into it right up to the hock if he made one wrong decision. Rank, pension and Boards of

Inquiry, the three Damoclean swords of the regular copper were very much to the forefront in his mind at this moment, and he was ready to be friends with anybody who might be able to help.

'You've got a few ears in Whitehall yourself, if I'm not mistaken,' he went on.

'Hallaby tell you that?'

'Well—sort of—and of course we hear things back there in London you know—and I can put two and two together with the next man.'

'Well, you just go ahead and do that, Mr Bayliss. Only for God's sake get your sums right,' I told him. 'If Hallaby said anything at all about me you probably misinterpreted it. He knew nothing about me, for the simple reason there's nothing to know. And the things you heard, or misheard, in Whitehall must have been about somebody else.'

'Oh, sure, sure, sure,' he said, and winked again.

That is one of the funny things about a singularly unfunny profession. You tell a layman that you have even the most tenuous connection with Intelligence work, and he will immediately put you down as a romantic liar, but try convincing the same chap that you haven't and that is the signal for nods and becks and wreathed smiles and promises that your little secret is safe with *him*. One of the other funny things is the mutual distrust between the spy and the copper—even when they're both on the same side. You'd think that there would be a certain empathy, if not sympathy, between them by the very similarity of their lousy jobs—but is there hell. They hate each other's guts instinctively. Bayliss was certainly hating mine. I could feel it emanating from him with his sweat, and his efforts to be friendly were as convincing as the smile on the face of the tiger.

We went down to breakfast then, but he could only stomach coffee, which made him sweat even more, and it was a relief to see Safaraz making signs to me from the door of the dining-room. I excused myself, got up and went over, feeling Bayliss's eyes boring into my back.

'The taker of bribes will meet the sahib at the police hospital,' Safaraz said. 'And he asks that you hurry because matters which were before confused can now only be described in English.'

'What did he say?'

'One bloody-damn-big-bugger-up, sahib. And he also says please not to bring anybody else with you.'

I sighed and made my way back to the table, concocting what I hoped would be a convincing reason for ditching Bayliss en route.

Chapter Five

BAYLISS wouldn't be shaken off at first, so I had to do it the rough way in the end. I said I had some private business of my own and that I'd rather be alone.

'The hell with you then,' he snarled. 'I'm seeing somebody officially and I'll tell them I want you taken off the job.'

'Splendid,' I told him. 'It's been nice knowing you, Mr Bayliss.' I didn't feel that it was much of a victory as I could quite understand his feelings. He was in a hell of a position. He'd been warned to tread softly, he had no official standing and he had not only lost his liaison officer but also his partner. I left him in the dining-room and made my way to the lobby, and I was foolish enough to look back. He was hunched in his chair glowering at the table in front of him—a very angry man, but also a bewildered and rather pathetic one. I went back and said, 'I'm sorry. I don't want to keep rubbing it in, but things are different out here. This contact of mine just wouldn't talk in front of a witness. It's as simple as that. I promise you I'll come straight back after I've seen him.'

'Where the hell's Thorlby?' he demanded. 'I'm entitled to know that, and I'm going to make a stink if I'm not told.'

'I honestly don't know. I'm hoping to find that out from this man.' I could see his face hardening in preparation for another donnybrook, and I had a brainwave. 'You could help things along quite a bit if you had a talk with that hippy who recognized Thorlby yesterday. Threlfall, wasn't it?' He brightened visibly and some of the droop went out of his shoulders. This was something he understood.

'You're damn right,' he said, and made for the door. 'I'll Threlfall the bastard.' I hoped he wouldn't find him, because I'd said it in much the same spirit as one would give an importunate child a job, just to get him out of one's hair.

54

Mukherjee saw me from the verandah as I came through the hospital compound, and gave me a quick sign to go round to the side entrance. He met me at the door and muttered, 'Somebody has talked. There are three newspapermen in the waiting-room. The rest will be on to us like vultures as soon as word gets round.'

'Is it Thorlby you've got here?' I asked.

'You tell me,' he shrugged, and led me through to a small private ward at the back of the main building. A man was lying on the single bed, an indistinct bulk seen through the mosquito net, and an Indian police havildar sat beside him wearing that bored expression that coppers of every hue assume when on bedside stand-by duty. He rose and lifted the mosquito net as Mukherjee snapped his fingers. It was Thorlby all right, naked from the waist up, a turbanlike bandage on his head and a drip-feed needle in his arm—and he was unconscious.

'Yes—that's him,' I confirmed.

'A mobile patrol fished him out of Tolly's Nala,' Mukherjee said, and I shuddered. Tolly's Nala is a canal that runs through South Calcutta to the Kidderpore Docks, where it oozes its filth into the Hooghly. It is, in fact, a ten mile long open sewer for one of the densest packed shanty towns in the world. 'Depressed fracture of the occi-occip—bashed on the head and he'd lost a lot of blood. He'd been dumped there for dead all right.'

'Now why would they dump one on the Maidan and cart the other across town?' I mused.

'Good sense,' Mukherjee answered. 'One dead European in either place might just get by—two together is asking too much. Whoever dumped them was unlucky that they were found, anyhow. Little bit darker when they picked up Hallaby and he'd have been six feet under in a communal grave now. And if Tolly's Nala had been flowing a bit faster the mud turtles round the Hooghly burning ghats would have had this one.'

'What is it, Shyam? An ordinary dacoity?' I asked, and he looked at me angrily.

'You know it isn't,' he said. 'Why ask a damn fool question, Idwal?'

'Probably in order to get a damn fool answer. Come on—let's start. It's not a dacoity. So what? Let's think aloud.'

'What the hell are you trying to do?' he asked suspiciously. 'Pump me dry? When I ask *you* anything you play silly buggers.'

'All right, I'm taking you up on your offer—levelling with you.'

'What have you got to level with?'

'Hallaby was in Intelligence.'

'What branch?'

'I don't know.'

'So you're not levelling.'

'I'm trying to, God damn you. He was in Intelligence, but I don't know which branch of it. That's the truth.'

'All right, so it's the truth. I knew that anyway. What about this fellow then?'

'Just a policeman as far as I know.'

'Not so.'

'All right, you tell *me*.'

'He's in Intelligence too.'

'You're absolutely certain of that?' I was asking a genuine question now.

'Aren't *you*?'

I took a deep breath and said, 'I told you I was levelling. As far as I know this detective and the other one are both narcotic squad men. They are after hippies—hippies who carry drugs in commercial quantities. If they know who is picking the stuff up this end they will be able to watch the exit holes the other end and know who to pinch. Simple as that.'

He looked at me for a long moment, then shrugged. 'Is that really what you've been told?' he asked.

'On my word, if that's any use to you.'

'Not a damned bit—no offence meant.'

'None taken, but it happens to be the truth. We're wasting a hell of a lot of time, Shyam. Do we come out into the open with each other, or break things off here and now?'

'Let's be open then. Both these people are Intelligence. British Far Eastern Bureau.'

I shook my head firmly. 'If they're BFEB men you're the Imperial Wizard of the Ku Klux Klan,' I told him, and I really meant it. 'They're coppers, pure and simple. Correction. Delete "pure".' It was a feeble little joke, but it served to lower the tension. He grinned sheepishly and went through and conned four ounces of medicinal brandy from the duty surgeon and brought it back. I moved casually towards the window so I could tip my half of it out secretly because I knew from past experience that it would be locally distilled stuff of the genus known as panther piss, but the subterfuge wasn't necessary because at that moment the havildar by the bedside called softly, 'Sahib jagna hai,' (the sahib is awake) and, turning, we saw Thorlby stirring feebly. We went across and Shyam motioned me into the closer position and sent the havildar away. It wasn't politeness—it was just that he probably assumed that Thorlby would talk more freely to another European than to an Indian.

But he wasn't talking to anybody at first. He lay flat on his back staring sightlessly at the mosquito net above him and didn't hear me for a long time as I spoke softly and reassuringly to him, but eventually I saw his eyes flicker and turn towards me and he muttered inaudibly. I bent over him. 'All right, Thorlby,' I said. 'Don't worry—you're being looked after.'

I had to put my ear right close to his mouth to get his reply, but the words were quite clear when they came. 'You bastard you won't get away with this,' he whispered.

'Sure, sure,' I replied soothingly. 'Just take it easy. You'll be all right in a while.'

He was recovering rapidly. Hate and rage in the correct proportions can be a powerful restorative. 'Take it easy my arse,' he snarled. 'I know where I am. This is the police hospital, isn't it?'

'It is, and they're looking after you,' I began. 'All you've got to do is——'

'All I've got to do is to file a complaint of attempted murder,' he said. 'I want to see a police officer.'

Shyam put his hand on my arm and gently eased me away. 'Certainly,' he said. 'I am Superintendent Mukherjee, Calcutta CID. You wish to make a statement?'

'You're damn right I do, but I want a uniformed man in first to vouch for you,' Thorlby answered.

'Surely Mr Rees can vouch for me,' Shyam said.

'In a pig's eye he can,' Thorlby shot back at him. 'It's against Mr Bloody Rees that I want to file the complaint.'

I said, 'Oh, cut it out, Thorlby. I know you've been through the mill but let's be sensible.' Then Shyam caught my eye and gestured towards the door curtly, following me up when I stalked out angrily, and calling to the havildar to bring in the Duty Inspector.

But I heard it all just the same, because I went round on to the verandah and listened at the open window of the ward.

Thorlby was saying, '——this fellow Hallaby called at a little after nine and said that he and Rees had something to show us. Bayliss, that's the Chief Superintendent with me, wasn't feeling very well so I said I'd go down and see what it was, and then come back. Hallaby was waiting in the lobby——'

'With Mr Rees?' Shyam asked.

'No, he wasn't there then, but Hallaby said we'd be meeting him at an ash—ashcan—it sounded like—a sort of a hostel for pilgrims——'

'Ashram,' Mukherjee said. 'Yes, that's right—but which one? There are hundreds of them in and around Calcutta.'

'He didn't say, except that it was in a pretty beat-up part of the town. He had a taxi waiting outside. I went straight off with him and didn't bother Bayliss. It was a ten minute ride —we passed a big railway station——'

'Did you cross the river?'

'I don't think so. I certainly didn't notice it if we did.'

'You couldn't miss it. There's only one bridge over the Hooghly—huge, half a mile long, brilliantly lighted——'

'No, we didn't cross a bridge.'

'So the railway station would be Sealdah—that's this side. The only other one is Howrah, the other side. Right—go on, Mr Thorlby.'

'I asked Hallaby what we were going to see, but he said he didn't know. Rees had called him, apparently pretty excited, and said he had something important that we ought to know about. Anyhow, we got out in a dark lane that stank like hell and Hallaby sent the taxi off and we started to look for this ash—ash——'

'Ashram—yes——'

'And eventually Hallaby found it—just a gateway between two buildings that opened into what seemed a sort of courtyard. It was as dark as hell, not a light anywhere, and we were ankledeep in all manner of shit, slipping and sliding, and Hallaby seemed to be looking for another gateway. I remember going under an archway and there was a chink of light showing through the crack of a door. Hallaby tapped at it and the light went out and I heard the door open. Hallaby spoke in Indian——'

'In Hindi? You're sure of that?' It was evidently news to Mukherjee that Hallaby spoke anything but English.

'Your bloody language, whatever you call it. Someone answered him in the same language and he seemed to go forward through the door—and there was a thud and a bump and he yelled, "Rees!—for Christ's sake!—it's me Hallaby!" in English—and another voice called out, "Get the other bastard, you bloody fools!"—also in English—and before I knew what the hell was happening they were all over me—seemed like half a dozen or more—and down I went. Never had a chance——' His voice was failing and the Bengali doctor came in at that stage and hoofed Mukherjee out of it. I went back along the verandah and met him at the door. He looked at me speculatively.

'Where were you last night, Idwal?' he asked.

'In the hotel. I never left it,' I told him. 'I certainly wasn't at that ashram, if that's what you're thinking.'

'You listened?' he said reproachfully.

'Of course I listened. It concerned me, didn't it?'

'It's not funny.'

'You're damn right it's not. It's just plain nuts.'

'What about witnesses? Somebody who could swear that you never left the hotel?'

'No difficulty at all. Safaraz would swear to anything that I told him to—and I could buy another dozen dedicated liars from among the hotel servants for five rupees each.'

He shook his head sadly. 'I hope you wouldn't do that, Idwal, because if you did, you would be forcing me to buy *two* dozen liars, plus a taxi driver, to swear that you *did* leave the hotel. What a pity we can't be honest with each other.'

'I am being honest. I didn't leave my room after dinner.'

'Then why did Hallaby call your name?'

'But *did* he call my name?'

'This man says he did—and he's too sick to lie.'

'And that's *bloody* sick for a policeman, I agree, but that's my story, and I'm sticking to it.' And there being nothing else for it I started to withdraw, but he said that he believed me at this point, albeit with reservations, and we went back to see what else we could drag out of Thorlby, but the doctor had posted a large and aggressive Eurasian nurse on guard, so we had to give it up.

I went back to the hotel and up to my room and sat down to compose a long coded cable to the Gaffer's cover address in

London, but I was less than halfway through when Safaraz came in grinning and told me that the police-sahib up on the next floor was lambasting the hell out of a gora. 'Gora' means literally, a low-caste white man, and Indians, who are among the politest people in the East, seldom use the term unless they mean deliberately to be insulting. 'Which gora?' I asked.

'One who wears Bengali clothes, has hair like a woman and behaves like the male whores of Ghor Khatri in Peshawur,' he told me with satisfaction. The hippies really offended his sense of propriety. They did mine too, but since I had probably been the cause of this one's grief, I thought I had better go up and get him off the hook, and, anyhow, I was fed up with wading through that damned codebook.

Three bearers and a sweeper were gathered in an awed knot at the top of the stairs, bending their ears towards the door of Bayliss's room. I went to it and knocked and listened at the crack, but I couldn't hear a sound. I knocked again, louder, but still got no answer, so I called to the bearers to use their pass-key. The head one said, with respect, that he'd rather not, as the sahib was undoubtedly mad, and the mad were the Protected of Allah. However, Safaraz had followed me up and he got the key without any sweat, and I went in. There was a small lobby the other side, with a bathroom opening off it and beyond that a further door into the bedroom which was closed but not locked. I went through, and then pulled up and stared at them. Bayliss was sitting at his ease one side of the room with the hippy standing facing the opposite wall, three feet out from it, balanced on his tip-toes and supporting his weight on his fingertips, in the peculiarly painful stance known as the riot cops' frisking position. He'd obviously been there quite a time because he collapsed on to his knees just as I came in, and started to whimper. Bayliss completely disregarded me. He got up and moved across to the hippy, grabbed a handful of hair and hoisted him to his feet, then slammed him against the wall again.

'Back there and stay there, you son of a bitch, until I tell you to move,' he said flatly and without heat. The hippy screamed and started to blubber, then slid down to the floor again. I got Bayliss by the arm and spun him round, and dragged him out into the lobby.

'What the hell do you think you're doing, you bloody fool?' I demanded.

'Watch it, Rees,' he warned. 'I've had enough of you people. I want to know where Thorlby is, and if this long-haired git knows anything he's going to spill it. Now get out of my way.'

'I know where Thorlby is,' I said.

'Where?'

'Turn that poor stiff loose and I'll tell you.'

'Why should I? I've got a lot out of him already. Keep your nose out of it and I'll get the rest.'

'Have it your own way,' I told him. 'I'm going to fetch the local law, and you're going to get done for illegal arrest, wrongful detention and assault.'

'For Christ's sake!' he yelled. '*You* told me to pick this louse up.'

'I'll deny it.' I went to the door and beckoned to Safaraz who was keeping a beady eye on the floor servants outside.

'Go and get Superintendent Mukherjee,' I told him, and repeated it in English for Bayliss's benefit. Bayliss said wearily, 'All right, all right, please yourself.' He turned back into the bedroom. 'Hop it,' he said to the hippy, who had dragged himself to his feet again. Like the rest of them he was bleached white, with shoulderlength hair, wispy beard, love-beads, browband—the whole weird regalia. He was wearing a once white dhoti and a grubby native shirt. His face was twitching and his nose and pale blue eyes were streaming. He said to Bayliss, 'Can I have my things back, please?'

'Hop it,' Bayliss repeated, tersely.

'*Please*——' the hippy implored.

Bayliss walked across to a table and picked up a small cloth pouch—the sort that Bengalis wear on a string next to their skin in lieu of the pockets their national dress lacks. He hefted it in his palm for a moment or so, considering, then he tossed it through the open window down into the street. The hippy shrieked and ran towards the door, cannoning off the end of the bed and falling over a chair in blind panic, and I heard him crashing down the stairs. I went to the window in time to see a half-naked opportunist pick up the pouch and take off with a howling mob in pursuit.

I looked inquiringly at Bayliss.

'About fifteen quidsworth,' he shrugged. 'Plus the works—needle, dropper, bent spoon and a stub of candle. He's going to have quite a shake on by the time he scores again. The bastard.'

'Was that Threlfall?' I asked.

'It was,' he said. 'Now suppose you tell me where Thorlby is?'

'In the police hospital. He'd been beaten up badly and dropped in the canal.' I could see that with the lifting of his uncertainty his arrogance was returning to him. He gave a twisted grin.

'That will teach him not to go haring off on his own—maybe,' he said, then, as an afterthought asked how badly hurt he was.

'He'll live,' I told him, and I could have sworn that he looked disappointed. 'What did you pick up from Threlfall?'

'One copper never asks another to disclose information obtained by unorthodox methods,' he quoted. 'First thing you learn as a rookie.'

'I'm not a copper, thank God,' I answered.

'You still don't get told though. Not until I think fit.'

'Don't bother. I'll tell *you*,' I said. 'You picked up nothing.'

'You want to bet?'

'Candy from a kid,' I matched his teasing smirk. 'Well, I've found your pal for you. You want to watch each other in future though. As I told you, things are a little different out here from pinching pickpockets in Piccadilly. Good morning.'

He had recovered his creaking humour fully now. He guffawed and told me that I was the one who would have to watch it if ever he bumped into me in Piccadilly. 'I'll have you for as much as spitting on the pavement,' he said. 'No hard feelings, Rees. Seriously though, suppose we even up, eh? I really was getting some stuff from that junkie when you came busting in.'

'Such as?'

'Looks like the flower children are getting organized properly. It's a rat-run from China through here, Afghanistan, Persia and the Middle East. A long line of dope carriers. Knock one off and there's half a dozen ready to plug the gap —literally, because they work in groups of six, apparently.'

'I know that,' I told him.

'Superior bastard,' he said. 'But I bet you didn't realize that the gent you just got off the hook was the head boy of one of the sixes. And he was just going to cough about who killed Hallaby.'

Chapter Six

IT WAS AT THIS POINT that I snapped out of the malaise that had been gripping me. It wasn't only to secure my passport, and it most certainly wasn't to oblige the Gaffer. It was just that this suddenly began to look like a job—one that had to be done by somebody, and since I happened to be the nearest—oh, what the hell. In spite of myself I just got interested, that's all.

'What did you find out?' I asked Bayliss.

'There's two mobs in charge of things here. One is Italian —smells awful like Mafia to me—the other is run by a gooroo. That right?'

'Guru. That can mean anything—holy man—teacher— healer. Who's this chap of yours working for?'

'Threlfall? The guru. He reckons the Italians killed Hallaby. Both mobs run on the Six system. Officially each bloke just knows the head of his Six, who in turn knows the head of his Six. They're not supposed to know anybody sideways, if you see what I mean.'

'And downwards?'

'Well, each of them knows the Six he is in charge of, naturally.'

'In other words each man knows his own Six and one man above him, who in turn is a member of the next higher Six, and so on?'

'That's it.'

'Well, how does he know that the guru is at the head of things if he, Threlfall I mean, is only supposed to know one man above him? Does that mean that Threlfall is second top man?'

'Hell no. He's only a tiddler. His Six would be about bottom according to him. The guru business is guesswork.'

'Did he name the man above him?'

'No, he bloody well didn't, because that's just about where you came horning in. If you'd left it to me I'd have——'

'Yes, yes, yes,' I agreed and beat a retreat. I needed to think this one over. I'd flung the wretched Threlfall into the ring completely at random, but it looked as if I'd hit on something by accident. At this stage I wanted only one thing—the identity of Hallaby's murderer. Having got it, I would hand it over to Mukherjee to deal with. But I had to be certain, and one can never be certain of anything in the way of information obtained by Bayliss's methods, because a man under extreme duress will often admit to anything for the sake of a few minutes' respite—recanting later when the heat was off—and this applied even more in the case of a drug addict. So Threlfall, except as a last resort, was out as a possible source of information. What had I got left? Thorlby's very vague lead—an ashram near Sealdah Station. As Mukherjee had said, there were hundreds of them in and around Calcutta. They ranged from clinically clean, properly run Brahminical establishments to filthy dumps that were little more than thieves' kitchens. Strictly speaking, an ashram is a sort of seminary for seekers after the Eternal Truth, and they are generally headed by a guru. Rest houses for pilgrims are either serais or dharmsalas, but lately, since the hippy boom, every pest-hole in India that could accommodate a few not too demanding bodies had become an 'ashram,' and the rogue who ran it, ipso facto, promoted himself to the guruship. All that was needed was some sort of enclosed space—courtyard, vacant lot, a derelict house—somewhere the clients could spread their sleeping mats under cover from the monsoon rain—a few idols swiped from a roadside shrine—a brass gong and an incense burner and they were in business. Real ashrams made no charge for accommodation; all a client had to do was to satisfy the guru about his bona fides as a postulant and he was admitted regardless of colour or creed. They were maintained by

66

donations from the pious and anything that grateful clients cared to kick in with when they left. The more respectable of the phonies did make a set charge, others, after a murderous bargaining session, took what they could get, while, at the bottom of the scale, they relied on what they could steal while the clients slept. The police sometimes ran a jaundiced eye over them, but there was no licensing system nor, as far as I knew, even a register kept of them.

Then I thought of Barney Giffard. No man knew the business as he did. It was outside this very hotel that he had seen the Light in 1945. Walking down Chowringhee as Regimental Sergeant-major of a British infantry battalion at the end of the war, he had been accosted by a leprous beggar who wouldn't be shaken off, so he had belted him hard, knocking him flat into the gutter, and walked on—probably a thing he had done unthinkingly a hundred times before. This time, however, delayed action hit him twenty paces along the sidewalk. He turned back and picked the beggar up, asked his forgiveness in his pidgin Hindi, and gave him what money he had in his pocket. The delighted beggar would no doubt have settled for the same terms as often as the gods in their wisdom chose to send a mad sahib his way, but Barney was a changed man from that instant. Changed in all respects that is, except for his sergeant-major's language. That, to his deep and abiding regret, he found impossible to do anything about. 'He looked into my heart and washed away all sin—God All-bloody-Mighty He did, brother—and I've been as happy as a sodding sandboy doing His work ever since—' he had once said to an astonished Anglican bishop who visited the mission he ran on his small Army pension and considerably larger fund of faith. The outcastes to whom he ministered called him, with awe, 'Gali sahib'. Gali means foul language, in which now, twenty-six years later, he was proficient in five different tongues.

I changed into loose Punjabi clothes and wound a pagri round my head because a European would have had no peace from the mob in the areas Barney moved in. Disguise with me fortunately not a matter of dark stain and crêpe hair so much as just thinking, moving and speaking like the locals, some of whom, particularly from the north, are no darker than the Mediterranean peoples.

I went on foot, because, at this hour of the evening one might run into him anywhere between the Municipal Market and the Beliaghata Canal which bounds the eastern fringe of the city. I was lucky, and I found him within the hour, working his sergeant-major's magic in the teeming square in front of the Jain Temple, in that he actually had the beggars squatting in orderly rows, with the women and small children in front, while he ladled out the last scrapings of boiled rice from a group of forty-gallon oil drums standing on bricks over a fire on the sidewalk. A police babu was telling him in English that he was breaking a city fire ordinance, and Barney was telling him in the same language to piss off. He told me to do likewise in Hindi when I touched him on the arm.

'It's me, Rees,' I said, and he peered at me through smoke-grimed eyes, then let out a roar of welcome.

"Halleluia, brother!' He wiped his streaming face on the tail of his Bengali khamis. 'Sweet Jesus—what I could do to a couple of beers at this moment, if I wasn't saved.'

'All right, backslide a bit and I'll buy you a couple,' I told him.

'Buy me one and put the price of the other in my rice fund. That'll feed ten of these poor buggers for two days.'

'You're as bad as Safaraz,' I said. 'He's always telling me how many starving Indians my whisky would feed.'

'He's damn right. How is the wicked bastard, God bless him?' He turned and shot a string of instructions at his helpers, in Bengali interspersed with Tyneside profanity, then joined me. 'The first class refreshment bar at Sealdah Station,' he said with satisfaction, 'where a black market beer will cost

68

you ten rupees, God forgive you. I hope their bloody icebox is working.' He was limping badly because he suffered from an oedema in both ankles, which were wrapped in dirty rags and hung dropsically over the busted pair of carpet slippers he wore. For the rest, he had on a dhoti, khamis and, incongruously, a frayed tweed golf cap. He had once been a big man, but his skin now hung on him like an over-large suit on a dwarf, because he fed, like those he ministered to, on a bowl of rice and a meagre handful of vegetables each evening. He had an untidy reddish beard, and his eyes, weakened by years of malnutrition, peered and blinked through steel-rimmed spectacles which were missing one sidepiece. And he was very dirty, because Calcutta pavements, when you live and sleep on them, tend to make you that way. Do I make him sound as if he were putting on a St Francis of Assisi act? He wasn't putting on any sort of act at all. He was a saint in his own right, but he'd have sworn horribly at anyone ill-advised enough to tell him so.

Recumbent bodies packed the assembly platform of that ante-room to hell which is Sealdah Station, because nowadays it not only serves the needs of genuine travellers, but it is also a favoured sojourning place for refugees. I followed Barney, who, in spite of his monstrously swollen feet, picked his way through the crowd with the certainty of a police horse, never once putting a foot wrong, and murmuring unerringly, 'Prahnam', 'Salaam aleikhum', or 'Khuda mehr-bani', according to whether he was stepping over Hindu, Muslim or a member of another of India's three hundred and twenty-two known sects.

We cleared a space for ourselves at one of the filthy tables in the bar, and three bearers brought up our two small beers, reverently like wine waiters at the Ritz serving vintage champagne. Barney's eyes glistened. He drank his slowly, savouring it drop by drop, then sat back and smiled beatific-ally.

'I love you as a brother, Idwal,' he said. 'But you didn't come down here dressed up like a bloody Punjabi just to tempt me from the path of righteousness with a beer. Spill it.'

'An ashram near this station where one European was killed last night, and another left for dead?' I said, and he shook his head.

'You're asking me to play police nark?'

'You know I'm not a cop, Barney.'

'A rose by any other name——'

'But there will be a net out for this. An awful lot of innocent people could be pulled in and put through the mill.'

'If they're innocent they'll have nothing to fear.'

'Barney, Barney, Barney,' I said reproachfully. 'You know better than that. If they're innocent they'll get put through it a damned sight worse—until one of them coughs in sheer desperation—or weariness.'

'The bloody bastards,' he swore. 'Yes—I know. But these people trust me, Idwal. If it ever leaked out that I'd split on one of them——'

'Your people wouldn't have done it.'

'I know that—but what you're asking me is to find out *through* my people, aren't you?'

'Something like that. Look—if I'm right this mob of goondahs are running dope. You surely don't side with that sort of filth do you?'

'Of course I don't side with them—but I don't hold a writ to bring them to judgement either. God will do that in His own good time.'

'Well, I wish He'd pull his finger out. These bastards are making an awful lot of money—and causing a commensurate amount of misery in the meantime,' I said, and he looked angry.

'Sorry,' I added hastily. 'I didn't mean to blaspheme—but they are doing just that, *and* murdering.'

He was silent for some minutes, scowling into space, and

I *was* sorry because I felt I'd spoiled his treat and soured his beer.

'Where are you staying?' he asked at length.

'The Grand.'

'Leave me some telephone money,' he told me, and swore viciously when I tried to make it fifty rupees.

'No, not even for the bloody rice fund,' he said. 'Stuff your Judas money. Two twenty-five paisa bits, that's all.'

Don't ask me how he did it, but the telephone was ringing as I entered my room on return.

'Sree Gurudas Lane, just behind the station,' he said. 'Left hand side—between a cycle repair shop and a Hindu bakery. But watch it, for God's sake, Idwal. They're bad people from what I could gather—really bad.'

I said, 'Thanks, Barney—and I—' but he had already hung up. I rang for Safaraz.

'We are poor men from Bangladesh,' I told him. 'Get some clothes.'

'We are too tall for poor men,' he said, cocking a thoughtful eye at me. 'And not fat enough for Bengalis. Perhaps farmers from Chandpur. The monsoon has washed away our crops and now the soldiers have descended like locusts, so we have run like the others. Only a Pathan stands and defends his home with his life.'

'Get the clothes then, and don't talk so bloody much.' I gave him twenty rupees and he departed happily, to be back in under an hour with a dubious-looking bundle of clothing.

He gloated as we dressed. 'To the very life, sahib. Coarse khaddar cloth woven by their wives, who are fat and lazy like all women of the south, smeared with cow-dung and stinking like an untouchable's billy-goat. A pity we shaved this morning. We men grow in one day the whiskers of a month for Chandpuris, who are weak in the balls,' he said, quoting a popular canard firmly believed by all northern bucks. 'Do we take guns or knives?'

71

'Neither. We are peaceful Hindus,' I said flatly. 'If you start anything tonight I'll see you grow less whiskers than a Chandpuri for the next year or so,' and he belly-laughed for a full two minutes. Coarseness and humour are one and indivisible to a Pathan.

We went out through the service entrance and walked to Sealdah, with Safaraz miffishly silent for once. He, like all his compatriots under ninety, could walk a full forty-five miles over mountains between one sun-up and another, and keep it up indefinitely, but a mile and a half on pavements hurt his feet and his dignity. He murmured that it was not fitting for a sahib to walk through filthy streets, and wanted to hail a taxi.

'We are poor men, owl-brain,' I told him. 'Go back if walking tires you,' and he gibbered with rage.

Finding Sree Gurudas Lane proved a tougher proposition than I had bargained for. Street names are hell to find in Calcutta even at the less seamy end, because they are invariably stuck on to buildings, usually under overhanging balconies, and then covered with ads for pile cure, vitality pills and the Indian Communist Party. To ask the way is fatal, because a crowd will gather on the instant, all eager to help and each shouting the others down until finally when one beats a retreat they form a procession and accompany the inquirer in the hope of a tip at the end of it. Added to that, down here there were no street lights.

Safaraz kept repeating with mealy-mouthed satisfaction, 'I told the sahib that men of substance, like us, should not walk like beggars. A taxi driver would have had no difficulty in finding it.' Until finally I was spitting obscenity at him in three languages. We found it in the end, a narrow gut between ramshackle buildings where one could have touched the walls each side with outstretched arms had one been willing to wade in the open sewer in the middle. It was lined on either side with 'shops'. You have to quote the word because they are nothing more than shallow recesses running along the fronts of the buildings, a scarce six feet wide and a little more than that in depth. In front of each of them is usually a wooden platform on which the goods are displayed by day, and where the entire family sleeps by night, with at least one member plus a mangy pi-dog awake and on guard. We could feel rather than hear their suspicious rustling as we passed. Two sacred cows with their calves blocked the entire width of the lane halfway down. They must have got our scent through the variegated stinks of the sewer, because they realized that we weren't Hindus and they got up and bolted, lowing with fear. Christians and Muslims eat beef; Hindus are vegetarians and the delicate sense of smell of these animals can detect the difference immediately.

We came upon the entrance to the ashram purely because they were baking at the bread shop, and the glow from the small charcoal oven fell upon a pile of rusty cycle wheels the other side of a narrow archway. I plucked Safaraz's sleeve and we went through. There was a muddy courtyard the other side and I could see the loom of dark buildings against the sky all round, unrelieved by the merest glimmer of light. I had to rely wholly on the superb nightsight of Safaraz now, and I was sorry I had needled him, because he is apt to get prima donna-ish when he is out of temper.

'Where are we, O-seer-in-the-dark-who-puts-the-tiger-to-shame?' I asked him. Believe it or not, there's one short word for that in Pushto.

'In the-shit-like-the-mud-turtles-of-Benares,' he growled. There's one word for that too, even shorter. But his Hillman's instincts were functioning now, and he could no more have sulked than a bird-dog when the pheasants are astir in the brushwood. He guided me to the nearest wall, and we patted our way along it to the corner, counting paces, then did the next wall, and the next, finding the expected archway in the third. We passed it and went on to the point at which we had entered, learning thereby that the courtyard was

73

about twenty yards square and the perimeter was unpierced except for the two archways. So far, so good. We crossed directly to the second archway, banging into the stone coping of a well in the middle—a handy thing to note in case of a hasty departure.

I whispered to Safarax, 'Through this second archway should be a door. Last night a light showed there, the door was opened and Hallaby sahib was killed and a Berlaity policeman badly beaten.'

I heard his breath whistle thinly in his nostrils—a nice balance of incredulity and disgust, 'And you said no guns or knives! Allah protects those who protect themselves.'

'I said no guns or knives,' I confirmed. 'I want to know who comes and goes here—and why. That and that alone at this point.'

We crept through the archway. Safaraz found the door on his side. He halted and I felt him kneel to put his ear to the crack beneath it. He straightened.

'No light there, sahib,' he muttered, 'but there is the breathing of a sleeping man.'

'One man?'

'One man only, sahib. A European.'

This was too much, even for me. 'Dogs that read the Koran-ji, elephants that fly, and clever Pathans,' I quoted a Punjabi proverb, the inference being that all are equally unlikely.

'He sleeps with his head clear of the blanket and snores like a camel in rut,' Safaraz said calmly. He had something there. Indians, even in the hottest weather, cover their heads when sleeping, though they may have to take off their loin-cloths to do it. The night is full of evil spirits which creep in through the open mouths and nostrils of the unwary, and take possession of their souls.

We went on. There was a smaller courtyard on this side and, facing us as we came through, there was a hideous six-armed manifestly female idol in a niche the opposite side with four votive lamps flickering before it, giving just enough light to see another door in the otherwise blank wall. We were tiptoeing towards it, keeping to the shadows round the wall, when we heard footsteps behind us.

Safaraz froze, then pulled me down into the gloom of the corner farthest from the idol.

The footsteps came on, two pairs it sounded like, and then, as the newcomers came in through the third arch, we heard voices.

One said, 'God, why'n hell doesn't somebody do something about old six-armed-Lizzie-with-the-tits there? She scares the piss out of me when I come back alone at night—if I ain't high.'

'Watch it,' somebody else said. 'The Swami don't dig taking the mike out of the gods.'

'Gods my arse—'

'Watch it!' angrily.

'What in hell's the matter with you? Something bring you down? Listen—I'm quitting.'

'You can't quit, you fool.'

'After last night I can. I got a stake now——'

And then they had passed and the mumbled voices were no longer intelligible. We saw them halt in front of the door near the idol, and one or other of them must have knocked or made some other sort of signal, because the door opened and a dim light showed for a moment, then they went in and the door closed.

Safaraz whispered, 'Did the sahib understand that?'

'Yes. An Americani and an Englishman spoke——'

'I know. One was the he-whore who the Berlaity policeman was beating.'

'You're sure of that?'

'In the dark my ears are even better than my eyes,' he boasted—and not vainly, because it was a simple statement of

75

fact. 'I may not understand the words, but I do not mistake voices.'

'Good. Now if I could but see what lies behind that door—' I began.

'Simple. Above the door is a flat roof—'

'How can you tell that from here?'

'I can see the line the top of the wall makes against the sky. Above there is nothing, therefore the roof is flat. I can also smell smoke, and the scented filth these idolators burn before their obscene gods—'

I was with him there—so could I.

'That means there must be a hole in the roof for the smoke to emerge and through which a man might look—' he went on.

Right again—that would be the nearest thing they would have to a chimney in a private house in Calcutta.

'So, if the sahib would wait here while I went to see——'

'QED.'

'Sahib?'

'That's French for "no—*you* wait here and *I'll* go to see".'

'But with respect, I am lighter on my feet and more agile.'

'Sure, sure, sure—like the goats of the Khyber Pass. Come and give me a bunk up on to the roof, and then—'

And then somebody shone a torch on us from behind and said, 'Hath uthao!' which means, 'Get your hands up,' in what the grammarians would call 'the urgent imperative.'

Chapter Seven

I THOUGHT SAFARAZ was going to be stupid so I shot a growled order at him out of the side of my mouth as I raised my hands above my head and turned into the light. Reluctantly he hoisted his then. Behind the blinding beam of the torch was an impenetrable wall of darkness which I guessed was defeating even Safaraz's nightsight, so I couldn't tell how many there were, nor if they were armed or merely bluffing. But the latter point was solved when a hand moved forward into the light and showed us a flat black automatic, then moved back out of sight again. I assumed an apologetic and conciliatory smirk and said in Bengali, 'We are poor men who seek shelter, O thrice-born.'

There was no answer, but the light came forward and a second man moved round behind us and gave us a quick but very expert frisking. Safaraz was carrying nothing at all, and I had only a few small coins tied into the corner of the dirty khaddar sheet I wore like a cape. They took these, and for a moment I had hopes that they were just a couple of goondahs on the prowl, in which case we might have expected a kick up the arse apiece and have been allowed to go, but I dismissed that immediately. That sort of petty criminal doesn't go heeled with expensive hardware.

The man behind me said, 'Gumao aur ek dum side jao' —(Turn and go straight ahead) which we did, to find that the door beside the idol was now open. We went through and I remember reflecting sourly that this was a hell of a way to finish up, and hoping, illogically, that whatever else they did with my carcass, they wouldn't dump it in Tolly's Nala. Safaraz was muttering that if I'd allowed guns and-or knives this wouldn't have happened, and I was wishing to God he would shut up, because he was using Pushto, and

77

if we had any hope at all it would be successfully to pass ourselves off for what we were dressed as—impoverished farmers from the delta that lay to the east of Calcutta, who spoke a low patois of Hindi-Bengali.

The room we found ourselves in was long and low and filled with smoke from a cowdung fire in the centre, that swirled in acrid wreaths before drifting out through the hole in the roof. It was completely unfurnished except for a few scattered bedding rolls and a row of brass cooking pots along one wall, and the far end of it was cut off by a tattered Bokhara curtain hanging on a sagging bamboo rod. The two hippies who had preceded us were already lounging on bedding rolls, and a European girl dressed in a grubby sari was stirring something in a pot over the fire. And Safaraz had been right, because the nearer of the hippies was Threlfall, and for a moment I thought I'd lost any chance I ever had of bluffing our way out of this, because he was bound to recognize me. But then I saw that he was engaged in the horrible ritual of the junkie—a strap round his left upper arm bringing up the big vein in the crook of his elbow while he boiled something in a spoon over a stub of candle on the floor. I hoped fervently that he would stay preoccupied for a long time. The other fellow looked up at us without particular interest and went on with a conversation he had been holding with the girl. She hardly wasted a glance on us either. She was the usual dirty little scrubber one found running with these people—long greasy hair, phony tilak and a generally un-washed appearance. He, unlike Threlfall, was a hefty, heavy-featured type with hair that was naturally fair and not dyed. Out of his Bengali garb and in clean jeans I'd have picked him as a Minnesota farmboy.

He was saying, '—gave me this crap about he thought Peace Corps did it for love, but I said to the interpreter guy, "tell the sunnervabitch I ain't driving no goddamn tractor for less than ten rupees an hour"—so in the end we settled for five and I came away after a month with six Cs, but I got rolled in this goddam ashram in Allahabad——'

She said, wearily, 'Yeah—you told me. Listen—did you tell Threlley that Swami-ji wanted him?'

'Wouldn't listen. Someone had swiped his works and he was as edgy as all hell till he scored again off Smiker.' He stretched out his foot and kicked Threlfall, who was now lying back on the bedding roll after fixing. 'Hey—hear that? The Swami wants you.'

'Up the Swami,' murmured Threlfall, eyes closed and face now relaxed.

'Sure—game as a piss-ant now you're turned on again, ain't you? Tell him that yourself,' the farmboy said, and the girl sucked her breath in sharply and pointed warningly at the curtain.

We were still standing just inside the door. One man remained behind us, unseen, and the other went forward to the curtain. He was dressed in the usual dhoti and khamis without turban or tilak on his forehead, so it was not possible to tell his caste. He paused at the curtain and said something in a low voice, then moved it aside and slipped through out of sight, and I remember thinking that if there was a Swami, which means Brahmin priest, the other side, he was a phony, because the man hadn't removed his sandals before going through. He reappeared and beckoned, and the man behind us prodded us in turn and we went forward. I nudged Safaraz, then bent and made the namaste sign, which is with the palms together as in prayer, head bowed reverently and nose touching the fingertips. It's about as humble an attitude as one human can assume to another, and upwards of three hundred and fifty million of the lower orders of Hinduism make it whenever they come within the shadow lengths of a Brahmin—that's if they know him to be a Brahmin. If they don't know it, they make namaste just the same, to be on the safe side. Out of the corner of my eye I could see Safaraz

79

doing it too, and hating it, but this way we could both keep our faces down—and with the dim light from the few oil lamps on the walls I was still hoping we might just about get by. The man at the curtain held it aside and we shuffled through, kicking our sandals off as we went. The space the other side was roughly equal to the other one—about forty feet in length by half that in width. There was another idol at the far end, lighted like the one outside with votive lamps, and a brass tray held smouldering sandalwood chips that sent up a sweet, heavy cloud of smoke that mingled over the top of the curtain with that of the cooking fire outside. I'd have given a lot at that moment for one good deep breath of clean, fresh air.

Halfway down on one side was a low desk like that of a bazaar letter-writer—and a man sat behind it in the so-called yoga-baithni posture, legs crossed with soles of the feet upwards. He was naked from the waist up, with the Brahminical thread of white cotton crossing his obese and sweating torso. His head was shaved and he wore the cobra tilak of the priest and law-giver, which is shaped like the 'eye' part of a hook-and-eye. I started my spiel even as the man behind prodded us forward—a long drawn-out wail, 'O Bahadur— O Swami-ji—O tisra paida—Hamlog nuqsan nahin irada—' (Oh Exalted One—Sir Swami—Oh thrice-born, we meant no harm—) until a swipe over the ear from behind brought me to snuffling silence. I was hoping that Safaraz wouldn't try to back me up in my supplications because he has a northern accent one could cut with a knife and he'd have sounded like a Yorkshireman trying to pass himself off as a Devonian. Fortunately he didn't—not at that point. The Swami, who I decided *was* a phony because he had not bothered to stub out a cigarette that smouldered in an ashtray beside the desk, said in Hindi, 'Which one?'

'The shorter,' answered the man behind us. That was me —Safaraz is just over the six foot mark—I'm just under.

'When he spoke with the gora at the station he was dressed as a Punjabi, but Asa Ram followed him back to the Grand Hotel and set Piyare to watch—then he came out again dressed as we see him now, together with this one. We have followed him ever since.'

So that was it. I felt like the sort of gent who would answer an ad in a pulp magazine, 'Be a Government Secret Agent in six easy lessons: Five Dollars—including badge and certificate.' And the really awful part of it was that Safaraz could understand what they were saying, and witness my humiliation. Quite obviously Hallaby had been blown right from the start, after which all his contacts had been watched. Jesus! This was a worse boob than any ever made by poor bloody Wainwright.

The 'Swami' looked up at me and grinned faintly, almost sympathetically. 'Too bad,' he said in accentless English. I started to wail in Bengali again but he just looked bored and made a gesture of dismissal—and it was then, with the best of all possible intentions, that Safaraz, who is quite unaware of his northern accent, decided I needed help, because he started to wail also, with the result that we *both* were belted over the ear this time. My iron will and magnificent training helped me to accept it with resignation, merely hunching like a ruptured camel and wailing the louder. But not so Safaraz, who doesn't like being belted over the ear, particularly by Hindus. He spun, dropped and kicked all in one and the man behind us, who I saw was a real Chandpuri, bore out the contention regarding genital weakness, because he howled, dropped the automatic he had been holding on us, and clutched himself in agony—and I had just enough wit to pounce on the gun. The other man was dragging one out from under his khamis so I pulled the trigger—and even then I boobed again, because I didn't slip the safety catch the first time and he almost had us—but I did beat him to the shot by a fraction of a second. The first man was in dolorous condition, because Safaraz really has a kick like a Mountain Artillery mule, bare feet notwithstanding.

'Shoot him too, sahib!' Safaraz yelled, but I didn't—not from any nice-mindedness on my part, but because I didn't want to waste ammunition. I didn't even shoot the 'Swami'. I didn't need to. He was running with amazing speed for a fat man, crouched double and making for a door behind the idol, and Safaraz split his shaven skull like a melon, with the perfectly thrown heavy teakwood desk, and then, quick-thinking, thieving bloody Pathan that he is, bless him, he found time to relieve the man I had shot of his pistol, and he tried to use it on the Chandpuri, but he boobed with the safety catch also, so he contented himself with a further kick to the crotch. Personally, given the choice, I'd have settled for a bullet.

We came out through the curtain like bats from hell. The farmboy was standing looking at us with fallen jaw, his reflexes obviously not meshing at all well. The junkie had more on the ball with his dope-sharpened sensibility now at its zenith, and he and the scrubber were making for the door, neck and neck, when we overtook them. I slammed Threlfall hard on the side of the head with the flattened gun, and he dropped. Safaraz, no gentleman under conditions like this, clobbered the lady, and then we were out in the courtyard, our bare feet slip-slapping horribly in all sorts of unimaginable filth. There was a light in the room under the arch, and a man stood silhouetted in the doorway with what looked like a rifle in his hands—at least Safaraz swore afterwards that he *thought* it was a rifle. He, Safaraz, had now mastered the intricacies of the safety catch, and I would like to think that this man was the one who had dealt with poor Hallaby. Anyhow, Safaraz got him in the belly as we sped past and he folded like a shot snipe.

We came out into the lane and ran like hares each side of

the central sewer, and doubled round the corner at the first crossing and waited for possible pursuit, but none came so, after a ten minute interval, we went on, and Safaraz started to moan about a taxi again.

'What do we use for money?' I asked him, and he slapped the butt of his newly acquired gun, so I took it from him and we walked the whole way, which I'd prefer not to dwell on. Ugh! Those pavements. Getting into the hotel brought further difficulties because the service entrance was now locked and barred, so we had to get past the hefty Sikh watchmen at the front door, who are armed with murderous bellmouthed shotguns. They naturally wouldn't let us in and in the end we had to disclose our identities. Safaraz explained matters in great detail by telling them that I had been paying a visit incognito to a brothel, and was being badly beaten up by twelve goondahs when he, Safaraz, had rescued me, singlehanded. It was losing nothing in the telling, and I could hear their guffaws as I crept up the stairs to my room.

I took a much-needed shower and a solid four fingers of scotch and then sat down to think about things—and they certainly called for some thinking. I was blown wide open in this town now—as a European, a Punjabi and a low-caste Hindu. I was known to hippies and Indians alike as an associate of the police, and, if that were not enough, we had left three dead men in the ashram. I couldn't picture any of the still living putting up an official squawk, but those shots must have been heard and the police might conceivably drop in on a routine visit in the morning—and if they started to question Threlfall, who they'd recognize as a junkie immediately and just treat to cold turkey, he'd be bound to talk, even if the farmboy and the girl didn't.

I made a long arm for the telephone.

Mukherjee wasn't at the station, and the night duty havildar couldn't tell me where he was, so I just had to leave a message for him to call me when he came in, then I slid into bed, but I didn't get to sleep because there was a soft but insistent knocking at my door some ten minutes later. I got up, cursing, and opened. Two of the four Sikh watchmen from below stood outside with the air of men who wished for nothing more than to render a service—and collect a tip.

'The lady, sahib,' said one of them, smirking lasciviously, and I gawped at the wench who I'd caught trying to rob the beggar in front of the hotel. She was lurking behind them looking nervous.

I said, 'These two your agents? Go and peddle it somewhere else—I'd rather have a good cup of tea.'

'Please—' she began, but I was giving the watchmen a dressing down—in English, so she'd get the benefit of it too. She started to cry then, which was probably an act, but it made me feel uncomfortable.

'What do you want?' I asked, with as little grace as I could put into it.

'My boy-friend is in trouble I think,' she snivelled.

'So what?'

'You're a policeman, aren't you?'

'God forbid. Who is your boy-friend, anyhow?'

'The one you pigs—policemen—roughed up this afternoon. His name is Ronnie Threlfall—and he's sick.' She started to cry again, louder, and doors were opening along the corridor and eyes peering through cracks.

I said, 'Hut jao,' to the Sikhs, and they went, tipless and sorrowful.

I motioned to her to come in, and pointed to a chair. She was still crying.

I said, 'All right, you can stop now and get on with it. What sort of trouble is he in?'

'He was let in for this by a boy called Les Horton—'

Ah, we were getting somewhere now. That was the lucky

84

lad the Gaffer had told me about, who got away with things in Istanbul.

'Yes—go on,' I said. 'Let in for what?'

'Well, Ronnie wasn't on the stuff at all—not even pot —until Les started him off. The dirty swine—he doesn't use it himself—just pushes it. Ronnie built up very quickly. He had to leave college——'

'Which college?'

'Willesden Art School—and he just hung about Piccadilly scoring wherever he could. I tried to get him to register——'

'Register?'

'You know—as an addict. You get a scrip to buy the damned stuff on prescription then—but it means taking tailing-off treatment at a clinic, and he couldn't face that—so he had to raise enough to buy from the pushers. He needed over ten pounds a day—and he was getting nothing— unemployment pay, supplementary allowance—not a sausage. And of course his education grant had stopped—and he couldn't work—so he started nicking things——'

'Like what?'

'Oh, anything—out of the back of delivery vans mostly, because he was too scruffy to go shoplifting. Then he got ambitious and he was pinched swiping a colour television out of a house in Croydon——'

'And got a two-year suspended sentence,' I said knowledgeably. It's sometimes a good thing to let a client who is telling all think that you know some of the facts already. It helps to keep them to the truth. 'Go on.'

She shrugged. 'Well, you know all about it then.'

'Yes—but let's hear it again.'

'He was in a bad fix now. If he was picked up and done for something else he would collect for that, plus the two years swinging over him. I was earning the horse money——'

'How?'

She shrieked at me, 'You know bloody well how, you stinking fascist pig. Wasn't I done for it under the Street Offences Act—twice?'

'That's right. I was just checking. Go on.'

'Well, I couldn't risk it any more—it would have meant prison the third time, and God knows what would have happened to him then. Anyhow, it was about now that Les Horton showed up. He'd been out here in India, and he came back to England loaded with money. He had good connections too, and he was getting Ronnie his full fix every day. Then he suggested that we came back to India with him. He had a truck and he got up a party of ten at a hundred pounds a head—but we were broke, so he said we could pay him later. Ronnie's passport had been withdrawn by the Crown Court, but Les got him a false one quite easily. So out we came——'

'Any bother in Turkey?'

'No. Why?'

'Horton had been arrested in Istanbul previously for drug offences—oh, yes, I know—he was acquitted——'

'I see what you mean. No, he got through without any trouble at all. He was on a false passport too, and he'd got rid of his long hair and whiskers and was dressing square like a couple of the others. He didn't risk carrying anything though—not until we got through into Iran—and then only transistors and a couple of Japanese cameras to bribe the police with—Oops, sorry—no offence meant.'

'My back's broad,' I said. 'Carry on.'

She fumbled in her loose skirt and pulled out a crumpled, half-smoked cigarette.

'Look—would you mind——?' she asked. 'I'm frazzled to hell.'

'What is it? Bhang?'

'What else? I don't touch hard stuff, thank God.'

'Then I *would* mind,' I told her, and poured a stiff scotch and passed it to her together with an ordinary cigarette. 'It would stink the place out and get me a bad name with the hired help. Go on.'

She took the drink gratefully, gulped and choked over it, and held the cigarette with a trembling hand while I lighted it for her. She looked up at me.

'I'm talking too bloody much,' she said. 'I may be dropping Ronnie in the crap with you bastards.'

'If you want help for him you'll have to be absolutely frank,' I said, and added, 'You haven't told me anything that isn't known. Right—go on.'

'We had a rough spin in Afghanistan. The three girls, I mean.'

'In what way?'

'You know what goes on in Afghanistan?'

I nodded. 'Yes, I know. The boys put you on the batter, did they?'

'Not Ronnie,' she said fiercely. 'You can't hold it against *him*. He got on to some bad junk in Herat and nearly died. He didn't know what was going on. That bastard Les said that he hadn't made anything on the trip because some of the others hadn't paid him yet, and we'd had engine and tyre trouble which had cost the earth to have fixed, and he hadn't been scoring or carrying on the way—so he had to get a stake to carry on to India.'

'So?'

'So, like you said—he put us on the batter.' She rubbed out her cigarette, balled her fists, and her face contorted. 'The bastard—the bastard—the dirty, kinky *bastard*. He didn't need the bread—he was still loaded. No—he used to watch. He used to bring these camel-stinking swine along to the truck, and watch through a hole in the back of the cab.'

'Three of you,' I said. 'Couldn't you have put up a show against him?'

'Not a chance. Five of the alleged men had dropped out along the road by this time. That left us three girls, and the

87

other two were just kids, fifteen—sixteen. How the hell they got past the police and passport control at Dover I wouldn't know—and then there was Ronnie, sick like I said—and Horton himself. He told us we either played ball and raised the money for the rest of the trip—or he'd drive on alone. God knows what would have happened to us then. We did try to latch on to a couple of other parties going through, but what a hope! The girls were mostly on the same racket —either because the boys were making them, or because they liked it anyhow. Jesus! I thought I'd met every type of slag in Piccadilly and Soho—of all three sexes—but if you really want the absolute, rock-bottom arsehole of humanity, black, white and khaki, try the fair city of Kabul.'

She was crying again—really crying now. Before it had merely been an expression of nervousness—a sort of whimper. Now the floodgates were open and I could see that when she stopped she'd be like a piece of chewed string, and any questions I put to her would be answered mechanically and truthfully for the simple reason that she wouldn't have the energy to lie, or even to keep anything back. It's a dirty business this. I was genuinely sorry for the wretched girl, but here I was thinking in terms of the Rules for Interrogation. I left her alone for some minutes, then I said, 'All right—you still haven't told me what sort of trouble he's in. I can't help until I know.'

'There's some pigs—police—coming out from London—I suppose you're one of them—and there's a mob here who want them killed. A *white* mob, not Indians—and they're working on a crowd of boys to do it for them—junkies, who would cut their own mothers' throats if you kept them off it for twenty-four hours, then dangled a fix in front of them.'

'Yes—and——?'

'That's all. I know that Ronnie, poor bloody Ronnie, has been elected as one of them. I want him out of it before he *does* kill somebody. They still hang out here, don't they?'

'They do,' I assured her. 'All right—quite simple. Tell me who is behind it all and I'll get your Ronnie off the hook.'

She looked at me, hope fighting with her natural hatred and suspicion of authority—authority in any shape or form. 'You're not—just saying that? You'll give him a break——?'

'Let's get this sorted out,' I said. 'First of all I'm not a cop——'

'Then what am I wasting my bloody time for? You said you were——'

'Shut up,' I told her sharply. 'I didn't tell you anything of the sort—but I *am* telling you something now. I have a certain official position that carries a bit of influence with it——'

'Which you'll use on Ronnie's behalf providing I'll listen to reason?' she sneered. 'Sure, sure, sure—anything you like, just so as Ronnie doesn't drop in for it.'

'What's your name?' I asked.

'Pewsey Darrell. Why?'

'Well, you listen to me, Pewsey. I'm promising nothing —but I'll do my best for him just as long as you come clean with anything you know. You'll have to take that or leave it. And as for listening to reason, you can forget it, because I wouldn't touch you with a long bamboo pole.'

'And I wouldn't blame you,' she said, and from such small things do human relationships spring. She said it without bitterness or self-pity. Quite obviously she hadn't a single illusion left about herself, and I suddenly felt a louse for insulting her. Whatever her shortcomings she certainly had loyalty.

'So what do you know?' I asked.

'Not much. We shook loose from Les after we crossed from West Pakistan, and came on down here. We've been living rough—sleeping on the Maidan most nights. A rupee a day covers our food. God, I never want to see a bowl of rice or a bloody chapatti again as long as I live.'

'What about Threlfall's habit?'

89

'Ten rupees a day sustains that out here. I raise what I can by panhandling the few tourists that come to this ghastly dump—scrounge from the European and Anglo-Indian Charitable Fund at the Bishop's House—beg—hustle—Oh, Christ, why go on? I raise it, that's all. We were getting by. I've got no silly ideas about Ronnie ever kicking the habit, but at least the poor little sod has some sort of peace here. But then Les turned up from Katmandu—that was a couple of days ago. I wasn't around when he arrived, but Ronnie told me about this crazy assassination thing that night. I talked him out of it, or thought I had—but then yesterday this copper—the old one from London—picked him up and put the heat on him—then he disappeared, that was last night—I don't know where he is now——'

'That's all you know?'

'Absolutely all—I swear.'

'All right—don't worry. I know where he is—or was a few hours ago.'

'Where?' she asked, in a fever of anxiety.

'Not far from here—I can't tell you more than that at the moment, but I'll put you in touch as soon as I am able. Where will you be?'

'Oh, I'll be around—outside somewhere——' she gestured vaguely.

I said, 'Have you got any money?'

She nodded, but not very convincingly, so I picked up a couple of tens and held them out to her. 'That's a loan,' I told her, 'but not for Ronnie's fixes. Get a decent meal, girl, and clean yourself up a bit.'

She grinned.

'Then you *would* touch me with a bamboo pole, eh? No thanks. I'll be grateful for anything you can do for him, but *I'm* not for reforming. I'm miles past that.'

'Who's trying to reform you?' I said. 'Take it, you silly little bitch, and get the hell out of here. I want to get some sleep.'

She hesitated, then nodded curtly and took it. 'Thanks. A loan, like you said.'

I saw her to the door, but it just wasn't my day because Mukherjee arrived at that moment—and well, I ask you? Here I was seeing a scruffy but pretty little trollop off the premises, me with a towel round my waist and nothing more—rumpled bed—two whisky glasses on the table—and her with twenty chips prominently displayed in her hand. He bowed to her gravely and came in, a model of polite discretion looking like all three monkeys who see, hear and speak no evil.

I said, 'It's not what it might appear to you at first sight, Superintendent-ji,' as I closed the door on her.

'My dear Idwal, do you think I have a mind like a sewer?' he asked, shocked.

'Yes,' I said. 'Only dirty. Any news?'

'I was thinking you should have some for me—about four corpses in an ashram near Sealdah.'

'Three,' I corrected. 'Two goondahs and a fake Swami. Self-defence, Superintendent-ji. I was hoping to claim your indulgence in keeping it out of court.'

'No sweat about those three,' he said, going all American. 'But I wish you'd taken that hippy Threlfall off my patch before rubbing him out.'

Chapter Eight

I SAID SLOWLY, 'The poor little devil.'

Mukherjee shrugged. 'He and his sort, they don't work—they take drugs. I'm afraid I have no sympathy to waste on them.'

'I wasn't thinking of *him*.'

'Then who?'

'It doesn't matter. Anyhow, I give you my word *we* didn't rub him out.'

'We?'

'Safaraz or me.'

'I see. But you do admit to killing the others?'

'Don't be stupid. I admit to nothing.'

'Of course not. I wouldn't expect you to. But off the record——?'

'On or off the record—we weren't there.'

'You don't trust me?'

'Just as far as I'd trust a tiger with a sweet little baa-lamb.'

'What's a bar lamb?'

'Forget it. Nothing personal, Shyam—but a copper in charge of a murder case—Christ, you don't start showing him your operation scars.'

'Two goondahs and a religious charlatan? You don't think we'd call that murder, do you? Or a hippy, if it comes to that. You ought to get a small reward under the Abatement of Nuisances Act.'

'Yes—but I'm still not risking it. You haven't told me how he died.'

Mukherjee grinned. 'Sorry. I forgot you weren't there. He was shot—deliberately. A close one in the back of the head.'

'Another one,' I said.

'Another *three*——'

'I was thinking about Hallaby.'

'Of course—yes, he was shot in the head too. The goondahs each got theirs in the belly—and the reverend gentleman had his head split open. Did they say anything before they died?'

'How the hell would I know?'

'I thought you might have heard—from a friend or something.'

'My friends are respectable, Shyam. They don't go round knocking people off at night. Although, now you come to mention it, I did hear a whisper on the latrine radio.'

'I would be grateful to hear it.'

'It would appear that a couple of Chandpuris went to a phony ashram behind Sealdah Station. They were found on the premises, and their story that they were looking for somewhere to sleep was not accepted by a couple of strongarm boys. They were taken before a man pretending to be a Swami——'

'You—I mean the Chandpuris, were certain that he *was* pretending?'

'Absolutely. Anyhow, you yourself just said he was a charlatan.'

'Quite so—but I was wondering how you—sorry—the Chandpuris knew?'

'The goondahs didn't take their sandals off before venturing into his presence—and he was smoking a cigarette.'

'Very observant of the Chandpuris. I wish some of my policemen were as wide awake. Please go on.'

'Well, the Chandpuris were a little bit phony themselves—and the Swami and the goondahs appeared to know this. They also appeared to have had the phony Chandpuris under surveillance for some time previously—and finally the Chandpuris were absolutely certain that they were going to be rubbed out after interrogation—so they took steps to prevent this.'

'What sort of steps?'

'Bloody long ones—through the bazaar.'

'Yes, but how did they get away in the first place?'

'One Chandpuri kicked a goondah, who happened to be a real Chandpuri, in the cods——'

'What's "cods"?' asked Mukherjee, who collects British and American colloquialisms like a philatelist collects postage stamps.

'Balls.'

'Thank you. Proceed please.'

'The goondah dropped his gun, whereupon one of the phony Chandpuris picked it up intending to hold the others at bay—but the other goondah produced a gun and—well, one thing led to another and he unfortunately got in the way of one. Then the Swami, who was buggering off——'

'Buggering who?'

'Running away—got clobbered by a desk——'

'Clobbered?'

'Hit. Then, finally, another armed goondah got in the way as the phony Chandpuris were making their exit. That was just sheer bad luck——'

Mukherjee nodded ponderously and pursed his lips. 'For him—yes. Um—I see. One way and another, a proper cods up, no?'

'It could be termed that, yes. Well, now you know everything from the Chandpuris' side—but I can assure you that they had no knowledge of the death of Threlfall. He was there, fixing——'

'Fixing who?'

'Taking drugs—and there was another hippy there, an American—and an English girl—but while the Chandpuris were there these people took no part in any of the action whatsoever—although one of the Chandpuris walloped Threlfall as they were making their getaway——'

'Walloped meaning——?'

'Same as clobbered—but it was only a relatively light tap on the head in order to stop his going for help. You say he was shot?'

'Yes. Thank you, Idwal—that fits in with what I saw round there a little while ago. The other two—the man and the girl could you, or maybe the Chandpuris, describe them?'

'The man—age twenty-five to thirty—height five feet ten inches or thereabouts—heavily built—naturally fair hair, a bit shorter than most hippies wear it—blue eyes—side and chin whiskers but no moustache—rather a Scandinavian cast of features——'

'Scandin—what caste?'

'Oh, hell—leave that. What I meant was that he looked like a Swede or a Norwegian——'

'Not American?'

'Yes, sure, American—but his grandfather was a Swede perhaps——'

'You know that for certain? Where did you meet his grand-father?'

'I don't know it for certain—and you're just playing the idiot boy in the hope of making me trip up. Stop it, or I'll heave you out on your ear—without offering you a drink first.'

'Crystal clear from now on,' he said, fixing his eye on the bottle. I poured drinks and he gave a sigh of content as he took his. 'Okay—mud in your eye. Give us a rundown on the broad. It's wonderful what a drink can do to one's command of the more idiomatic forms of speech. I thought you were never going to take the hint.'

'She looked a scrubber. That means——'

'A mare that runs wild in the scrub country, copulating indiscriminately with stray stallions. Derivation Australian, but also applied to women of similar propensities in other parts of English-speaking world.' He held out his glass. 'Give me another drink and I'll give you the bloody Latin root of it.'

I topped his glass up, and went on, 'Small, five feet I should say, thin, blue eyes, hair that would probably be fair if it was washed—cheap cotton sari which also could have done with a wash, in which case it would have been blue—Rajput tilak and a lot of imitation silver bangles, ear-rings and things.'

He nodded. 'That's right. Mr Ashley Ahrlberg and Miss Sandra Smith to the life.'

'Have you got them?'

'No—and I don't intend to take them—not yet. They didn't do it.'

'But they would know who did, surely?'

'Damn right they would—and a lot of other things as well. When I pull them in they're going to cough the lot. I don't want to spring the trap too soon though.'

'Do the Press know about these latest killings?'

'They don't know of *any* of the killings.'

'How the devil have you managed to keep them dark?'

'My God, man—you ask that in Calcutta? What the hell is one death, two deaths, two hundred deaths in this poor tortured town?'

'Maybe—but you said that European deaths *were* news.'

'Except when the European dies of enteric—and is cremated. That's what happened to Mr Hallaby—yesterday evening—at the Christian crematorium. We've got a medical certificate and an entry at the Municipal Office to prove it.'

'You mean to say that the High Commissioner's office accepted that?'

'Bloody High Commissioner's office asked for it to be done that way. That would have been arranged away up on the New Delhi–Whitehall level. It suits both sides and doesn't hamper inquiries.'

'What about Threlfall?'

'He was gathered up with the Swami and the goondahs. They'll all be burnt at the ghats tonight—in the ordinary way of business.'

'I didn't know you were allowed to burn Christians in a Hindu ghat.'

'We're not—and the real Swamis are very particular about

that—but Threlfall, who incidentally had a passport in the name of Bowman, is not a Christian according to papers found in his wallet. There's a so-called Hindu sect in London—the Haré-Krishnas or something—that will make you a Brahmin while you wait. It's not recognized out here, because you can't join Hinduism like you can Christianity, the Muslims or the Buddhists—you've got to be born into it—born three bloody times at least to be a Brahmin too. Anyhow, he appears to be one of them, so we accept him at face value, with tongue in cheek—Mr Ronald Threlfall—Bowman, alias Ram Dass Yogi.'

I remembered seeing these weirdies on one of my rare visits to London—nuts of both sexes dressed in saffron robes, the men with shaven heads, thumping tomtoms and yowling gibberish purporting to be mantras in Oxford Street.

I said, 'I see. Well, now, I've told you everything I know about the Chandpuris. Is there anything else I can do?'

'Yes—tell me who that scrubber was you were just showing out.'

'Threlfall's girl-friend. She was worried about his disappearance and came to see me.'

'Um—I'd better have her in to see if she can add a little grist to the mill.'

'I don't think she can,' I said. 'I got everything out of her, and it didn't amount to much.'

'Suppose you pass it on to me.'

'It was little enough. He was an art school dropout——'

'Dropout?'

'You know bloody well what a dropout is. You have them out here.'

He grinned. 'Yes, but we call them sunyassis. When a man gets fed up with his wife, mother-in-law and bloodsucking children, he puts on a loincloth, takes up a staff and begging bowl and buggers off into the jungle. Very holy. I often feel tempted to do it myself. All right, so Threlfall was a dropout —yes?'

'That's all—except that he was a junkie, and he had a conviction for theft in England.'

'Pretty typical in other words?'

'Yes.'

'And the girl?'

'Pretty typical also. She strung along with this fellow and did what she could for him. She's going to feel bad about this.'

'That is why I think I ought to pull her in. The court would then deport her to England. That would be better than staying out here and living in the gutters.'

'I suppose you're right—but please don't do anything until I've seen her again. I'll try to talk some sense into her, and get her to go home voluntarily instead of with a copper's writ stuck on her. With this fellow out of her system she might make a fresh start at home, given a chance.'

'You are interested in her?'

'Only as a sign of the times, poor little bitch. There are too many of them coming out here with stars in their eyes, Shyam. Some are genuinely seeking something—they're not all junkies, thieves and incipient whores—not at first, anyhow, but that's how most of them finish up.'

He rose. 'All right, Idwal. I'll lay off for twenty-four hours. If you can get her a ticket from the High Commissioner and see her off the premises—fine. If you can't, she's got to be picked up as an undesirable and turfed out. Sorry.'

'I'm not blaming you,' I said. 'You've got enough problems without importing them. How's Thorlby, by the way?'

'Recovering. Can you repay my little favour by getting both of them off my back?'

'I wish I could. Are they worrying you?'

'Not them—not directly, I mean—but our higher-ups are riding me a bit hard. Bad image. Two Scotland Yard men come out here, and we can't protect them.'

'*They* are going to be ridden a bit hard when they get home,' I said. 'Two Scotland Yard men come out here, and they can't look after themselves. All right, I'll do what I can, but I can't promise anything.'

There was no point in going back to bed now as it was broad daylight. Safaraz came in so I sent him down for some breakfast and I had it in my room in order to dodge Bayliss, then I went out to see if I could find the girl.

The refugees were beginning to move from the Maidan, and I stood for a moment in front of the hotel and was immediately surrounded by wailing beggars who pulled at my sleeves, knelt and clasped my ankles, thrust pitiful little monkeylike babies into my face and generally subjected me to the routine treatment. It was stupid to stand there even for a moment, no doubt, but I wanted to see whether she was in her usual place in the shelter of the portico. She wasn't, so I moved out into the roadway, like a swimmer in the Amazon trying to shake free from piranhas. It's difficult to do it short of sheer brutality. Give them something and you're stuck with them for the rest of the day, and the next, because they'll wait for you outside any building you duck into. There seems to be an invisible point though at which, if you can get past it without weakening, they accept defeat and melt away. Up north, a beggar who doesn't collect from you will give you a mouthful of abuse— but in Calcutta they haven't the strength even to call you a heel. They just look, and Christ it's hard to take.

I made it across the tram tracks and on to the Maidan where I could see a small group of hippies waking, sitting up and scratching themselves. The beggars were still with me, but they pulled up short and made off when they saw where I was heading, and I could hear them muttering among themselves that the long-haired White Devils would beat them if they saw them panhandling a sahib. There were five of them— three men and two girls. But she wasn't one of them, so I walked past, and one of the men, dressed like a Hollywood mahatma, called out, 'Peace and love, brother. Come and join us,' then, when I didn't answer, he yelled, 'You can bang one of the birds for two rupees—or me for three if you're a fairy,' and the whole gang went off into shrieks. I went on to another group without success, and finally made a complete circuit of the Maidan, right down as far as the Birla Planetarium. If she was not in an ashram somewhere, this place and the covered portico of the Grand and the shops each side of it would be where she would normally spend the sweltering hours between mid-morning and sundown, when it was too stiflingly humid to walk about without half drowning in one's own sweat.

I turned back towards Chowringhee. I'd done what I could. She would have to take her chance with the police now. Perhaps it was the better way anyhow. She'd be collected up and put into the Remand Wing of Alipore Prison until a deportation order was made out. It wouldn't be luxurious, but surely anything was better than this——

And then I saw the farmboy. He had seen me too. He was standing some little distance off when I turned—as if he had been behind me originally. He hesitated, obviously wanting to speak to me, but uncertain how I'd react. I wheeled and went straight over to him.

He said, nervously, 'Say—I didn't mean no offence.'

'None taken,' I said. 'But what are you talking about?'

'You *are* the guy who came to the ashram last night—with another guy?' I nodded, and he peered into my face. 'You look kinda different dressed like this. Last night I'd have sworn you were an Indian——'

'You're Ashley Ahrlberg, aren't you?' I said, and he looked really worried.

'Sure—but I don't want to get mixed up in none of this —I never had trouble with the police, either here or back home——'

'You could be in plenty right at this moment,' I told him. 'What happened to Threlfall?'

He seemed to go white under his mixture of grime and tan.

'Look Mr Rees——' he began, but I gave him no time to think.

'How do you know my name?'

'Well—I guess—someone must've told me——'

'Who?'

'I—I can't remember—some guy, somewhere—Look——'

'You said you've never been in trouble? You're heading straight for it. Now, come on—the truth. What happened to Threlfall——?'

'I tell you—I don't know——'

'You want to be charged with his murder?'

'Are you out of your skull?' he shrieked. 'I had nothing to do with it——'

'Do with what?'

'With what you were talking about for Cri'sake——'

'What was that——?'

'Ah, shit—look, I'll tell you everything, but I need help right now——'

'You mean a fix?'

'Fix hell—I don't use it. No, I need help with this dame——'

'What dame?'

'Threlfall's chick—Pewsey Darrell——'

'Where is she?'

'In a dump in Dilkhusha Street. She tried to knock herself off——'

'When?'

'An hour ago—maybe a bit longer——'

'Why?'

'Someone told her Threlfall was dead.'

'How did she try to do it?'

'She had a fistful of those small black pills they use here—da—dak——'

'Daquirity seeds——'

'That's right—man, they're just plain sudden death if you don't know how to handle them. Anyhow, she came along to this place—it's a friend's pad where I'm staying with another chick while the heat's on the ashram—Well, she turns up looking like hell, and says can she stay there for a while and my friend says sure, and the next thing we know she's swallowing these things like they was candy. My chick gets them away from her and we shove our fingers down her pipe and make her sick some of them up—but there's sure as hell a lot still down her——'

'Did you get a doctor?'

'With what? These stinkers out here want the dough first.'

'Who's with her now?'

'Just my chick.'

We had been walking during this exchange and we were now back on Chowringhee. I called a cab. 'What number?' I asked him.

'Twenty-three——'

'Get in,' I told him.

It was only a five-minute run along Park Street, passing rapidly from the semi-respectable rundown area that is central Calcutta today, to the howling wilderness of the bustees. The driver took one look at the end of Dilkhusha Street, which was about six feet wide, and shrugged hopelessly, so I paid him off and we went on per boot.

Number twenty-three was just a doorway between a grain shop and an Indian Christian undertaker's parlour. We went with Mr Ahrlberg leading, and I followed him up some filthy narrow stairs to a dark landing at the top, where he stood to one side while someone unseen clobbered me cold with a club.

Chapter Nine

BUT HE WASN'T very good at it. Your real professional uses half a sockful of damp sand in preference to a hard club, which tends to bounce off a skull like mine. It knocked me cold all right, but I wasn't out for very long, because they were still roping me up when I came to, and I had enough muzzy wit left to play possum and keep my eyes closed.

Ahrlberg was saying exultantly, '—just fell for it. No sweat at all. Boy, you shoulda heard me——'

'We have,' someone said sourly. 'Belt up, for Cri'sake. Pull that bloody rope tighter or he'll be kicking himself loose.'

I risked the merest flicker of an eyelid. The small and completely bare room was dimly lighted by one dirty window high up in the wall. There seemed to be three of them—the two who were tying me, and this third fellow who was speaking. He was English from his accent, dressed in the universal dhoti and khamis, and he was sitting in the corner across from me, on the floor but in European style with his legs stretched out in front of him, which looks peculiarly ungainly and out of place with Indian costume. These bums will never learn from observation.

They finished tying me, making a better job of it than of club-wielding, then they moved round and joined the first gent, who said, 'Come on, this isn't a mothers' meeting. Move yourselves and wake the bastard up.' Ahrlberg pulled a face and said, 'You do it, Yonni. The smell of burning hair makes me sick.'

Yonni was apparently blessed with a stronger stomach, because he fished a lighter from under his khamis, knelt in front of me, flicked it alight and held the flame under my nostrils. I've seen it done before—and it's a bloody sight quicker in reaction than smelling-salts. I woke with a roar, which amused Yonni, a tall willowy youth, very much indeed. He was about to do it again, unnecessarily, but the first man reached out and kicked him aside.

'No time for that,' he said. 'Right, you Rees—I've got a few questions for you——' But I never heard what they were. Instead I heard, with a certain measure of relief, a thunderous hammering at the door, and a voice yelling, 'Pol-liss hai— Yeh darwaza kholo, ek dum!' (This is the police. Open this door immediately!)

Things happened quickly after that. The man in charge pointed to the window and muttered something to Ahrlberg who made a back for him to hop on to and then spring for the window. I yelled in Hindi that they were escaping, but Yonni put a stop to that by kicking me in the mouth before following close on the heels of Ahrlberg who was second through the bolt-hole. The door was good, hefty and solid, as doors, interior as well as exterior, always are in India, and the law wasn't making much headway on it in spite of a lot of noise. I managed to struggle to my knees, then my feet, and bird-hop across to it and somehow turn and work the rough iron bolt loose with my hands, which were tied behind me. The door burst open and Safaraz came through with a rush. But there were no police.

He cut me loose in a matter of seconds and I dashed for the window and he gave me a bunk-up. It opened on to a flat roof, and across a narrow alley there was another flat roof— and then another and another—maybe ten square miles of them—none of them with chimneys, but all with shanty penthouses, chicken and goat pens and piles of miscellaneous junk, and, as everywhere else in Calcutta with its highest square-mile density in the world, people. Just thousands and thousands of people. I didn't even start to give chase. It was hopeless. I restrained Safaraz from mounting a one-man flying column, and we climbed back into the room.

'How did you know I was here?' I asked. Then as I saw,

and heard, him take a deep breath, I realized that this was going to take some considerable time. It always does when Safaraz starts telling one how clever he is. 'Tell me as we go along,' I told him, 'and make it short.'

'As short as a rooster's nuptials, sahib,' he promised. 'Oh, off and away with alacrity. Yes, sahib—I was tidying the sahib's room when he left, as he will no doubt remember—and thinking, by the way, it is time he ordered some new shirts and——'

'Get on with it, for the sake of Allah the Compassionate.' I begged of him.

'I am doing so, sahib. I happened to be glancing out of the window when I saw the sahib in the road beneath, surrounded by beggars. He crossed the tram-tracks, as he again will no doubt recall, and passed close to a group of goras and dirty miss-sahibs, who called out to him, although at that distance, due to the noise of the trams and the people beneath, I could not hear the actual words, but I have no reason to believe that they were anything but ribald, because all then started to laugh like hyenas—but the sahib, with his customary dignity treated them with contempt and walked on, and——'

It took a full fifteen minutes, but at the end of it I learned that Safaraz had seen Ahrlberg rise from under a tree across the tracks from where he had obviously been watching the door of the Grand, and slip on to my trail. He, Safaraz, was out of the hotel and after us much quicker than it took him to tell it. He saw us talking together, then kept us in sight back to Chowringhee, but the taxi caught him short and all he could do was to memorize its number and wait for it to return to the rank, which, fortunately for me, it apparently did without too much delay. It took Safaraz, who was not carrying any money but did have his Khyber knife under his cummerbund, a further three minutes to terrorize the driver into taking him to where he had dropped us, and divulging the address we had given him and he had arrived on the scene in time to hear me roaring with pain when Yonni had applied his restorative. He did not know how many there were in the room or whether or not they were armed, so he used the police stratagem.

'Son of Suliman,' I called him, and he looked modest which comes as easy to him as fine needlework does to a camel. Suliman, from the Koran, is one and the same as Solomon, from the Bible.

We arrived back at the Grand—and Pewsey Darrell was in her usual place. I caught her eye and gestured to her to follow me, and she was on my heels as we got to the door of my room. Safaraz drifted off, looking a model of diplomacy.

She had obviously made some effort to clean herself up, because she was wearing a new cotton sari, and her hair had been washed. But I was puzzled by her general demeanour. For a girl who had gone in to bat for her wretched boy-friend as she had, she was singularly unmoved by his death. And then it suddenly came to me. She quite obviously didn't know.

She grinned at me impudently and said, 'Hallo. Changed your mind, have you? Fine.' She pirouetted in the sari. 'I spent nine of your rupees on this—and another on a bath at the YWCA. Oh, God—it was gorgeous. A tub *full* of scalding water and a huge lump of carbolic soap. I looked like a lobster when I climbed out.'

I said, 'Sit down. Have you heard anything of Threlfall?'

'Not a blind word,' she said, and her face clouded. 'Either he's on one hell of a jag, or he's sick again. Have *you* heard anything?'

'Yes—I've heard,' I said. 'I'm sorry, Pewsey—I'm afraid I've got bad news for you.'

She looked at me and I could see that she was making a fight to keep on top of things.

'Go on,' she whispered. 'You—mean—he's dead?' I nodded. 'How?' she asked.

'He was shot.'

I poured her a whisky but she shook her head. She was back in some sort of control now.

'Did you have anything to do with it?' she asked dully.

'No.'

'The police?'

'Nor the police. Both the police and I would like to know who *did* do it. Perhaps you could help.'

'I could make a couple of inspired guesses.'

'Such as?'

'Horton—or one of his bloody Six.'

She broke then, and it was terrible to watch. To these kids, emotion, except for the ritualistic ecstasy of the pop rave or the phony anger of the 'demo', is something indecent—worse, it's square. This was terrible because it was silent. She just sat with her face screwed up as if she were having a limb amputated. I left her alone and walked to the window and looked out across the Maidan. After a time she said, 'All right. Sorry about that.' I nodded at the whisky, and she took a small sip and asked me for a cigarette.

'You mentioned Horton,' I said as I held a match for her. 'Can you describe him to me?'

'Dark—very bushy eyebrows, and his nose—sort of—well, thickened at the top and—you know—like a boxer's. He used to be a boxer once—not up to much, but——'

'That's fine,' I said, because she had fingered the top boy in that room with absolute accuracy. 'Now what about this Six of his? Did *he* tell you about that?'

'Oh, God no. Worse than my old man used to be about the Masons. Cut your throat if you breathe a word, and all that sort of thing.'

'Then where did you hear about it?'

'From Ronnie——'

'He was one of the Six?'

'Not properly. He just carried for them. Nobody who was on the stuff ever was a full member of a Six.'

'I see. Could you tell me the names of any of the people who were?'

'Some of them. There was an American called Ashley something or other——'

'Ahrlberg?'

'Right—and a Swede called Yonnie——'

'Yes.'

'And an Australian they used to call Tumba-bloody-Rumba. That's all I know for certain. Others used to come and go— They could have been in the Six or not—I wouldn't be knowing.'

'What did they do, Pewsey? I mean, what was their object —their—their——?'

'Their raison d'être?' said this surprising girl. 'Oh—watching the carriers. They have to be organized—two or three people watching one—the one who is actually carrying at the time—and dealing with them if they ever slipped up, or stole any of the junk or gold.'

'How does gold come into it?'

She looked at me in some surprise. 'Well, that's the whole thing. They carry junk north and gold, that pays for the junk, south. I thought everybody knew that. All the *hippies* know it.'

I said, 'Let's be honest for once. I didn't know that bit of it. Thanks.'

'Don't mention it,' she said dryly. 'I never thought the fuzz would ever turn me into a stool pigeon.'

'I'm not the fuzz—and you're not a stool pigeon. A stool pigeon is one of *them* who gives information to the law "for purposes of monetary reward or other favourable consideration". Have I promised you anything?'

'No—you paid in advance. Twenty rupees—and you've treated me decently and made me feel human again. I'm afraid I'm a sucker for that.'

'You're under no obligation for either. Listen to me, Pewsey. I have no particular grouch against a youngster just because he wears his hair long, grows whiskers, doesn't wash and scrounges for a living instead of working. That's his affair, and as long as he doesn't interfere with my way of life, I haven't the slightest desire to interfere with his. All right?' She nodded, and I went on, 'Now the majority of those weirdies out there in Chowringhee, and in a line stretching right back to London, are just that. Feckless, idle bums, or, in some cases, phony mystics—both equally harmless. Do you agree?' Again she nodded. 'But according to what you, yourself, have told me, some of them are being used by some pretty powerful forces higher up—or am I talking through my hat?'

'You're dead right. The Barons.'

'The what?'

'That's what the boys call them—The Barons.'

'Is that so? Interesting. Have you ever seen any of them?'

'You've got to be joking. Of course I haven't seen any of them. I don't know anybody who has.'

'Any more inspired guesses?'

'Not a one. You sometimes hear people talking about them, in whispers, but that's all. Ronnie had a couple of theories——'

'I'd like to hear them.'

'Two mobs—one Indian, one Italian. Both organized along the same lines—the Six system. Down at floor level they get mixed up—and some of them don't even know which crowd they're working for. All sorts of things go on—hijackings, murders—ugh.'

'Had he any idea which of them Horton was working for?'

'It varied—Ronnie's guess I mean. Sometimes he thought Horton was "Curry and Rice"—other times "Spaghett".'

'Is that how they're known?'

'I don't know. That's how Ronnie used to refer to them when he discussed it with me, which wasn't very often.'

'I see.'

'I'm not being very helpful, am I?' she said.

'Pewsey,' I said, and meant it, 'you've given me the only

leads I've had so far. Damn it all, girl, add them up for yourself—the carriers are junkies——'

'Most—not all.'

'Good. The Sixes are the traffic police——'

'Only they don't hand out just tickets——'

'So we've seen. There are two crowds——'

'Or so Ronnie thought——'

'Which he labelled "Curry and Rice" and "Spaghett".'

'Correct.'

'The top people are known as "Barons". Did they differentiate between "Curry and Rice" and "Spaghett" Barons?'

'I've no idea. You've got to remember that Ronnie and I talked about it very little between ourselves. Some of it I've picked up listening to the boys talking at night round the fire —when they thought there weren't any Six-men about.'

'The Six-men would pipe them down, would they?'

'I'm pretty damned certain of that, although I've only ever seen it actually working once.'

'When was that?'

'On the way out—just north of Lahore. We camped for a few days at the side of the road—Horton, Ronnie, the other two girls and me. A couple of other parties joined us, one coming south, the other going north. About ten in each— quite a crowd together. Horton didn't like the others being there, but there was nothing he could do about it. Ronnie asked him why he didn't move and he said he couldn't as we were waiting for somebody—then they turned up on a native bus—Yonnie and Tumba-bloody-Rumba. That was the first time Ronnie and I met them. It was too late to move on that night—and there was a party—lots of pot and some hard stuff —most of them stoned out of their skulls. One of the boys in the party going north started to shoot off his mouth about the Barons. He said he knew a couple of journalists in London and he was going to sell them one hell of a story. I had dropped out of the party by this time and I'd dragged my sleeping bag some distance away. These two, Tumba and Yonnie, who don't use anything, came out from the firelight and stood quite close. They didn't realize I was there. Yonnie said, "Yes —what do you want?" and Tumba said, "We've got to shut that drongo up." Yonnie said, "What drongo?" and Tumba said, "The one who was beefing about stories to the papers, you bloody fool. Who else?" "How do we do it?" Yonnie asked. "That mob won't be sleeping before daylight." "I'll get next to him and tell him I've got a couple of ounces to sell cheap—and lead him off towards the truck——". They moved away then and I didn't hear any more—but next day the boy had vanished. His party searched all around—it's open country there—just the road running across flat fields. We even helped them. There's a big river nearby, the Chenab I think they call it, and everybody thought he must have wandered off and fallen in—and they all agreed to say nothing, in case there was trouble with the police. But I know damn well what happened to him.'

She finished with a shudder.

I said, 'Has it occurred to you that you might be in danger yourself?'

'Why me?' she asked. 'I haven't done anything to the bastard, much as I'd like to.'

'Two very good reasons,' I told her. 'One, you were Threlfall's girl-friend, so whatever they had against him might well have rubbed off on to you. Two, they've had a couple of goes at me—the second only an hour ago, and I know they've had me under observation for some time. That being so, they'll know you've been in here with me for long periods. They'll put two and two together——'

'And it will add up to a screwing session—nothing unusual in that,' she shrugged.

'I wouldn't bet on it,' I said. 'Anyhow, I'm afraid Calcutta is out for you from now on.'

'I'm not in love with the ghastly dump, but I'm not giving

Horton the satisfaction of driving me out of it——' And she really looked as if she meant it. I sighed inwardly.

'Pewsey, listen to me,' I said firmly. 'I happen to know that the police are going to pick you up and deport you to England.'

'What have *I* done?'

'Legally quite enough to get yourself on the sling-out list. The law books call it "wandering abroad without fixed abode or visible means of support".'

'Yes, but why me in particular? That applies to every hippy in India.'

'Because they, too, know of your connection with Threlfall, and they think you might be in danger. They don't like European murders—they've got more than enough of their own.'

'I'm not going back on a deportation order——'

'If you're sensible you won't have to. I'll be able to get you an air ticket from the High Commissioner.'

She looked mutinous for some minutes, then she caved in. In actual fact it was more than obvious that all she wanted was to shake the dust of the place from her feet, but she had to put up a show of resistance first.

I said, 'Good, then that's settled. You had better stay here until plane time. I'll fix a room for you——'

'What do I use for money?' she asked.

'It will be on the house.'

'Which means that you'll be paying for it? No thanks.'

'Why? Do you think I'd be round to collect the rent?'

'I know perfectly well that you wouldn't. That being so, I don't want any more bloody charity from you.'

'I don't follow the logic of that,' I said. 'But calm yourself —it's on the poor old British taxpayer. All right, make yourself comfortable here. I'm going down to the desk, then along to the High Commissioner's office. I should be back within the hour. Have you had any breakfast?'

'Yes—Bengal caviar—a bowl of rice.'

'I'll send you some up. Bacon and eggs, toast, coffee and orange juice all right?'

'Satan you bastard—get thee behind me,' she said.

I went out, and once again it happened. I met Bayliss in the doorway. I tried to close the door but I couldn't short of actually slamming it in his face. He looked past me at the girl and shrugged. I said, 'Come on—I'll tell you all about it as we go down.'

'No need,' he said. 'My dad told me about the birds and the bees on my fourteenth birthday—unless, of course, it's different in India.'

'Funny man,' I snarled. 'That happened to be Threlfall's girl.'

'Hiring her out, is he? The dirty little get.'

'He's dead—like Hallaby—shot through the head.'

'Oh, Christ,' he said. 'De mortuis nil nisi bonum—even when speaking of villains. Poor little bastard.'

'The local police think they might have a go at her, and I've been asked to fix up an air ticket at the High Commissioner's Office.'

'I'd like to have a talk with her before she goes,' he said. 'She may be able to put us on to a thing or two about Threlfall's associates. Any chance of an arrest yet?'

'None so far—but we've got a few leads,' I told him, then, because I didn't want him to go crashing into my room and upsetting the girl further while I was away, I added, 'Would you like to walk down to the H.C.'s place with me, and I'll give you a rundown on things so far.'

He nodded and I stopped at the desk and booked another room on my floor for the girl, then I rang through to the servants' quarters for Safaraz and told him not to go to my room for the next hour, much to his mystification—and finally I sent a late breakfast up to her.

But I hit a snag at the High Commissioner's office. There is one man there who is authorized to grant without question any request I make while actually working for the Gaffer—but only one man. And, naturally, he had to be on leave and wasn't due back for fourteen days. It wasn't the damnedest bit of use trying to work the oracle with anybody else there because, officially, I have no standing whatsoever. I have, of course, a link back to the Gaffer, but it is for use only in extreme operational necessity—and it involves elaborate coding. I could imagine his reaction if he was dragged out of bed at three in the morning to work with the cipher templates for a couple of hours on a request for an immediate air passage to London for a flower floosie who wished to avoid the embarrassment of deportation—not to mention the motives he'd impute to me.

I rejoined Bayliss in the H.C.'s compound, swearing softly. He asked if he could help through police channels back home, and I thanked him nicely.

'My pleasure,' he said. 'Three things in life that are very hard to get rid of—mothers-in-law, stray cats and obsolete bits of crumpet.' The older they get the dirtier their minds.

We went back to the hotel then. We'd only been away a little over half an hour—but it had been more than enough for them.

Chapter Ten

THE ROOM looked as if it had been hit by a China Sea typhoon—furniture was overturned, a window broken and coffee, eggs, toast and broken crockery littered the floor.

Bayliss grunted, 'This is getting monotonous. Where's the body?'

I went over to the bathroom door. It was locked on the other side. I kicked it and Pewsey yelled, 'I'm warning you, you bloody swine, I've got a razor here.'

'Put it down and come out,' I told her, and she opened the door the merest crack and peeped through, then, assured, she emerged.

'What happened?' I asked.

'Tumba-bloody-Rumba came up,' she explained. 'He told me it was all codswallop about Ronnie being dead, and that he was in the Methodist Mission Hospital, and he wanted to take me there. I said I'd go down later and he got tough and tried to manhandle me. I got away and hopped into the bathroom.' She looked around. 'I'm sorry about all this. They won't make you pay for it, will they?'

'How long ago was this?'

'Ten minutes—quarter of an hour—the racket brought a couple of servants along and he must have beat it.' She looked at Bayliss. 'Who's this?' she asked.

I caught Bayliss's eye, and he nodded, so I introduced him by rank and name and she pretended to look impressed.

'The highest I've ever been moved on by is a sergeant,' she said. 'I never thought little me would be hobnobbing with the Bigpigs like this.'

'Ah, just goes to show you,' said Bayliss profoundly. 'Tumba-bloody-Rumba, eh? Otherwise known as The Grin—said to have been christened William Theophilus Hasseltine. A pity the officiating clergyman didn't drown him in the font. Ever have any professional dealings with him?'

She went scarlet. 'No,' she snapped. '*I'm* not a professional, whatever he might have been.'

'A ponce,' Bayliss explained to me. 'He's been done three times in London for living on the immoral earnings of a string of women. Used to kick the daylights out of them if the revenue ever dropped off.' He turned back to Pewsey. 'Any other names you can come up with?'

'No. What do you think I am? A copper's nark or something?' She seemed thoroughly put out.

'Come on, Pewsey,' I said. 'You don't owe these lugs anything. Arhlberg, Yonni the Swede—any more? It will all help.'

'Help who?' she asked. 'Not me. I've got to live in London when I go back. How long do you think I'd last if word got round that I'd been snouting?'

'I never disclosed a source of information in my life,' Bayliss assured her.

'Who'd trust one of you blokes,' she said scornfully. 'I don't mind talking to Mr Rees—but not to a Yard stiff.'

'You wound me,' said Bayliss, and winked at me. 'All right, Pewsey——'

'Miss Darrell to you.'

'Miss Darrell. Ahrlberg?—Yonni? No, not on my books—but thank you for Tumba. I didn't know he was out here. And I understand you've had a bit of bother with Horton, so Mr Rees tells me.'

'Yes—but I didn't know Mr Rees was going to tell *you*——'

'Now look here, Miss Darrell,' I began.

'That's all right. *You* can call me Pewsey,' she said, and Bayliss winked at me again—archly.

'You say you've got to live in London—well, the more of these people caught and put where they belong, the safer it's going to be for you. You can see what you're up against.' I might have got somewhere, but then Bayliss butted in.

'They think you've grassed on them already,' he said. 'Finger 'em, girl, and give yourself a chance—before they stick a nasty one on you.' He looked around the room. 'You don't think this bugger was playing "catch-me-kiss-me", do you?'

'I don't know any more names,' she said sulkily.

'Well, anything else of interest?' he urged. 'Take pushers, for instance.'

'What about them?'

'Well, it would help us considerably if you could identify out here anybody you knew for certain to be in the junk business at home. See what I mean?'

'No.'

'Pushers——!' he began, explosively.

'Don't shout,' she said coolly. 'Pushers—they've got to live like anybody else I suppose——'

'You don't mean to tell me that you're on their side?' I said angrily.

'I'm not on anyone's side—pushers *or* pigs,' she shrugged.

'Just watch it with the "pigs",' Bayliss growled.

'Why? You've got no authority this far from Piccadilly.' She was over her temper now and was deliberately needling him.

'Which means you've got no protection either,' he said. 'You're heading for a clout over the ear'ole, my girl.'

'You just try it, Bigpig,' she warned. 'I'm not a sick junkie to be pushed around by anybody who just happens to be feeling strong. Yes—I know who you are now. It was you who put the frighteners on Ronnie Threlfall—so that he panicked and ran off, and they killed him and——' She stopped and gulped and I realized that all that had gone before was the merest camouflage for the poor little devil's real feelings. I signed to Bayliss to get out, and he winked again and went. Unfortunately she saw this exchange because when I said, 'Sorry about that, Pewsey,' she almost spat, and told me to get stuffed.

'What have I done?' I asked, really taken aback, because it was such a complete reversal of her previous reaction.

'I've been wet-and-dried before,' she said. 'Think I don't recognize it?' And a great light dawned upon me. Have you ever seen one of those gimmicky barometer things they give away as prizes in fairground shooting galleries—in the form of a cottage with two doors? When it's going to rain, the farmer comes out of one. When sunshine is predicted, he backs indoors and his wife comes out. They are called Wet'n'Dries, and the term is also applied to one of the cruder techniques in interrogation. There are two men on the job—an absolute stinker and a decent, sympathetic type. The former shouts, bullies, threatens and finally storms out of the cell with promises of worse to come at the next session unless the client has seen the error of his ways in the meantime. Then the nice bloke comes in—'Christ, I'm sorry about all that. He's a bastard. I don't approve of these methods myself, but unfortunately there's nothing I can do about it. Have a cigarette'—etc. The client, unless he's been very thoroughly trained in contra-interrogation, often falls for it out of sheer gratitude, and tells all.

I said, 'Well, if you really think you're getting the treatment, there's nothing more I can say.' I tossed the key of her room on to the table. 'That's yours—number twenty-five. I'm afraid your flight to London will take a few days to arrange. You'll have to stay in your room the whole time. Keep your door locked and don't open to anybody unless Mr Bayliss or I are there to vouch for them. Good-bye and good luck.'

I opened the door for her but she decided to sit down and weep then. I closed the door again, and stood looking at her in complete exasperation.

'What the devil's the matter *now*?' I demanded.

'It's not you I've got a hate on,' she sniffed. 'It's that bloody old fuzz.'

'It's me you accused of wet-and-drying.'

'But I didn't mean it.'

'Then why say it?'

'I don't know—I was feeling lousy about poor old Ronnie. I don't have to go to that other room do I?'

'You can't stay here.'

'Why—you queer or something?'

'No, but nymphos jar me.' I said it deliberately to jar *her*, and it did.

'I'm not a nympho!' she screamed.

'Then stop behaving like one,' I told her. 'One minute you're going all dewy-eyed over "poor old Ronnie", the next, you're trying to crawl into the sack with me. I prefer to pick my own bedmates.'

'Honestly,' she said earnestly, 'I wouldn't get in your way. It's just that I'm dead scared of being on my own. You hadn't been gone a few minutes before that Tumba-bloody-Rumba arrived—and I tell you, he meant business.' She shuddered. 'You heard what the pig called him—The Grin. He's got this fixed smile when he's going to—to—do something to somebody —and yet, at the same time, his face and eyes are dead. He's a nutter—not a junkie—I could understand that—but a nutter —ugh!'

'Don't worry,' I said. 'The room is just down the corridor and I can keep an eye on you.'

'But you're not here all the time,' she insisted. 'Don't you understand? There must be dozens of them—inside this place and out—just watching. I know the way they work.'

'Then why the hell don't you come clean to Bayliss?' I said, really angrily. 'You may not like pigs, as you call them, but if you want people like The Grin off your back you've got to co-operate.'

She gestured hopelessly. 'I've been anti-pig all my life. You can't just change overnight.'

'But *why* are you anti-pig? I mean, have you, yourself, any real reason for it—other than the fact that you've been running around with a bunch of no-good bums?'

'Four bloody good reasons,' she said. 'Probation, Approved

School, Junior Delinquents' Detention Centre and Borstal. I only need prison to make it a full house.'

'Whose fault is that? *You* must have made the choice originally.'

'Ah, what the hell's the use?' she said. 'If I told you all about it you'd think I was pulling a hard luck story. You're all the same, you mob—the magistrates, probation officers, the do-gooding old cows that hang round the juvenile courts and the toffee-nosed bitches that run the Centres. Did I say "bitches"? Correction—butches—because that's what most of them are. There's You and Us. Well, bugger you, Rees—I'm going back to Us. I was a fool ever to think of coming over to You.'

She made for the door. 'Take your key,' I told her.

'Stuff it,' she shot at me over her shoulder and went out. I followed her and grabbed her by the arm.

'Come back, you little fool,' I said, shaking her, and I was so angry that I didn't see Bayliss leaning against the wall a few yards down from my door. But she did, the little devil, because she drew herself up and said, 'Oo, I'm not a girl like that, Mr Rees. Besides, you're old enough to be my father.'

That was too much. I gave her a shove that sent her spinning down the corridor and she lost her footing and sat flat on her backside. Bayliss followed me back into the room. 'Trying to jack the price up?' he asked innocently.

'Listen, Bayliss,' I told him. 'Just one more heavy-footed cop's witticism from you and I'll put *you* on your arse outside also.'

He sighed. 'How I'd love you to come to London for a little holiday when all this is over, Mr Rees. I'd have you inside the day you arrived.'

'Actually I was trying to talk her into co-operating with you, and she accused me of wet-and-drying.'

'In those words?'

'Yes.'

'Um—so she's got a record too, has she?'

'The lot, less prison.'

'I wish I'd known it. I wouldn't have been so polite.'

'Anyhow, she's refused protection and says she's going back to her pals—and we both know she's in danger.'

'Can't you get her pulled in?'

'I didn't want to if I could help it, but I have no option now.' I picked up the telephone and got through to headquarters, and for once Mukherjee was in his office.

'I'm sorry, Shyam,' I said, 'but that air passage is likely to be delayed, so I think the law had better take its course.'

'I'll see to it,' he promised.

'She's just left here,' I went on, 'so she should be somewhere in Chowringhee——'

'Jawaharlal Nehru Road, you out-of-date Imperialist,' he kidded. 'All right, I'll send a couple of women officers along and you can point her out.'

'I'd rather not figure in it personally,' I said anxiously.

'But Idwal, how else do we do it? There are lots of lady hippies in Calcutta—and you people all look alike to my people. They wouldn't know her from a bar of soap.'

And it was then that I had my bright idea. 'One of the Scotland Yard officers is with me at the moment,' I said. 'If you don't mind, I'll send him with them.'

'Just so as he realizes that he has no official standing,' Mukherjee said firmly.

'I promise you that. Thanks, Shyam.' I hung up, and Bayliss, who had been straining his ears to catch the other side of the conversation, said, 'Christ! Whore-frosting at my seniority. They'll never believe it back home.'

They came round promptly and I went down with Bayliss to meet them in the lobby—two capable-looking Hindu girls from the Child Prostitution Control desk, who a few short years before would have had no career outside purdah.

'Do they speak English?' Bayliss asked.

'We'll do our best,' the elder said, straightfaced.

I left them questioning the hall porter, and went back to my room to compose a report to the Gaffer, although Lord knows I had little enough to tell him. Hallaby dead and one of the Yard men beaten up on our side, with a few of theirs off the board also, but not a step forward in our investigations. It made pretty arid reading *en claire* and even worse when it was compressed and pruned for coding. I winced as I thought of his probable answer.

Bayliss came back after a couple of hours, growling and cursing.

'Not a sign of the little cow,' he said. 'Tramped our goddam feet off up and down this street in front and over that king-sized prairie thing opposite. Loads of hippies around, but she's not one of them.'

'Did you ask any of them if they'd seen her?'

'I'm not *that* dumb. Two local women cops and a pig from Piccadilly asking one hippy if he'd seen another? You must be joking. You wouldn't be having a couple of beers on ice anywhere, would you? I'm sweating like a June bride.'

'Did the hall porter remember seeing her go out?'

'Yes—she turned left and some bloke came up and spoke to her, and they went off together.' He grinned impishly. 'The hall porter wanted to know if he could get you another one in her place—very nice, very clean and not too expensive, he said.'

I almost cancelled the beers that I had ordered up from the bar.

She'd turn up again, I told myself, but later on, when Bayliss had taken his aching feet off to soak them in a hot bath, I started to work things out. She never slept in ashrams, she had told me, because they were generally lousy—literally—and the same thing went for the Maidan, where the dust was alive with fleas. No, the portico outside the hotel was her favourite spot, even when Threlfall used to wander off on his own. That's where she'd come again eventually. I went down on the off chance that she might have returned, but a couple of male flower children were caterwauling folk songs to the plunking of an out-of-tune guitar in her usual corner. I saw the hall porter and tore a ten-rupee note in two, giving him one half and the promise of the other if he let me know as soon as she got back.

But she still hadn't arrived when I went down the following morning, and now I started to worry. There was an old ruined serai out on the Barrackpore road that hippy vehicles always made for on arrival in the city. It was here that battered mini-vans and beat-up Land-Rovers used to be bought and sold and cannibalized, and it was from here that the return convoys used to set out. Blankets, heavy clothing and blackened cooking utensils changed hands here, and it had become an unofficial post office. It was a two-way funnel, in other words, that they all had to pass through. I changed into local clothes and went out there with Safaraz, to find that nothing had left for the north in the last seven days, and that nothing was now likely to until after the monsoon, because bridges along the frontier had not been rebuilt since the war ended, and the flooded rivers were already impassable. So that bolt-hole was denied to her. The only way out was by air—highly unlikely in the absence of a ticket from the HC—or by train to Bombay from whence she could fly on, if she had the funds, or go by infrequent ship via the Cape.

No, I told myself, she was still in Calcutta—and as soon as I laid eyes on her I would have her locked up until she could be shipped out in safety. What happened to her in London was entirely her business, and that of Scotland Yard—at least *I* would be off the hook. Yes, that's what I told myself—and also Bayliss and the battered Thorlby who was now sitting up in his hospital bed looking alternately savage and sorry for himself, according to how badly his fractured skull was hurting him.

'Unless she's been rubbed out already,' Bayliss said, putting into words that which, deep down, I was fearing.

'I don't think so,' I said.

'Why not?'

'They wouldn't risk it.'

'They risked Hallaby—and this bloke here.' He jerked his head at Thorlby. 'He'd be dead too if he didn't have a reinforced concrete skull.'

'Maybe—but that was more or less a natural reaction. They stumbled on their headquarters in the dark, and got laced up by the sentries. Wouldn't you read it that way, Thorlby?'

'Dunno,' he grunted. 'All I want is to get out of this nigger dump and get back to London—and if the top brass don't like it, they can upward shove their job asswise. That's me.'

'Threlfall?' said Bayliss.

'Threlfall was one of their own.'

'So's the bird.'

'Yes—but they know that you Yard men and I are interested in her——'

'*You* are. I never got the chance.'

'Cut out the clowning. They know we have a professional interest in her and that there would be one hell of a stink if anything happened to her.'

'She's disappeared, and if anybody, other than you I mean, has been raising a stink about it, I certainly haven't heard. Kee-rist! There's more stink kicked up at home over a kid who disappears for a few hours on his way to school than there is here for half a dozen murders in one night.'

'Anyhow, I don't think they've done anything to her.'

'You *hope* not.'

'Oh, get stuffed,' I told him, and heard him chuckling as I left the ward.

I went round to see Mukherjee then, and he was rather uptight about things, because he was still being ridden into the ground over Hallaby and the assault on Thorlby.

'And then you made me lay off the girl for twenty-four hours, and now she's disappeared. My God, Idwal, if anything has happened to her and it leaks out, my job is not worth a Pathan's chance of going to heaven.'

'Your people didn't bother much about Threlfall's murder,' I said. 'Why would the girl's disappearance worry them?'

'The Press would whip it up. White slave traffic—wicked rajahs buying innocent virgins, and all that sort of thing. Huh —poor bloody rajahs can't keep themselves in socks nowadays, let alone virgins.' And then he was called over the intercom, and he came back after a couple of minutes, looking relieved.

'The policewomen have got her down below now,' he told me. We went down to the charge-room but it wasn't Pewsey. It was a tall and very dirty girl in tight jeans, swearing like a Liverpool fireman and threatening the entire Indian law enforcement establishment with the full consequences of her father's wrath—daddy apparently being a political life peer of progressively liberal views, prepared to fight to the death for his daughter's right to smoke pot and copulate where the hell she pleased, from Soho to the pavements of Calcutta.

I gave it up and went back to the hotel, and there was a long signal in from the Gaffer which took me an equally long time to decode—and it was just what I expected, and more— finishing up with a personal message from the passport authorities to the effect that my application was being considered and a further communication 'would emanate in due course'—which in our jargon means a bloody long time, if ever.

So I wasn't feeling so good when the telephone woke me in the early hours, and a weary Mukherjee told me that they'd picked her up off Baghbazar—dead.

Chapter Eleven

I COLLECTED BAYLISS on the way down as I realized that there would be an inquest on this one, if only because of the fact that she had already been registered as a missing person, and they wouldn't be able to hush it up like the others. That being the case, somebody would have to give formal evidence of identity, and I didn't want it to be me.

Mukherjee picked us up in a squad car at the front door. 'Any details?' I asked.

'Sheer chance,' he answered. 'She fell or jumped from a car on the Grand Trunk Road, the other side of the river just after midnight. A foot-constable saw it happen and went up to her. She was alive then, but badly hurt. He went to find a telephone, and that took some time, and when he returned to the spot she had vanished. Unfortunately he wasn't able to get the number or description of the car. All he realized was that she was a European and that there had been an order round to all stations to look for an English girl. When the mobiles got there with proper lights they found drag marks and bloodstains from the road to the river, only a few yards away at that point. I think they came back after the policeman was off the scene, and dumped her. A water police boat fished her out two hours later, a couple of miles downstream. She was dead this time.'

'You're sure about this one?' I asked. 'The women police made a mistake last time.'

'No mistake. She has a tattoo on—' he coughed 'on the upper part of her thigh—"Pewsey—Ronnie—True Love". I did not know European women did that.'

'Borstal-bait, gaolbirds and whores only,' Bayliss said, and for some totally illogical reason I could have driven my fist into his face.

126

We rode the rest of the way to the morgue in silence. It is in a dirty side street in the shadow of the Howrah Bridge. A young Parsee doctor was washing at a sink in a corner of the gloomy, slab-lined chamber that was lit by a solitary low-powered bulb. He nodded to Mukherjee and went over to a muslin-covered form on a table under the light. He drew the sheet back. Both eyes were bruised and blackened and one side of her mouth was badly cut, but for all that she looked strangely at peace. A clean white sari covered her, her damp hair had been combed and arranged, and a rosary was twined round her crossed hands.

'Who did all this?' I asked.

'The women police officers,' the doctor told me. 'They were sorry because she was very young and a long way from her home. They were also worried about the cross and beads, not knowing if she was a Catholic or not. They got them from the Lost Property Office next door. Is it all right please?'

'It's all right,' I said, and marvelled inwardly that people with as much on their own plates and surrounded by death as are the Calcutta Police, could find time to afford this pathetic bit of human flotsam these last small courtesies.

Mukherjee was filling in an official form. 'Cause of death?' he asked. 'Drowning?'

'Not drowning,' the doctor said. 'No water in the lungs.'

'Then what?'

'Severe beating first. Those injuries to the face and—' he turned the sari down, '—marks on throat were not caused by fall from the car. Shock and distress would lower the vitality so that the fall and then the immersion in the river would precipitate death rather than directly cause it, particularly with condition already lowered by malnutrition as I think this girl's was.'

'So—murder?' said Mukherjee.

'I would say so.' The doctor turned to me. 'And if you, sir, will excuse vulgar and intemperate language, I hope Mr

Mukherjee catches the bastards and, after fair trial, hangs the bloody lot.'

'So do I,' said Bayliss, surprisingly, 'because that will mean doing 'em out here and not back home where they'd get a couple of years' suspended sentence and something out of the poor box.'

We came out into the darkness.

'Which direction was the car going, Shyam?' I asked.

'North.'

'Him—hippies going north? Not many of them now as they're afraid the monsoon will catch them. Can you stop and check every carload of Europeans?'

'The order has already gone out. They've got three hours' start but we can still stop them this side of the Pakistan border.'

'How far does your authority run?' I asked him.

'Officially only in the Calcutta area, but there won't be any difficulty with the other Forces,' he told me.

'Which are they?'

'West Bengal, Bihar and Uttar Pradesh.'

'What about the Punjab?'

'I'm hoping we will have got them before they get that far, but if they do manage to slip through, the Punjab Frontier Force will co-operate. No sweat.'

'I know three possibles who might have done this, Shyam.'

'Good. Then you won't mind going north with me to identify any likely fish we get in the net?'

'I'm entirely at your service—but it might be a good idea to have a look round town first, just in case one or more of them are still hanging about.'

Mukherjee nodded gravely. 'A very good idea indeed, Idwal,' he said. 'The only disadvantage being that I don't know who the hell we would be looking for.'

'I do,' I said.

'Will you do the looking then?'

'Sure—but I'd like to clear things first. I have no authority to make an arrest——'

'The freedom of the city,' Mukherjee said. 'If you see any-body, anybody at all, you think I ought to have a little talk to, pull him in, Idwal. I'll have word sent round to every—what is it you call police stations in England——?'

'Nicks,' said Bayliss.

'Thank you—every nick in Calcutta to co-operate.' He bowed towards Bayliss, 'and the same courtesy is extended to you, my dear colleague.'

'Thank *you*,' said Bayliss, 'but what about the politicians?'

'*Something* the politicians,' said Mukherjee succinctly.

'In spades, doubled,' Bayliss agreed. 'From Delhi to Down-ing Street.'

It is a cardinal rule in this business that personal involve-ment, sentiment or, in fact, any emotion at all is to be kept out of things. Anger and hatred particularly are luxuries one just cannot afford. They are energy-consuming and they cloud the judgement. It is all a matter of self-discipline, I remember telling myself as we drove back to the hotel. But somehow it wasn't working. I was in a cold, murderous rage. I didn't want to talk and I certainly didn't want to listen to Bayliss and Mukherjee exchanging professional chit-chat, so I told them that I had to see somebody and I got out in Dalhousie Square and walked the rest of the distance. But the respite wasn't for long, because Bayliss was waiting for me in my room when I arrived, trying to make conversation with Safaraz, without marked success. Safaraz doesn't speak English but he knows cops in any language and is as kindly disposed to them as a mongoose is to cobras.

Bayliss said, 'So you know what we're up against now.' There was an 'I told you so' note to it that enraged me still further.

'I already knew,' I said shortly.

'Did you? Well, I'll be honest. I certainly didn't know. I

thought Hallaby's case and this were quite apart—that it was something to do with you Intelligence people. I've never known hippies to go in for murder before. They haven't the guts.'

'It doesn't take guts to kick a girl to death.'

'Perhaps not, but it's still out of pattern.' He looked puzzled and worried. 'I didn't believe they'd shot Threlfall either. I'm not so sure now though.'

'I've been a bit closer to them than you,' I said spitefully.

'Out here maybe. But I've been dealing with the young punks for a long time. Sure, they're violent—but only in mobs —demos in Trafalgar Square and round the London School of Economics—sitting on their arses in the roadway—a dozen of them jumping on a bobby, that sort of thing. But guns— strangling—no. That's for the villains.'

'The ones I've seen *are* villains,' I said flatly. 'Horton, Ahrlberg, the Swede, Yonni——'

'Tumba-bloody-Rumba?'

'No, I haven't seen him.'

'He's about the only one I would have said had a criminal potential. I'm not talking about small-time drug-pushing, shop-lifting and other petty larceny. Real crime.'

'Is he a junkie?' I asked.

'No.'

'Nor are any of the others I've seen, other than Threlfall, of course. So there's your pattern for you. The real criminals using the junkies and the genuine, dyed-in-the-wool hippies. Do you agree?'

'Looks like it. But we're still only dealing with the tip of the iceberg. Who, in your opinion, would the Big Boy be?'

'I'm not a policeman.'

'So you keep on saying—but Christ, you know the form out here. I'm asking for your help.'

'I'm sorry—I wouldn't be knowing—not unless there was a political angle to it.'

'And there isn't to this——?'

'I didn't say that. In fact I know damn well that there is, or the Simon Legree I work for wouldn't be interested in it. What I am saying is that I can't see the link-up from where I'm standing at the moment. This is a case where one needs to get in on the ground floor and burrow upwards.'

'Sure,' he said gloomily, 'if only one knew which building the bloody ground floor was in.'

'I'm going to have a walk round town,' I told him, 'and I'm taking up Mukherjee's invitation. The first one of them that I see I'm pulling in.'

'Can I come with you?'

'I'm afraid not. I'm going in local clothes.'

'Couldn't I also?'

'I'm sorry, but I don't think so. You'd be in the soup if anybody spoke to you. Anyhow, I'd be obliged if you'd stay close to the telephone in case Mukherjee rings through with information about that car.'

He saw the sense of this and didn't attempt to argue further. I said to Safaraz after he had gone, 'Would you know any of the goras who have given us trouble, if you saw them again?'

'In a million faces, sahib,' he assured me. 'The two in the ashram——'

'Only the fair one still lives. The other was shot.'

'No loss to the world—then there was a dirty miss-sahib there——'

'Correct—and yesterday?'

'Three of them—the fair one from the ashram who the sahib met on the Maidan and two others——'

'Whose faces, unfortunately, you did not see, because they bolted through the window as you came in through the door.'

I was only testing him, and it worked. He looked at me reproachfully. 'Sahib, has living in this accursed city given me the eyes of an owl? One with the face of a pahlwan who fights in bazar boxing booths—the other also fair like the one from the ashram, on whom scent and a rose behind the ear would not have been out of place. All in Bengali clothes.' No, he hadn't become owl-eyed.

'Good,' I said. 'We go into the bazar, separately, to look for these people. Both as Punjabi Mussalmans.'

'Ha, sahib. And if we find them?'

'You will point them out, with discretion, to a policeman and ask that they be taken into custody and that Superintendent Mukherjee be informed immediately,' I told him, and he looked at me in sheer horror.

'I ask a policeman to do what I am more capable of doing myself? Sahib! Sahib!'

'I want no tamasha or disorderly conduct, Safaraz,' I told him. 'Do you understand?' He nodded glumly and went with the air of a man asked to jettison his family honour.

I grabbed a cup of coffee, then changed and went out into the morning heat. I had no set plan, so I made my way the full length of Chowringhee in the first instance, crossing from side to side and scanning the small groups of hippies who each morning sought the shade of the banyan trees that lined the edge of the Maidan and the tram tracks. They weren't there, any of them. I hadn't expected them to be, but the thing had become so insistent now that I had to exhaust every possibility before moving on to the next stage.

I finished up at the bottom of Chowringhee near the Anglican cathedral. There was the usual breadline of poor Anglo-Indians and native Christians in the compound of the Bishop's House, and I saw Barney Giffard arrive with the beat-up rickshaw in which he used to collect handouts of rice, stale vegetables or anything else he could add to the evil-looking but nourishing witch's brew he made up each day in the oil-drums. I waited at the gate until he came out, then I fell in beside him at the shafts. He didn't recognize me for a moment, and thanked me courteously in Hindi.

I said, 'Hallo, Barney. I need your help again.'

He peered at me, then scowled and told me to sod off.

'Three Indians and a poor devil of a hippy dead, and the word going round the bazar that I'm a police informer,' he said. 'I never thought you'd let me down like that, Idwal.'

'I'm sorry,' I told him. 'There are more dead now. That's what I'm trying to stop.'

'How about leaving it to the Lord? *You* don't seem to be doing so good,' he advised.

'You're damn right,' I said ruefully. 'But there is something somewhere about the Lord helping those who help themselves isn't there?'

'There is—and something more about fools rushing in where angels fear to tread. You made a proper balls-up of that one, lad.'

'Don't rub it in,' I begged. 'I *must* make contact with one of them though, Barney. Help me.'

'What can *I* do?'

'Four names—Horton, Ahrlberg, a Swede called Yonni and an Australian known as Tumba——'

'—Bloody-Rumba,' he supplied. 'All right, what about 'em?'

'Are they still in Calcutta, or are they heading north?'

'Ahrlberg was here two days ago—I saw him in Chittaranjan Avenue. I don't know about the others.'

'Where does Ahrlberg usually hang out?'

'Ask the sparrows and the crows. That ashram you buggered up was their usual stamping-ground. He may have moved into another. Sorry I can't help you.'

'Or won't?'

'Can't. It's no good being peevish, Idwal. I stand in a sort of special relationship to these bums. If they thought I was stooling on them—well, you see what I mean?'

'No, I don't see what you mean—and I don't see that putting me in touch with Ahrlberg could possibly be construed as stooling. I'm not a policeman.'

'No, but you are Authority—capital A—and as such *you*

133

stand in a special relationship to them too—that of a tiger to a bunch of woolly little innocent lambs—or that's how they see it—and I'd be a right sort of bastard if I delivered any of 'em to your red fangs and claws.'

'I'm sorry you weren't with me at three o'clock this morning,' I told him after a long silence. 'You'd have seen some red-fang-and-claw handiwork for yourself. Not mine. Theirs. A girl—seventeen, eighteen or thereabouts—beaten up, strangled and finally fished out of the Hooghli, dead. They thought, wrongly, that she'd been talking—to me. Of course I can understand your being a bit scared of what they might do to you if they thought you'd been doing the same thing. It perhaps wasn't fair to ask you.'

It almost worked. We were picking our way through the pot-holes of Shakespeare Sarani by this time. He dropped the shafts of the rickshaw and slapped me clean across the mouth, then he stood with his head bowed and shoulders dropping. I reloaded some mouldy potatoes and half a pumpkin that had spilled out on to the ground and picked up the shafts again.

'I'm sorry, Barney,' I said. 'Come on—I'll help you back with this lot.' But he shook his head and took the shafts from me and plodded on. I stood watching him go, then, feeling a complete louse, I went back to the hotel.

I let myself into my room and staggered back as something hit me—something that clawed and swore and spat. Safaraz was yelling, 'Peace, shameless one, or I'll show you how we deal with strumpets in my country,' in Hindi, and the shame-less one was calling him a stinking black bastard in Billings-gate, and it took a little time to sort things out, but finally he flung her into a chair, raging and breathless, and I saw it was the girl from the ashram.

'I saw none of the men, sahib,' Safaraz explained, 'but this dirty one sat with others of her kind on the Maidan. Since the sahib had not told me that I had to hand *women* over to the police, I thought it better to bring her back here.'

'I said I wanted no disorder,' I said sternly.

'There was none, sahib. I merely plucked her from their midst and put her under my arm, and they, thinking no doubt that I was taking her for some purpose of my own, made much ribaldry, which fortunately I did not understand.'

'Then how did you know it was ribaldry, you fool?' I asked.

'From the lewdness of their gestures, sahib,' he said primly. 'There was some slight misunderstanding with the hall porter, but I told him that I was bringing this one here on the sahib's orders.' I was certainly stacking up a reputation in this pub.

The girl was watching us closely. The fight had gone out of her and I was pretty certain that it had been replaced by fear, because a muscle in her face was twitching and her breath was quick and shallow. I said to her, 'You needn't be afraid. I've got a few questions for you. If the answers are satisfactory you can go.'

The English seemed to reassure her, but only marginally.

'Who the hell are you?' she demanded. 'You'd better let me go, or my friends will have the British consul round here—damn quick.'

'I doubt it,' I said. 'Anyhow, there's no such animal—only a High Commissioner, and he's fed up to the back teeth with you people. He'd probably hand you over to the Indian police as a vagrant.'

But she didn't seem to hear this. She was looking from one to the other of us, and her nervousness was increasing.

'You—you're not an Indian?' she said.

'Who and what I am doesn't matter. Your answers to my questions *do*——' I began.

'You're the men who came to the ashram and—and—the Swami—and Ghosh—Oh, my God——' She was almost passing out.

'Good,' I said. 'You remember us. That should save a lot of time. Now come on—Horton, Ahrlberg, Yonni and Tumba-bloody-Rumba—where are they?'

'I don't know,' she breathed, her hands were twisting the front of her grubby sari.

'Too bad,' I said. 'You can't say I didn't give you a chance. I'll just have to leave it to this man then. It won't be pleasant.'

'Durao lekin ke chot mat lagao,' I said to Safaraz (Frighten but don't hurt her) and I never saw him look so silly before. If I'd told him to cut her throat, he'd have understood and no doubt complied, but just to frighten—well, it was completely outside his experience. He didn't quite scratch his head, but he did stand on one leg and look bashful, then, realizing that it was an order, he conjured up the most bloody awful grimace I have ever seen, took his knife from under his shirt and advanced on her.

She screamed, 'They'll kill me if I tell!'

'They won't,' I said, 'but *he* will if you *don't*.'

'Aurungabad,' she babbled. 'Please—I don't know any more than that——'

'How are they travelling?'

'By car——'

'When did they leave?'

'Last night——'

'What's the number of the car?'

'I don't know—I really don't know. I never saw it—just knew they were going in a car——'

'Their names?'

'You just said their names yourself——'

'I want them from you. Come on—who were they?'

'Les Horton and Yonni and Buddy Ahrlberg——'

'Yes—come on——'

'I—I—That's all—I——'

I signed to Safaraz and she screamed again.

'He told me what he'd do if I talked——'

'His name? The fourth one?'

'You know him—you know him——'

'Come on—you've named the others——'

136

'Tumba——' She couldn't get the rest of it out. I thought she was going to be sick.

'And who else?'

'That's the lot——'

'One other—who was it?'

'P-Pewsey—Oh God—I saw what they did to her—She —she talked——'

'Who did it?'

'Les—and——'

'Tumba-bloody-Rumba?'

She just nodded. It was peculiar this inhibition his name seemed to set up in her. She was on the point of passing out again, but I couldn't let up now.

'Where are they going in Aurungabad?'

'I don't know—you've got to believe me—I really don't know—except that—that——'

'Except what?'

'They go there a lot, but never all at one time before—It's an ashram near some caves——'

That was sufficient. I knew Aurungabad and the Ellora Caves nearby. I was glad it was over—but she still presented a problem. She had undoubtedly been seen being brought here, and although the main ones were out of town, there were others still about who could make things uncomfortable for her. For her own sake she had to be taken care of. I told Safaraz to stay with her and I heard her wail of dismay as I left the room. I went along to No. 25 and got on the telephone to head-quarters. Mukherjee wasn't there, but he had left orders that got me quite a lot of priority and they switched me through to the radio room and I eventually got him in a car the other side of Kidderpore. I told him the score and said I wanted the girl taken into protective custody.

'No sweat,' he said. 'I'll send the women officers for her.'

'Make it the rear service entrance and get them to bring a burqa along,' I told him.

'Good idea,' he said. 'I'll do that—and I'll be round to see you myself as soon as I can get off my present commitment.'

The same two women were round in half an hour, and the sight of their neat uniforms had a peculiar effect on her. They calmed her terror, but increased her resentment.

'You dirty bastard!' she yelled. 'You said you'd let me go.'

'How long do you think you'd last?' I asked her. 'You'll be all right—three squares and a flop per diem—nice air-conditioned nick—free flight home, and this time next week you'll be in London. Lucky girl.'

'Fuzz!' she said, screwed up her face and spat. Then she refused to put the burqa on, but the deceptively gentle little policewomen coped with that admirably. It is a head-to-foot all-enveloping white cotton cloak with a Ku Klux Klan type of hood, which is worn by orthodox Muslim women in the Punjab, but is common enough in Calcutta. They whipped it over her and led her off, and I think, all in all, she was glad to go.

I sent Safaraz down to the news-stand for a road map and I studied it while I waited for Mukherjee. Aurungabad is in the province that was until recently the princely state of Hyderabad, but has now been annexed by India and renamed Maharashta. It is about two hundred miles from Bombay, off the beaten track except for a metre-gauge railway that meanders through the hills from the main line at the junction of Manmad. What the devil would they be doing there, I wondered? It was a military cantonment in the days of the British, but I had heard that except for an occasional influx of tourists when an American cruise liner happened to be in Bombay and a visit to the quite phenomenal caves of Ellora was arranged, the place was now a haunt of the panther, the chital deer and the jackal.

I consulted the Indian Airlines handbook and found that there was a flight there twice a week—the next being two days away. I checked the distance roughly by road and made it a shade over twelve hundred miles—up the Grand Trunk Road then a turn off westward through Nagpur, the geographical centre of the sub-continent. Say three days driving over really bad roads. I wouldn't save any time, but there was always the chance of my catching up with them by road, whereas if I flew I would have to pick up their trail afresh— and in any case I would most probably need a car there, and I did not know what the hiring facilities might be. I looked at my watch. Ten o'clock. They had a ten hour start. That could be made up.

I sent Safaraz to collect my car from the hotel garage and told him to prepare for a long, hard drive. He turned his eyes skyward and murmured a prayer of thanksgiving. He hated Calcutta. 'We camp,' I added. 'Light scale. We are men of Jullundur who buy wool.' Punjabis are ubiquitous in India, and their clothes are light and comfortable.

Mukherjee arrived then. I gave him a quick rundown on what I had gathered from the girl. He rubbed his chin ruminatively. 'Aurungabad? Now what do they want there? Hm—I'm grateful, Idwal. Very best of luck. You'll keep me in touch with things?'

'Of course,' I promised. 'Not only keep you in touch—I'll hand the damned lot over to you as soon as I've squeezed out what information I can get from them. Will you let the Maharashta police know I'm coming?'

He shook his head. 'Too much red tape that way,' he said, 'and probably too much talk before you even arrive. If you'll stop at headquarters on your way out of town I'll give you a letter to my opposite number over there.'

'Much better,' I agreed. And then Safaraz came back and started quickly to get the few items together that even Punjab wooldealers, pretty Spartan characters at all times, would require on a fast dash across India at the hottest time of the year.

Chapter Twelve

I HAD A FEW MISGIVINGS about Bayliss as we crossed the Howrah Bridge to join the Grand Trunk Road the other side. I had just driven off without telling him. But what else could I do? Safaraz and I merged into the background without conscious effort, just two Indians going about their lawful occasions—but we would have become immediately conspicuous if we had had a European with us, and he'd have stood out like a whore in a nunnery if we had attempted to disguise him. No, it was better this way.

My car, a Rover, is a little dated but I don't use it much and it is well-maintained. Once clear of the city limits we cruised comfortably at 65 mph on the narrow but splendidly surfaced main road, slowing down and side-slipping into the deep dust on the shoulders only when overtaking bullock carts plodding along in the middle with their drivers usually asleep on top of their loads.

Whether one is ultimately going north, west or east, there is only one route out of Calcutta for the first fifty miles, and that is this road that was old when the Moghuls first came south from the Khyber on the heels of Genghis Khan. It runs arrow-straight, parallel with the Hooghli, shaded by ancient peepul trees, north-west, until, with dramatic suddenness, the junction of the Hooghli with the Ganges is reached, and the whole scene changes from flooded rice paddies, bamboo thickets and rain forest trees to rockstrewn, flint-hard open country where the murderous heat dances in a visible haze over the plain, and neither mad dogs, Englishmen or even the locals, come out in the midday sun.

We drove for ten hours that first day, stopping only for gas and a few discreet inquiries, and knocking off over five hundred miles, before arriving at a hotel in a small village. It was quite the lousiest and smelliest dump I've ever had the misfortune to sojourn in, but we had no choice. A sudden drenching pre-monsoon downpour caught us and put sleeping in the open out of the question. But at least we had our first small gleaning of information here. Over a meal in the chaikhana we started an argument between ourselves about the number of mythical goras—low-caste Europeans dressed in native style—who were in the car which had broken down fifteen miles farther back—and who had borrowed a large and equally mythical wrench from us which they had conveniently forgotten to return before driving off, the bastards. And, inevitably, we soon had an audience.

'Four of them,' grunted Safaraz.

'But three, brother,' I corrected.

'Four,' Safaraz insisted. 'One had a sickness of the belly and had to squat among the bushes.'

'And you have a sickness of the eyes, flea-brain. I say three —as do ten of my rupees to ten of yours.'

'Done—but how can it be proved?'

'They came this way. If Allah wills we shall overtake them again.'

'You are right, hadji,' an old man said to Safaraz. 'Four there were—Angresi goras dressed in Bengali clothes.'

'But how do we know they are the same ones?' I demanded. 'There may be others travelling this way by car.'

'No other goras have passed through here this month or more,' the old man said. 'I sit here each day from dawn to sundown, for there is naught else to do in this accursed place.'

'I shall take from you my ten rupees,' Safaraz chuckled, hand outstretched. 'Then I shall buy the eagle-eyed and venerable one a cup of coffee.'

'Not until I know what manner of car it was,' I yelled. 'Its colour, its size, whether it is old or new. I must know before I part with my money.'

But there things fell apart. The entire audience got into the act then. It was, we gathered from one, a large grey car of surpassing speed and beauty. He was a liar said another—small, black and beat-up it was. Like hell—it was Americani and blue—and so on, although most agreed that there were four goras in it and all demanded coffee from Safaraz. I left him to it and went up to bed, if you call a Pachmina blanket on a crumbling mud-and-cowdung floor bed. He came up later grumbling and swearing that it had cost him two rupees, but he had managed to get a fairly accurate description of them from one man of rather less risible imagination than the rest. It seemed that they were our people all right, though here again, there was much divergence of opinion, as there always is with an Indian crowd. But all agreed more or less on the time. They arrived at midday, fed and rested some two hours, then went on. They were getting low on petrol it appeared, but there was no supply in this place. None of the goras spoke Hindi, but the village schoolmaster knew enough English to be able to tell them that there was a garage in Bhalisgaon, fifty-five miles on.

Se we reduced their lead from ten hours to six. That was satisfactory. Tomorrow, with luck, we would have them in sight, then it would be a matter of tailing them without being seen ourselves, because I was determined to see what the Aurungabad connection was before tipping my hand.

We set out at dawn, still with a comfortable margin of petrol left, because we were carrying three five-gallon jerricans. The road had deteriorated now and speed had to be reduced accordingly, so it took us over two hours to reach Bhalisgaon. We tried the stolen wrench spiel again at the garage and learned that the goras, also, had left at dawn, having stayed in the serai overnight, so the lead had been reduced to two hours. Safaraz was worried.

'The rain last night has laid the dust, sahib, so that it does not rise over the trees at the passing of a car,' he said.

'So what?' I asked.

'So I will have no warning on this winding road if we overtake them.'

I saw his point. The transverse, east-west, roads are little used nowadays. Yesterday we had passed a bare handful of vehicles going the other way, and had not been passed ourselves by anything travelling west—nor had we overtaken anything. So a dust cloud in front of us would almost certainly be them, and Safaraz's sharp eyes would pick it up high above the trees long before we actually came up with them. But no dust cloud, no warning.

I thought it over for some minutes, then said, 'It doesn't matter. If we overtake them without warning we will just pass them and carry on until we come to a place where we can turn off and remain under cover until they have gone by.' And I had hardly spoken when we came up with them.

They were just round a blind bend, slewed diagonally across the road, and for a moment I thought it was a hold-up, and my hand shot under my shirt to my gun, but then I heard Safaraz chuckling.

'The gora-log have a flat tyre, sahib,' he said with malicious satisfaction.

I had a passing glimpse of them standing round the car disconsolately. Two of them tried hopefully to flag us down, but I pulled the wheel over, skittered through the dust and came back on to the hard surface the other side of them, and in the mirror I could see them making rude and angry gestures after us. It removed any lingering doubts I might have had because I recognized Horton and Ahrlberg without a shadow of uncertainty. The other two I didn't see clearly, and in any case I wouldn't have known the Australian if he had been one of them. I wasn't in the least worried about their recognizing either Safaraz or myself. We had come on them too suddenly, and were past them too fast in a cloud of dust for that. I handed the wheel over to Safaraz a few miles up the road, while I looked out for a suitable lay-by, and I found the ideal spot. It was a bullock cart track debouching off to the left and leading to a high wooded bank that overlooked the road. I got out and tested the ground underfoot, and found it firm, so we ran the car up into a patch of dense jungle and then went back and blotted out our wheel tracks in the roadside dust.

The sun had climbed up to the zenith and was halfway down its slide to the western hills before I started to worry. If it had only been a matter of changing a wheel they should have passed our position hours ago. Safaraz suggested going back to check on them, but I said that I didn't want them to see the car again if I could help it.

'I shall go on foot, sahib. Two miles each way—one hour.'

'You might be seen and recognized,' I said, and he looked scornful.

'The sahib knows better than that,' he said, so in the end I let him go, and waited another nail-biting two hours before deciding that something was very wrong indeed and that I had better go back myself.

I met him a mile down the road, crawling on his hands and knees and streaming blood from a horrible wound that ran from his ankle to a point midway between his right knee and his groin.

'A panther trap, sahib,' he said sheepishly. 'Of a type that should not have deceived a blind Bengali, let alone a man of the Hills.'

I did the best bandaging job I could with half a dirty turban and went back and got the car, then I got him into it and continued on to Bhalisgaon. We stopped at the spot where they had been halted—but there was no sign of them or the car.

'I saw that they had gone, sahib,' Safaraz explained. 'And I was coming back along the path through the jungle I had followed on my way out. I left it for a moment to drink from a waterhole, and fell into this cursed thing——'

144

They dig these pits near waterholes and bait them with young goats when there is a particularly troublesome tiger or panther around. They are lethal—twelve feet deep, smooth-sided and bristling with fire-hardened, upward-pointing stakes at the bottom. They are then covered with a light bamboo framework and realistically camouflaged with brushwood and dried grass. He had indeed been lucky only to have been spiked on one stake, although the wound it had made was certainly bad enough.

I saw their car outside the garage as we drove into the village, and I expected to see the men either at the chaikhana or the serai, so I didn't stop, but drove on a little way and then came back on foot in the fast gathering gloom to find the local doctor. There wasn't one, but there was a government dispensary in the charge of a medical orderly who I suborned with twenty rupees to come out and attend to Safaraz, hinting that we would rather not be seen by the lone policeman who was stationed here. He knew his job and he washed the wound, then stitched it quickly and neatly, bandaged it afresh and gave Safaraz a prophylactic shot, all in the space of ten minutes. I bribed him further then and told him that we were on the trail of four goras who owed a brother Punjabi a large sum of money and were absconding. Yes, he had seen four goras, he told me.

'They are men of wealth,' he said. 'Whether it is honestly come by or filched from your brother.'

'Of wealth?'

'Aye—they are not of this new race of white beggars who plague us. They came through last night and stayed at the serai, paying their way like honest travellers. They went on this morning, but their car broke down, so they walked back and made arrangements to have it towed into the village.'

'And they stay at the serai again?'

He shook his head. 'No. The part that is broken cannot be replaced here, so they sold the car to Jhoti Prasad, who owns the garage, and bought another from him. Ai-ee, it must be good to be wealthy. That damned rogue Jhoti Prasad has made five hundred rupees profit.'

'So they have returned the way they came?'

'No. They go on to Nagpur.'

'But Nagpur lies to the west of here,' I protested. 'We waited for them to come that way, but they didn't.'

'The main road to Nagpur runs west from here, agreed,' the medic said. 'But I told them of a shorter way—by which they will save over fifty miles.'

My jaw dropped. 'What shorter way is there?' I asked.

'Men of wealth,' he repeated, ignoring my question, 'but tight with it. I translated for them from English to Hindi and back again, for I am a man of education—not like that ignorant bastard Jhoti Prasad—and I saved them from being robbed of too much over that heap of rusty iron they bought —but got little thanks——'

I rubbed my nose with another ten rupee note. His hand shot out and it disappeared. 'Go back east some five miles and you will see it on your right—just a cart-track at first but it opens out into something better a few miles farther on. But drive with care. The road is shorter, but dangerous in parts.' He went off then, warning Safaraz not to put too great a strain on his leg for some days, and to have the stitches removed after a couple of weeks, and I sat cursing. I had a map, of course, but I had not thought it necessary to consult it up to now as I knew the road and the distances between salient points—or thought I did.

I got the map out and studied it in the light of a torch. Yes—there it was. A tiny dotted track, as unnoticeable on paper as it had apparently been on the ground when we passed it. I drove back into the village, since there was no further need to avoid being seen, and we ate at the chaikhana. I sat and puzzled then, whether it would be wiser to press on along the longer but better main road and hope to cut down the six hour start they had re-established, or to follow them over the shorter route. Both had about the same number of advantages and drawbacks. I could probably still beat them to Nagpur along the main road, six hours' start notwithstanding —but that could possibly mean a long roadside wait because they might halt for the night somewhere. A dangerous road, the medic had said—and the likelihood of the 'heap of rusty iron' packing in altogether. No, I couldn't afford to lose them at this stage. Nagpur was a pretty large city—the main crossroads and railway junction of India—east-west the Bombay Calcutta road and rail routes—north-south, Delhi to Madras. Possibly two hundred hotels, ranging from the reasonable to the louse-trap—serais, dharamsalas and God knows how many ashrams. Let them out of my sight once in the city and I'd probably lose them for good.

I discussed it with Safaraz as we slogged through a curry which at least made up in bulk what it lacked in epicurean properties. Being Safaraz he was all for pressing on immediately —on their heels, down the shorter route.

'Your leg——?' I said doubtfully.

'Is as good as new, sahib,' he said firmly, flexing it. 'That hakim was a thieving son of a whore, but was possessed of great skill.'

But I was still doubtful. He had lost a lot of blood and neither of us had much sleep the last couple of nights. But he overrode my scruples, and we started out.

It was a hell of a job finding the turn-off—one that taxed even Safaraz's eyes on that moonless pre-monsoon night, but we hit it eventually, and we slid and spun and churned our way through five miles of axle-deep dust that rose and choked us even through the tightly closed windows, before coming out on to a relatively solid road that had once been tarmac but was now a mass of potholes.

And then it happened again. One minute we were in the clear, with our headlights cutting a white swathe through the blackness of the overcast night, the next we were submerged in a solid downpour. It often happens that way at the break of the monsoon—without the faintest rumble or a flash of lightning as a warning. Rain, just rain, in an impenetrable sheet blotting out everything, reducing visibility to zero feet, turning the drainage ditches each side of the road into roaring torrents, flooding dried watercourses—and all in a space of minutes.

I slid to a stop, thanking my lucky stars that we happened at that juncture to be on an upward slope and not in one of the many valleys this by-road crossed. It poured for a couple of hours, and there was nothing for it but just to sit it out. It didn't worry me unduly because the chances were that they were being held up also—and we had been driving as fast as the road allowed and I was tired and welcomed the enforced rest.

It stopped as suddenly as it had commenced, like the turning off of a tap, but it was a long time before the surface water drained away, and I knew the road would be a river of semi-liquid mud for some hours yet, so we just sat on, dozing, until daylight, then I got out and waded to the top of the hill in front of us.

The road dipped sharply the other side to a river in the bottom of the valley, before rising again to yet another crest directly across from us—and there, in the middle of it, in the exactly equivalent position to ourselves a quarter of a mile on, was another car. I dropped flat in the wet undergrowth at the side of the road and wriggled back until I was below the skyline, and fetched my binoculars from the car. I returned to the top with Safaraz, as curious as a monkey, hard on my heels. I swore at him and told him to go back and rest his leg, but he grinned impudently and lay down on the crestline and recited a string of things he could see with his naked eyes that I was missing with the glasses.

'Ha, the three low-castes we have seen before, sahib, with a fourth we see for the first time. He is taller than the others, and as skinny as a rabid jackal—but he is strong. See that? He lifts the back of the car alone while the others struggle to put branches and bundles of undergrowth under the back wheels. The fools. Don't they realize that they will just churn that stuff into the mud when the wheels start to revolve? Ho, this is good. I love to see rogues and badmashes put to discomfort——'

And they certainly were being put to discomfort. They should have waited. The sun was shining brightly again now, and in an hour or so the mud would have dried and they could have driven on without difficulty. But they obviously didn't realize this, and they toiled, hamfistedly, like beavers—steadily making their position worse, because the car, under the furious gunning of Ahrlberg was slipping back and losing more ground than it was gaining. It slewed right round finally and slid slowly into the ditch. Slowly, but still too fast for Yonni to get out of the way, because he lost his footing and even at that distance we could hear his piercing shriek as it pinned him underneath.

Somehow they pulled him clear. Not even Safaraz could see the extent of the damage at that distance, but I could read from their expressions that it was pretty bad. They gathered round and stared helplessly at the injured man as he lay on the ground twitching jerkily from time to time—then they withdrew some distance and appeared to be having a consultation.

They got the car moving in the end and crawled up to the crest, and over it out of sight, with Ahrlberg at the wheel, and the other two pushing. The injured Yonni was still lying on the ground and I assumed that a couple of them would come back for him once they were on the downslope the other side. But apparently Yonni had his doubts about this because we could clearly see him rising feebly on one elbow and looking anxiously after them.

It was the fourth man who eventually came back, alone. This, obviously, was Tumba-bloody-Rumba, I decided, and I got my first good look at him full face. Tall, thin—not bearded like the others—a lanky, good-natured, open-faced boy— freckled. Eyes blue or grey—one couldn't be certain through the binoculars. An unremarkable face. It was the grin that impressed itself on me. Wide and ingenuous. A decent, warm-hearted guy coming back to help a stricken pal—one strong enough to carry him gently to the car unassisted.

He came right on up to Yonni and stood looking down at him, smiling whimsically. One could almost hear him gently joshing the other—'Well, you silly old so-and-so. What a hell of a thing to go and do to yourself. Never mind—we'll soon get you to a doctor——'

Then he felt under his loose Bengali khamis, brought out a pistol, took careful aim, and unhurriedly shot the other straight through the head.

He bent and removed a pouchbelt from round the dead man's waist, glanced through the contents, then took a couple of strings of love beads and a bracelet from him and finally pulled him by the ankles out of the ditch and into the under-growth out of sight. The whole thing took a matter of minutes and it put me in mind of a kindly but unsentimental motorist coming back to put a dog he has run over out of its misery.

Safaraz expelled his breath softly. He said, 'Sahib, even in Waziristan we take an enemy's sandals off and turn him to face Mecca before despatching him. The Smiling One lacked compassion. It would be a great pleasure to cut his throat, slowly, if the sahib would kindly give me leave to do so.'

I said, 'In the fullness of time, Safaraz. Either you, I or the hangman shall deal with that one, I promise you.'

Chapter Thirteen

I GAVE THEM fifteen minutes' start, then I walked forward, leaving Safaraz with the car. I passed the spot where they had bogged down and went on up to the next crest. Far in the distance below me I could see their car moving beetle-like across the plain. I walked back then and went into the scrub. High above already the 'sentry' vulture was poised on motionless wings, and a circle of specks showed others converging.

He lay on his back just as the Smiling One had dumped him. One could see now why he had been rubbed out. Both legs had suffered badly under the weight of the car, and he would undoubtedly have been a drag on them—but even so there was nothing wrong with him that couldn't have been put right with proper medical attention. Nothing, that is, other than a heavy bullet through the skull. I debated for a few moments on whether or not to delay further and bury him, but the ground here was rocky and I knew perfectly well that the jackals and hyenas would have him up again from anything less than six feet, and that they and the vultures between them would leave nothing but a heap of whitened bones by this time tomorow, so I just left things as they were and went back to the road and signalled Safaraz to bring the car forward.

They were a bare hour ahead of us now and it called for care. If we caught up with them before they reached Nagpur they would know with certainty that we had been behind the whole way because there wasn't as much as a hut on this road let alone a village. On the other hand we could quite easily lose them in the maelstrom of Nagpur's traffic if we were too far behind them. I decided, therefore, to keep my distance until we came in sight of the fort on top of Sitabaldi Peak which dominates the city, then to step on it and pass them in a cloud of dust on the outskirts and wait up some convenient side road until they in turn had passed us.

But it just didn't work out. The road enters the city proper through the old part where the streets are too narrow to allow a couple of bullock carts to pass—but they still try. It was that which was our undoing. I was behind their car, with a convenient country bus and a bullock cart between us giving good cover. The bus turned down a cross street and a second bullock cart came round the corner and locked wheels with the one in front of me, and then began a 'gali larai' or battle of abuse between the drivers. They are meticulously governed, these things. Each contender insults the other in turn, both being too polite to interrupt while his opponent has the floor, and the inevitable crowd that gathers becomes the umpires. It's all very amusing, unless they happen to be blocking your way in a narrow street. Miserably I watched the quarry drive through the crowd and turn a corner, and it was a good ten minutes later before both the insulters had run out of steam and it had been called a draw. They pulled aside finally and allowed me to inch past, and Safaraz leaned out and added a few phrases of his own which had both the crowd and the protagonists gasping with admiration, but it was too late then. We had lost the quarry.

I drove slowly through the native city and the old cantonment section, and then tried the suburbs of Sitabaldi and the railway colony of Craddock Town before, tired, hungry and savagely angry, giving it up and finding a serai. But my car, being a fairly good one in this land of beat-up jalopies, would have been conspicuous parked in a serai, which are for the humble and impecunious, so I dropped Safaraz and then went off and parked it in a lock-up garage. Then I found a pharmacist's shop in the bazar, and I went in and bought some sterile gauze, bandages and disinfectant—and Ahrlberg walked in behind me.

I felt acutely vulnerable for a moment until I remembered

that though he had seen me twice before, I was wearing Chandpuri clothes the first time, and European the second. Now I was a Punjabi, and a very hairy and dirty one as I had not shaved or washed for three days, and I was plastered with dust.

I waited, counting my change and stowing my parcels in various folds of my flowing shirt and baggy pantaloons, while he bought some aspirin. One of them must have had a headache, poor fellow. I hoped it was the Smiling One. That's how I was thinking of him now. 'Tumba-bloody-Rumba' had a smack of Falstaffian jollity about it, of good fellowship, belly-laughs and amiable clowning. Safaraz's name, which, in the vernacular, has a sinister sibilance—muskaranawala—fitted him much better.

I went out in the bazar. There was no street lighting as such in this part, but traders were now putting up naphtha flares over their stalls, and Arhlberg's white Bengali clothes, dusty though they were, stood out among the darker Central Indian garb, so he was easy to follow from a distance. He went back towards our serai, and for a moment I thought that that was where they were staying, and I was worried, but he passed the entrance to it and went on right through the bazar and into an area of close-huddled little bungalows on the fringe of Craddock Town, through these and into the old military cantonment. It was pitch dark now, for which I was thankful because the crowds had dwindled and it wasn't so easy to remain inconspicuous.

He stopped eventually at a dark gateway let into a high wall and disappeared under an archway. I waited for some minutes undecided. The gate itself was out of sight from where I was standing, and I couldn't see whether he had gone through it or was still waiting in the shadows. In the end I sauntered past and saw that he had evidently gone through. I circled right round the wall, which obviously enclosed a large courtyard, but it was windowless and no light was reflected over the parapet. I came back to the gate and risked sneaking up to it to peer through the crack, but again I could see nothing.

I was in a fever of impatience. So near to where they were but up against what appeared to be an insuperable barrier. I circled the wall again, this time studying it closer, and on the far side found it to be rather dilapidated and some of the blocks of stone had fallen away. It was the sort of thing that Safaraz, unhampered by a game leg, would have shinned up like a cat, but I wasn't quite so nimble. Still, there was nothing for it, so I tried a tentative finger-tip hold, then a foothold in a chink, and gradually I worked my way up to the top, which was about fifteen feet from the ground.

There was a quarter moon, but up to now it had been skulking behind the monsoon clouds. Fortunately it came out just as I got to the top and fractionally before I might have cut my hands to ribbons on the broken glass chevaux de frise that surmounted it. Somehow I managed to get over it without completely emasculating myself and drop down the other side on to the roof of a lean-to shed, and from it to the overgrown garden below. There were a couple of typical servants' godowns across the courtyard. I say typical because the whole place was completely traditional—the house of a well-to-do Muslim, where the women would have been kept in strict purdah behind windowless walls. A dim light showed through a grating in the nearer of them. That would have been the guard-house in older days, marking the limit that any non-castrated male, other than the lord and master, might go in the direction of the harem. They are little used for their original purpose nowadays—women's lib and the high cost of imported eunuchs tending to make plural marriage unpopular —but they are ideally suited to people who value seclusion for other reasons.

I realized at once that there would be no way into the main building in the centre of the courtyard other than through the godown, so I went round the other side of it and looked for the same sort of thing I had found in the outer wall—a tumble-down bit that I could climb—and amazingly I found one, where a fretted marble screen had broken away leaving a jagged fringe still cemented to the basic stonework. I climbed this and got on to a flat roof which overlooked another court-yard—in other words the layout of the place was a circular outer walled area containing a building in the form of a hollow square.

A couple of lighted windows looked out on to this inner space, and I could also see a chink of light round the edge of a badly fitting door the other side.

I edged along the roof until I was above the first window, and then leaned out and over until I was head downward and could get an inverted view of the inside of the room. It was quite bare except for a few faded rugs and a big ironbound chest, and the light came from a glaring petromax lamp. A door opened from this room into one beyond it and I could hear a babble of voices, tantalizingly just below the sound level that would have made the words intelligible, so I moved along farther to the second window and did another upside down balancing act. There were quite a lot of them here. I counted ten and there were a couple that I couldn't see fully just out of my line of sight. Horton was directly beneath the window and Ahrlberg was across the room facing him. They were sitting in a circle on the stone floor eating from a couple of big brass bowls of rice and curried vegetables, Indian style with their bare hands, but without the skill and grace that is needed to avoid messiness. Most were in local dress, dhotis, pantaloons, and the ubiquitous khamis and, in a couple of instances, the high-necked Hindu shirwani. There were a few traditional hippy styles there also—weirdo fringed shirts, head-bands, love beads—and all of the mob were long-haired—with a majority favouring beards ranging from the merest anaemic fringe to the full-flowing piratical. They were, in short, about as unsavoury a bunch of love children as I have ever seen congregated in one room.

They all seemed to be talking, but there was a marked paucity of listeners. And it was strictly a stag session, which surprised me because hippy gatherings tend to be co-ed. I tried to pick up the thread of what some of the nearer ones were talking about, but it was almost impossible to make sense of any of it, particularly when hanging upside down like a hibernating bat, and I was just about to give it up and swing back on to the roof when the Smiling One's voice rose again over the hubbub.

'For Chri'sake will some of you urgers pipe down for a minute and let a bloke hear himself think!' he yelled, then, in the resultant silence, he went on, ruefully good-humoured, 'Sorry, blokes, but I got to talk to a couple of you. Business.' He rose and came into full view from a position to one side of the window. 'George, Steve, Mike and Arthur in next door, and the rest of you can go on magging all night, you noisy lot of bastards.'

He went through the door into the other room and four of the others followed him, together with Horton. Ahrlberg sat on, however, and continued eating and talking simultaneously.

I eased myself along the roof again to the first window in time to see the six of them settling down on rugs and lighting cigarettes, but I knew I wouldn't be able to swing here upside down for any length of time, so I went on farther and lowered myself to the ground. I didn't like this new position because there was no exit except through the building, and if anybody came out and caught me here I would be flatfooted—and it wasn't much good as a listening post either as the window was about seven feet clear of the ground. But then I stumbled over a pile of chatthis—the porous clay water jars used throughout India—so I carried a couple across and they raised me to eyelevel with the window sill.

'—just a straight exchange,' the Smiling One was saying. 'What's biting you, Mike?'

'Who the hell wants to exchange this place for Calcutta?' Mike asked querulously. He was a whiskery gent who favoured the straight hippy garb.

'Somebody's got to do it over that side. You can't expect to sit on your arse here for keeps,' the Smiling One said. Yes, the name suited him. The smile was pasted on. It hadn't faded since I first saw him on the road.

'Who's sitting on his arse? Two trips a month right through to Bombay—two short hauls to Aurungabad. You call that loafing on the job?'

'Then Calcutta will be a rest cure, won't it?' The smile broadened.

'I don't want to go,' Mike said.

'And I don't want to listen to any more wails.' The smile threatened to explode into a gurgling laugh. 'Be nice, Mikey boy. We don't want any bother, do we?'

'I don't——'

'Nor me. Anything I hate it's bending a bloke—because when I bend 'em I bend 'em good. I bend 'em for keeps sometimes—and I don't like that—honest I don't.' He winked and leaned across and poked Mike playfully in the ribs with two stiffened fingers. Mike yelped. 'No sweat, is there, Mikey boy?' the Smiling One asked anxiously.

Mike swallowed and shook his head. The Smiling One looked round the others. 'Any more questions?' he asked. There weren't, so he went on, kindly, reasonably, 'Goodo— that's what I like—blokes pulling together. Right—I'll give you the full story. There's these two Scotland Yard pigs out from London, see? They know a few of us by sight—Les here, and me and Yonni and Ahrlberg—so it's best that we drift for a bit, see what I mean? We come over here and run your scene—you go over there and run ours. Like I said, a straight exchange.'

'How long is it going to be before they know a few of us?' one of the others asked.

'Good question,' the Smiling One said approvingly. 'That depends on how you use your loaves. None of you have got records, so you should be able to keep your noses clean until the cows come home. You're just four of the kids—part of the scene. As far as the mob's concerned you smoke and fix——' He looked round at them intently. 'None of you *has* picked up a habit since I saw you last I hope?'

There were four emphatic headshakes.

'Goodo. We don't want none of that nonsense, do we? All right then—Les'll tell you the new set-up in Calcutta. Okay, Les.'

Horton said, 'Much the same as before except that East Pakistan is now called Bangladesh and things haven't settled down properly yet. We're doing a long haul round from the Burma border, but that won't concern you blokes. As far as you're concerned, Quentin is still receiving and despatching from the old dump. The bums carry it in—you collect in the Howrah place——'

'That still safe?' one of the others asked.

'Yes, and it better stay that way,' Horton told him. 'It cost us a lot of bread to square the fuzz there—and then it's only on the understanding that we don't do anything *too* naughty. That's why you blokes must never carry anything yourselves —not a quarter ounce. If one of the bums gets pulled in, he's on his own. Unless a Six has been busted lower down he can only finger one of you—and that one had better be on his way —but quick.'

'Where to? The Sealdah ashram?'

'No—that's been busted. You go to the Barrackpore Road serai and act like you're trying to thumb a lift north—you're getting the hell out of it. They'll usually wear that and help you on your way, with a boot up the ass—but if they do pull you in, you stick to the same story. A bloke on Sealdah station gave you a parcel to deliver to the bum and paid you ten rupees. You did just that and no more. In other words you keep to procedure. If you do that they can never make anything stick—they can only pull in the odd bum carrying a parcel. We lose that parcel, but there's a lot more parcels we *don't* lose. Any more questions?' There weren't, so he went on, 'All right—you get away by train tomorrow morning. One of you will contact Quentin—that'd better be you, George, because he knows you—and things should be running smoothly by next Monday at the latest.' He looked at the Smiling One.

'Right,' said the Smiling One. 'What's been happening here? You, Mike.'

Mike said glumly, 'No change—and it's not easy. We collect from the bums when they come in on the Calcutta train or by bus, then carry it across to Aurungabad ourselves by road.'

'No bums going across yet?'

'No, it's off the route. That's why we look conspicuous. Why can't the bums carry it on from here by train themselves?'

The Smiling One winked and chortled. 'You know something? I believe you're getting just the littlest bit dim, cobber —because it's been explained to you all before—so very, very carefully. Explain again, Les, in case the gentleman ever comes back to this station.'

'Unsquarable railway cops at Bhusawal and Manmad,' Horton said. 'Always the chance of a spot search. And if you'd done what you were told and put up a tourist front instead of a beat one, you wouldn't have been conspicuous, would you?'

'The both of us wear ordinary suits when we're travelling——'

'But the whiskers, cobber, the whiskers——' the Smiling One said softly, 'You told him about that last time, didn't you Les?'

'I did—and about the long hair. But it didn't seem to get through to him.'

'Lots of tourists wear whiskers and long hair,' Mike protested. 'Christ, you don't want us to look like a bunch of squares, do you?'

'No—not square, cobber—just like you said—inconspicuous,' the Smiling One said kindly. 'Okay—wait here for a moment. You others can go.'

Three of them filed out, and Horton carefully closed the door after them. He looked across at the Smiling One, who nodded amiably. Mike was flat against the wall, gibbering.

'Look, Tumba—I'm sorry—I didn't understand—Look—I mean—well—you see——' And it ended on a blubbering moan as Horton hit him in the belly, then brought his knee up—then came down with the chopping edge of his palm—but why go on? It was as comprehensive and as sickening a beating up as I've ever seen administered. Done by an expert who loved his work, and watched by an aficionado who appreciated every nuance. 'Nice work, Les—lovely—lovely—Kidneys, Les —don't forget the gentleman's kidneys—*That's* the stuff. You *will* remember what you're told next time, won't you, Mikey boy? No—careful of the gentleman's face, Les—we don't want him to be conspicuous when he arrives in Calcutta, do we?'

They left him lying on the floor, a quivering, twitching heap, and went out into the other room. I considered I had garnered as much as I could conveniently digest for the moment, so I decided to move, as I could imagine the semi-immobilized Safaraz back at the serai just about blowing a gasket.

I slid away from the window and collected another couple of chatthis and made a jumping off platform from which I could grab a handhold on the low parapet that ran round the flat roof.

I managed that all right, with not too much noise, and I was tiptoeing across to the outer side when a square of light appeared bang in front of me as a trap door was lifted from below. I froze as someone pushed a bedding roll up, then climbed out himself—to be followed immediately by two more people. They were preparing to go to bed up here and, curiously, they didn't notice me for a few moments and I thought I was going to get away with it. Then the first guy looked up and said, 'Hallo, Lennie—how long you been up here?'

I half turned away and muttered something non-committal and another of them said, 'I came up after *you*, you clot——' This one was dressed more or less as I was, in Punjabi khaddar, and the mistake was understandable. I might still have got away with it, but the first speaker was of an inquiring turn of mind. 'Then who the hell's this?' he said, and straightened up from the bedding roll he was laying out and peered closely through the darkness at me. I moved away to the outer edge. 'Hey—just a minute,' said the other, and came after me. I didn't wait any longer. I ran to the edge and tried desperately to see what I was going to land on, and I was in the act of jumping when he grabbed me. I belted him hard and swung him round and heaved him at the other two, which gave me half a split second to get under way again. I landed hard and jolted myself badly, but it didn't slow me up any and I pounded across the outer courtyard and came up against the surrounding wall. There was, I knew, only the one gate here, and the lean-to shed I had climbed on to when coming in. I made for this by memory. Behind me I could hear a rising racket as those on the roof spread the news to their pals below, but fortunately they retained an element of caution which restrained them from jumping down off the roof after me, so it was some minutes before they streamed out carrying lights and by this time I was up on the roof of the shed.

I lay flat waiting for an opportune moment to shin over the top. I heard the Smiling One call out softly, 'No shooting, boys, or we'll have the cops round,' and I blessed him for it, but had second thoughts when he followed it up with, 'A knife in the guts is the best thing, but not too deep at first until I've had a talk with him.'

'It was a wog,' I heard someone say, and another said, 'Wog my arse. Did you see the way he belted Harry?'

'I tell you it was a wog. Big sod in a nightshirt thing and a turban——'

They'd got a couple of fairly powerful electric torches now, and the light was stabbing into all the likely corners, and I knew it would only be a matter of minutes before they got to the shed. I wouldn't have stood a chance against them once they knew definitely where I was, so I got my pistol out reluctantly. One past someone's ear would undoubtedly hold them long enough for me to get over the wall, but it would also bring the police, and would certainly tell this crowd that they weren't dealing with an ordinary sneak-thief who had broken in on the off-chance of snapping up the odd unconsidered trifle.

But once again my luck appeared to be in the ascendancy, because the torchbearers went past with no more than a cursory stab in my direction. I waited another couple of minutes while they poked around a pile of junk some yards away, then I rose and made a tentative jump for the spot where the cement embedded broken glass wasn't quite so thickly spread, but I missed the first time and came down on the tin roof with a heavy thump, and somebody yelled, 'There he is, the black bastard—on top of the shed. I told you it was a wog!'

I disregarded the glass and really took it fast. I was up, over and in mid-air all in one, and I landed in some scrubby undergrowth round the base of the wall, and ran like hell for the main road and the bazar the other side of it. I made it just as the gate opened and they came out—the original dozen I had seen, with perhaps a few more, but by this time I was in the fringe of the crowd. Somebody must have seen me crossing the road, because several of them came over and started a miniature dragnet operation, and then, to my joy, one gent seized upon a big Baluchi—the very last of the sub-continent's population to take liberties with, with the possible exception of a Pathan or a Gurkha. I heard him yelp, 'Here he is—this is the sod!' followed by a roar of rage from the Baluchi, who was about six-feet-six and built accordingly. He bellowed 'Soor ka bacha! Bahin chut—teri ma' ka——' which I won't translate—and a peroxided hippy came flying through the air like a rocket, to land in the middle of a stall selling cheap Japanese glassware. The whole thing collapsed with a crash, and there you had the makings of a first class bazar charivari.

I left quietly just as the fight was developing nicely—Muslims versus Hindus—with Sikhs yapping round the fringes as usual —and nobody knew what had started it—again—as bloody usual.

Chapter Fourteen

AS I HAD FORESEEN, Safaraz was pretty steamed up when I got back to the serai. He was worried, he told me, fearing that I had fallen into taklif, which is untranslatable because it doesn't entirely mean trouble, danger or misfortune, but something between all three, and is usually caused by one's own stupidity. Knowing Safaraz, I was completely certain that all that was really worrying him was that I had been mixed up in something that he had missed. We had a meal and I renewed the dressing on his leg. The wound was healing nicely, but I expressed deep concern over it and questioned the wisdom of taking him on farther, which had the desired effect of shutting him up.

I was thoroughly tired but I was unable to get to sleep for a long time. I lay on a charpoy on the flat roof of the serai and mulled over what I had learned that night. They were running junk in quantity. That we knew already. But it was invariably run from south to north—up through India, smuggled over the Pakistan frontier, carried openly into Afghanistan—care was needed to get it across Iran—no problem in Iraq that a little judicious bribery couldn't overcome—then the real obstacle—Turkey. The Turks hated junk and the people who trafficked in it. They didn't hesitate to apply the death penalty to their own nationals—and absolutely swingeing sentences on others—ten, fifteen, twenty years, according to the amount carried. There was no way of by-passing Turkey. It lay right across the ant-run. And there was talk now of applying capital punishment to foreigners also. That had curtailed the supply of carriers. Junkies would still take the risk if there was no other way to obtain supplies, but they were unreliable. Yes—we knew all this, and I was merely reiterating to myself. This new puzzle was why were they carrying it *across* India from east to west? Where did it go then? There were small seaports on the Malabar Coast, a large one at Marmagoa, a very much larger one at Bombay—then nothing until the West Pakistan border was crossed and the port of Karachi reached. Were they shipping it out by sea from any of these? Unlikely, because of the difficulty of landing it again. Customs were notoriously efficient in the seaports of Europe and America. No—they didn't like shipping it in bulk any more than sending it by air. A thousand carriers each with half a pound of base morphine concealed on his person incurred far less risk of detection than did a five-hundred-pound crate labelled farm machinery. Carriers, if the heat suddenly went on, could ditch their loads at the last moment. If one carrier was uncovered he took what was coming to him without a squawk. Anywhere other than Turkey the sentences weren't very heavy—but the consequences of talking too much could be fatal. Hadn't we been seeing that in operation?

No—the carrying was being done as before, by the hippies —or bums as these people called them. And 'these people'— the Smiling One, Horton, Ahrlberg et al? Who and what were they? On the surface, hippies, indistinguishable from the genuine article—but actually something very much tougher and more vicious. The hippies were the sheep—the others the sheepdogs—or wolves in sheep's clothing. To keep them in line—to control the picking up and dropping points. To do the bribing where necessary. To maintain discipline.

Yes, all this was quite clear, but the real question still remained unanswered. Why was it travelling at right angles to the accepted logical route?

Well—there was only one thing for it. I had to stay on the trail of the Smiling One, if he went farther west. That meant that I had to keep that depot of theirs under constant sur-veillance, and be ready to jump when they did. I hoped they weren't moving tonight. And having reached that point I went to sleep.

We were up at dawn and I led the way round to the bazar where the shindig had occurred the night before. There were still signs of it—one or two stalls were overturned and there was a lot of broken glass lying around. I asked a sweeper what had happened, and he told me that there had been a slight theological disputation between the Hindus and Muslims, then someone had tried to murder a Baluchi moneylender but had unfortunately not succeeded, and that things had built up from there. Safaraz looked really deprived. There was nothing he enjoyed more than a good communal riot.

There was a chaikhana in the bazar just across from the house, from where we could keep the gate in view. We settled down there and drank endless cups of sweet, lukewarm tea and munched ghee-soaked chapattis, and within an hour the first move occurred. The gate opened and a hippy came out and hailed a tonga—the one-horse carriage that does duty as a taxi in inland Indian towns. The tonga went inside, and shortly afterwards came out again with four passengers and a miscellaneous collection of baggage weighing the poor brute of a pony down. I had whistled up another tonga by this time, and I sent Safaraz in it to follow the first one. He came back in about an hour and told me that they had gone off in the Calcutta Mail which passed through every morning on its way from Bombay. They had taken second class tickets, and one of them was obviously recovering from some sickness, because he had to be helped along by two of the others. Evidently Mikey was still under the weather.

We waited again, and I paid a taxi driver ten rupees as a retainer, and a further five as a mouth-shutter, and told him to tinker with his engine and refuse any other business that might happen along. I assumed that if our three were going on from here that they'd go by car. There were three roads other than the one we'd come by—south, west and north-west— and they could normally leave by any of them—but I didn't want to get straight on their tails from here with a car which they could recognize again so I briefed Safaraz on a 'slipper'. And for once it worked. They came out in the car at mid-morning and drove off through the bazar, and Safaraz followed in the taxi and I went to the post office and gave the babu two rupees to call me when a telephone message came through for one Mohammed Ishaq. It came an hour later and Safaraz said, 'I wait at the twentieth milestone on the Wardha Road, sahib.'

So things were working out. Wardha was along the main road to Bombay—and to Manmad, where the Aurungabad road branched off. All I had to do now was to overtake them before they reached Manmad, taking care that they didn't lose me as they did yesterday. I collected the car, picked up our meagre luggage from the serai and got going—fast.

Safaraz was squatting at the side of the road winking lasciviously and making improper suggestions to a group of giggling village women who were dibbling rice shoots into the monsoon-flooded paddy nearby. Their husbands were congregated some distance away, scowling frightfully and making threatening noises, but doing little else about it. Even against odds of seven to one, a Pathan is still treated with a certain circumspection in those parts.

'Not quite two hours ahead of us, sahib,' he said as I picked him up. 'And travelling slowly because their car runs like a pregnant camel.'

We overhauled them comfortably, well short of Manmad, and I hung back until I judged they were clear of that drab little town before pushing on and catching sight of them again just before reaching the Aurungabad turn-off. It had become an exercise in fine judgement, this business of keeping them in sight without, I fervently hoped, their becoming aware of us, or on the other hand, falling so far behind as to lose them up a side road without realizing it until too late.

The turn-off ran straight across a bare plain for some miles before shooting up with dramatic suddenness between two great columns of sandstone, and climbing three thousand feet on to the Deccan Plateau at the top. It was dark now and we could see the reflection of their headlights far in front of us. The quarter moon faintly illuminated the dusty road, so I switched our lights off and trusted to luck.

On we went, climbing steadily through the Satmala Hills, the distant pinpoint of light ahead of us vanishing at times—then reappearing without warning. I was finding it hard to keep awake and Safaraz kept begging me to hand the wheel over to him. It would have been the sensible thing to do. There's nothing wrong with my eyesight, but his is phenomenal, especially in the dark—but the melancholy fact remains that he is a lousy driver and he scares the pants off me when he's at the wheel. To spare his feelings I pretended my refusal of his offer was out of consideration for his foot, and he grunted something about rather driving with a sore foot than a broken neck, and that's what we were both going to incur if I went over the edge. Things were becoming somewhat acrimonious when, over to our left, I saw the outline of Daulatabad etched starkly against the night sky. I've seen it several times, but the sheer wonder of it never fails to grip me. It's a column of basaltic rock a bare quarter mile in circumference, rising a clear thousand feet straight into the air—a needle surmounted by a tiny fort that was built by the Moghuls nearly five hundred years ago, and to which there is no way up except by a winding staircase tunnelled out of the living rock.

Safaraz stopped bellyaching and said, 'The gora-log have turned off, sahib. They go towards the fort.'

I stared at the lights but they seemed to be in the same juxtaposition to us as they had been for the last half hour. However, as usual he was right, and after some minutes I realized that they had taken the branch road that led first to Daulatabad and then on to the Ellora Caves, where it ended. Aurungabad itself, a fair-sized provincial town, lay some twenty miles farther along the main road we were on at present.

I stopped. This presented difficulties. There was, I remembered, a small government guesthouse at the caves, and another one at the foot of Daulatabad, but there was no village here, so anybody turning off had, of necessity, to be going to one or the other of these two places. Both were visited by tourists, particularly when there was a cruise ship in Bombay, but they usually stayed overnight at one of the two quite modern hotels in Aurungabad and came out here on day trips. By night, as I remembered it, the whole area was deserted. It was superstition. The history of this place was particularly bloody. Ten thousand Mahrattas had once been massacred here at the foot of Daulatabad—the Moghuls used the fort itself as a place of execution, taking prisoners up the stone staircase and pushing them off the parapet above—there was a small lake near the caves said at one time to be a breeding place for crocodiles which were fed on the discarded wives of some legendary maharajah—and so on—a welter of fact and myth that was believed and feared by the local population to an extent that even the drivers of the tourist cars and coaches from Aurungabad would not stay here a moment after sundown, no matter what the monetary inducement might be.

Why were these people going there? Aurungabad itself I could understand, because that was where the hippy line recommenced after the break at Nagpur. But here was nothing. Even the two guesthouses were only used by day, for the simple reason that servants wouldn't stay here overnight—and servants in India are like cars in Los Angeles—something the average person cannot survive without. The average person? But hippies weren't average persons. Was there a colony of them up this short valley? I'd never heard of one.

I sat and pondered. Daulatabad was two miles up this road, Ellora a further three. Not such a slog—but it would be beyond Safaraz at the moment. I therefore told him to drive two miles along towards Aurungabad and to pull up and wait for me.

'Where is the sahib going?' he asked.

'On a reconnaissance,' I told him, 'and I want no argument or insubordination. Take the car away and try and behave like a soldier and not a recruit who questions orders and thinks he knows better than his officer. Go!' A bit hard, I suppose, but it is the only way with Safaraz, who can stand anything but inactivity. He went, growling in the back of his throat.

I set off up the branch road, walking noiselessly in the soft dust on the verge. It was very dark and the huge banyan trees that lined the road met overhead, cutting off the uncertain light of the moon that appeared only intermittently from behind the scudding monsoon clouds.

I arrived at the fort in something under the half hour. There is a cleared area to one side of the road that is used as a car park during the tourist season, surrounded by souvenir shops, refreshment booths and enclosures for guides and dandiwalas —the coolies who carry shoulder-high sedan chairs for those too bone-lazy to explore the fort on foot. I skirted round this, keeping to the shadows at the perimeter, and came to the first wall that surrounds the foot of the column. There are three of them, and a ditch which was flooded in the old days and, like the maharajah's lake, kept full of crocodiles. There was once a drawbridge across it, but that has given place to a modern monstrosity of box-girders, and the old cobbled road that leads through the inner bastions to the entrance of the fort proper is now tarmacked. I remembered seeing, last time I was here, two eminent Cambridge Orientalists crying gently on each other's shoulders over this. I went through the first gate and stood listening for a few moments before venturing farther. A faint breeze rustled the leaves of the banyans overhead, and in the far distance I could hear the howl of a hyena-led jackal pack, but otherwise there wasn't a sound.

I went on through the next two gates and came up to the

tunnel that leads to the winding interior staircase. Here there *was* a noise—a hollow, sobbing moan coming from the pitch darkness, and I was glad I had heard it before under less eerie conditions in the full light of day. It is merely the wind entering the top of the stairway a thousand feet up in the fort, and funnelling down like an inverted trombone. In front of the tunnel is another small car park. It is for visiting VIPs who are about to brave the seventeen hundred odd steps to the top. This is all I wanted to see—just to make sure that they weren't holed up here before I went on to the caves at Ellora. They weren't here, so I turned back and started to walk on up the valley—and saw the lights in front of me just in time.

It was a car running on its parking lights, and it was just turning into the outer car park.

It came on slowly towards me, so I dropped into the ditch at the side of the road. It passed me and went on into the inner car park and stopped in front of the stairway tunnel. I went back up the ditch to the wall and crept round it until I was abreast of the car. I couldn't see a thing but I could hear them quite plainly. As usual it was the Smiling One who was holding the floor.

'—sure we're tired, cobber, and we'd like our supper—but business first as the whore said to the bishop. One little look at it and we'll all go back.' His voice was plummy, jocular and good-humoured.

'It's going to be a bit hard to find right away,' another voice answered. 'I mean, George put it here, and he'll be back from Bombay in the morning——'

'But you said *you* put it here,' the Smiling One said. 'Come on, sport, we're wasting time.'

'No—it was George. I was with him, but I didn't see the exact place——'

There was anxiety in this voice.

'That's what I can't quite understand,' the Smiling One said kindly, reasonably. 'You're in charge—you're responsible

—you're the bloke that has to answer to me for it—but it's all "George" this, "George" that and "George" the other.'

'Well, it was his idea——'

'But *why*? Fifteen pounds of horse isn't all that big, and you had ten square miles of caves up there to stash it in. Why bring it all the way down here?'

'In case the other place ever got busted——' They had gone inside now and the voices had become a receding mumble. I had only heard the two of them, but I had the impression that there were more people present. I edged round to the tunnel and peered inside.

There was nobody there, but I could hear shuffling footsteps climbing the stone stairs, and the voices once more had become audible.

'Sure, sure, sure—we don't want all of our eggs in one basket,' the Smiling One was saying. 'I've got all that—very sensible—give you full marks for it. But this seems a hell of a place to pick. I mean, you get lots of rubber-neckers, tourists and all that here, don't you?'

'Yes, but—Just a second. It's about here somewhere—Give us the torch, will you——' I could see the faint reflection of a light filtering round the spiral of the tunnel above me. Then there was a yell and the light disappeared.

'Stop the bastard! Stop him!' the Smiling One shouted. Footsteps came pounding down towards me. I turned and ran like hell, and hard on my heels somebody else came out and almost cannoned into my back. I jumped to one side and lay flat against the verge of the cliff at the mouth of the tunnel, and the other fellow ran straight on. I could hear him panting and whimpering with fear. Then the others came shooting out, so close that somebody trod on my hand, and the Smiling One was screaming, 'Get the torch on him! Get a light, you bloody zombies!'

Lying on the ground and looking up I could see much more against the sky than at my own level. There were four of them chasing one man and I heard his despairing wail as they caught him at the next gate.

'Where's the torch?' the Smiling One demanded, and cut loose with a blast of filth when somebody said that they had dropped it. 'Bring him back to the car then,' he snarled. All jocularity had soured now. I was in an awkward enough position as it was, but when somebody switched the parking lights on it was hair-raising, because I was lying against the wall not five yards in front of the car.

Fortunately all of them except the gent in the hot seat had their backs to me and I started to edge away an inch at a time.

'All right, Driff,' the Smiling One said. 'You've had your little joke. Where is it?'

'Tumba—please—listen—You gotta believe me—it—Tumba—look——' He was past coherent speech—in a miasmic welter of fear.

'Nine five pound packs,' the Smiling One said, 'and three of 'em's missing. You give us this line of crap about it being stashed down here—we take you at your word—you pull this George story—and finally you try to take a powder on us. Now suppose we have a little bit of truth with it, eh?'

'The runners—the bums—they've been nicking a bit here —a bit there—I didn't know——' the other gasped.

'They lifted fifteen pounds off of you?' the Smiling One said incredulously. He leaned forward and his face came into the light, and when he turned to look at one of the others I could see his smile—as twinklingly good-humoured as ever—his momentary spat of peevishness now past. He winked and chuckled. 'Aw—come on now, Driff boy—you can do better than that—It's *horse* we're talking about—not horse *manure*. Valuable stuff. Come on—I just cracked a little joke. You should be laughing. Laugh, Driff—let's hear you laugh——'

I saw his fist come back, but obviously the wretched Driff didn't, because he made no attempt to dodge it or cover up.

The blow exploded full in his face and his nose spurted blood like a busted fire hose.

'Yeah, you should be laughing—because it's the funniest thing I ever heard of. The bums lift fifteen pounds of horse off of a captain and he doesn't know—so he tells *his* captain a lot of wicked little fibs—and tries to shove it on to somebody else—then he tries to run away. *To run away!* From *me*! How much did you get for it, Driff?' His fist came back again.

'I didn't get anything,' Driff moaned. 'It was the Italians——'

'I see,' said the Smiling One understandingly. 'Get that, you others? It wasn't Driff, it wasn't the bums or the little leprechauns—it was the *Italians*. The *Italians*—the bastards. Now who'd a thought it?'

'They knocked the whole consignment off last month—down in Bombay,' Driff gasped. 'I didn't know for a long time, because some of the bums never turned up again—so I got scared—scared of what you'd—you'd—think when you found out—I was going to make it up over the next few months——'

'How?'

'Cutting——' The fist went in again, in earnest this time, sickeningly.

'Cutting? You were going to *cut* it? Pure stuff for the Marseilles factories—and you were going to *cut* it? Oh, no —no—no.' The others were holding the man up now, a sagging inert weight. The Smiling One stepped back, feeling his knuckles tenderly. 'Okay, that's it,' he said. 'Just what I thought. Carpenini up to his little larks again—but you can never get the truth out of this drongo until you belt it out of him. Right—bring him along.'

They picked him up—by wrists and ankles—and went into the tunnel.

I moved farther under cover. This was working out quite well. Obviously they were going to dump the unfortunate Driff somewhere inside, and it seemed a ready-made wet-and-dry situation for me. I'd go in when they had left, and come the Good Samaritan—and possibly learn more in half an hour than I'd garnered in the last month. But they were gone quite a long time and I found myself nodding off to sleep again.

It was the shriek that snapped me back to the present. High overhead and getting louder—until it ended with a thud some yards in front of my new position. I lay there in a cold sweat, sick with the sheer horror of it.

Chapter Fifteen

THEY CAME OUT of the tunnel and switched the car lights on. One of them moved forward into the beam and I saw that it was Horton. He stood looking around in some bewilderment.

'Where's the bugger gone?' he called out.

'Maybe proving that some fairies *can* fly,' the Smiling One answered with a fat chuckle. 'Farther over, you drongo, in the bushes.'

'Driff wasn't a fairy, was he?' Horton said.

'Figure of speech,' the Smiling One answered. 'Come on for Chri'sake. I want my supper.'

'Here he is,' I heard a voice I recognized as Ahrlberg's call out from the thick jungle the other side of the car.

'Fine, so now we know he arrived safely,' the Smiling One said. 'Are you coming, or do you want a long walk back?'

'But aren't we going to bury him?' Ahrlberg asked.

'Hell no,' the Smiling One said. 'If he's found there he's just another hippy that got stoned and fell off the top. Try and hide him and somebody might get suspicious if the jackals and vultures ever dug him up.'

'Makes sense I suppose,' Ahrlberg grunted, as he got back into the car.

They drove out then. I stood and watched their lights until they turned left at the entrance and went back towards the caves. I debated for some time. I was tired and hungry. The sensible thing to do now would be to return to the car and drive on to Aurungabad and put up somewhere for the night. But then I might miss them. They could turn right or left when they came back to the main road—or, on the other hand, they might remain at the caves indefinitely. Obviously there must be others up there. I sighed. No, the only thing for it was to push on up to the caves and nose around for a bit.

I've never walked a longer three miles. I'd got to that state where I was in a sort of semi-somnambulism—where over-hanging trees were assuming the shapes of animals—and there were some damned nasty ones round those parts—actual ones —without having to imagine them. Panthers, I remembered, were a particular scourge—and I kept hearing their character-istic coughing growl. I understood fully the locals' superstitious dread of this place by the time I reached the plain where the caves started.

There was, as I have said, a government resthouse here—servantless and unattended—and across from it there used to be a ruined serai—a huge place of tumbled walls and overgrown courtyards that had once been the crocodile-owning maha-rajah's summer palace. I came upon it suddenly—and for a time I didn't recognize it, because it had been tidied up some-what and there was a big banner over the gateway, and a couple of flaring naphha lamps enabled me to read in the Hindi and Telegu scripts, 'The Ashram of the Seven Imponderables'. So this was it. What a hell of a good idea. A natural stamping ground for hippies, but one which outsiders would keep away from, particularly at night.

I sneaked round the resthouse, but it didn't avail me of much. Half the roof seemed to be off it, and it looked, generally, as if it hadn't been occupied for years. The compound was completely overgrown with bamboo and wild bananas, but there was a small stream running through it, for which I was thankful as I had a burning thirst. I looked at my watch and was surprised to see that it was already after two o'clock. That meant another four hours of darkness. I pushed through the jungle of undergrowth and came across a small summer house. Like the resthouse itself, this place was a ruin, but at least it had a couple of marble benches in it that lifted me off the damp ground. I stretched out and, after slapping mosquitoes for some minutes, drifted off to sleep.

I woke as the sky was lightening towards the east. Minahs

and hoopoes were chirping in the trees overhead, and a monkey was sitting on a broken window sill across from me, scratching itself. It chattered angrily and made off as I stirred. I went back to the stream and pulled some bananas and mangoes on the way. They made a healthy, vitamin-packed breakfast no doubt, but I'd have traded them willingly for one small cup of coffee. Bacon and eggs I didn't let myself think about.

I went to the edge of the compound and laid up under cover in a spot from where I could look into the courtyard of the ashram. A girl was moving round collecting twigs, and another was drawing water from a well near the gate. They both wore saris, but were unmistakably European. They got a fire going and put some water on it in a brass lota. The twig gatherer then went across to a shed and milked a tethered goat while the other spooned instant coffee into a collection of mugs, glasses and tin cans. Somewhere an unseen gong was struck and a thin chant went up from an assembly of male and female voices—a chant with a sort of pop beat to it—and then a not unmusical tenor intoned a prayer in bad Hindi, and another voice yelled, 'For Christ's sake pack it in until the bloody sun comes out.'

A procession of shaven-headed men and sari-clad girls came into view round the corner of a building, thumping drums, banging cymbals and shouting, 'Hari Krishna—Ah—eeee!—Hari Krishna' over and over again, working themselves into a frenzy. Other figures were coming to life now, rising from sleeping mats under rough bamboo shelters—hairy, bearded men and maxi-clad girls. One of these started a counter-melody that was taken up by the rest of them in opposition to the chant. It was a very dirty ditty that I'd heard British and American soldiers sing on the march, and the two of them merged in an impressive din. There were quite obviously two factions here—earnest postulants to Hinduism and common-or-garden hippies, distinguishable by hair or the lack of it as far as males were concerned, and saris as distinct from maxis for the girls.

The earnest ones did two rounds of the courtyard and then disappeared again behind the building at the other end, leaving the field to the hairies who sat around the fire drinking coffee. Then I saw the Smiling One and Horton appear from one of the bamboo shelters with a couple of girls, and later on Ahrlberg showed up. The girls brought a table out from somewhere, and a large safari box with a portable stove and proceeded to get breakfast under way, which I found a little hard to bear. I noticed that apart from the girls, the hippies kept a respectful distance. They finished breakfast, and the girls tidied things up while the three men sat on at the table going through some papers. I was too far away to hear normal conversation although their words were quite plain when they raised their voices. The Smiling One called out, 'All right, you blokes, gather round where you can hear, will you. And one of you go and give the spooks a yell.'

There was a general shuffling around, and the shaven types reappeared. This, I decided, I just had to hear. I pulled back into the undergrowth and crept closer to the serai wall, but I was still separated by the width of the road and I'd have been in plain view from the gate if anybody looked out while I was actually crossing. I was in a ferment and was on the point of risking a quick dash across into the shelter of the wall when I noticed that the stream which ran through the garden came under the road through a culvert. I dropped into it and crawled through knee-deep slime to the other side and found myself right under the serai wall, but still not within proper earshot as they were gathering the other side of the courtyard. I crept round under the wall and came to another gate, diametrically opposite the main one, and immediately inside was one of the bigger bamboo shelters. I ducked through and found myself a well-hidden niche between the shelter and the stonework of the wall itself.

There was a lot of banter and chiacking from the hippies, directed at the earnest ones, who received it in silent and miffish dignity. Then the Smiling One stood up and there was an instant hush, without his having to call for it, which surprised me. The smile was wider and warmer than ever.

He said, 'Some of you bastards'll never learn, will you? I can talk and talk and talk to you, but I might as well put me bloody hat on a stick and mag to that. Well, this is the last time. Any more arsing around like there was this morning and the blokes or birds concerned deal with *me*. ME. Got it? I hope you have, because it'll save a lot of misunderstandings later. We've got a good set-up here—no real wogs to bother us, but the Hari boys to give the joint the proper atmosphere when the tourists start arriving. Give them a chance to do just that, and stop ribbing them. The hippies will be coming and going between here and Bombay—same terms as last season—'

'What were they last season?' somebody asked. 'I wasn't here and all these bloody liars tell you something different.'

'Good question,' answered the Smiling One. 'I'll tell you once again. Ten trouble-free runs in ten months and you're back in England with five thousand quid in your skyrocket.'

'And one slip-up and you're eating curry and rice in Thana Jail for the next ten years,' a hippy shouted, and the Smiling One beamed.

'Yeah, you got something there, cobber,' he agreed. 'You'll be doing *that* all right—if you're lucky, and the cops get to you before *I* do. You see, slip-ups can only happen if you're silly——' There was a murmur of dissent.

'I'm *telling* you,' he went on. 'You stick to the drill and there *won't* be any slip-ups. You're each carrying a dead kilo, packed in a nylon body belt, nice and flat——'

'Which gives you prickly heat for a start,' called the first interrupter.

'Not if you wash occasionally,' cracked the Smiling One. 'Well, as I was saying—you travel quietly and inoffensively.

Anybody speaks to you you give him the "peace and love, brother" routine. Cop tells you to move on, you move on without backchat. You travel in pairs—*one stays awake while the other sleeps.* You smoke nothing but tobacco—got that? None of you's on hard stuff or you wouldn't be here—but if anybody *has* picked up a habit you'd better say so now, and we'll take you back on the eastern side and put you on work where it doesn't matter——' There was a long pause as he looked round. 'Nobody? Good. You'll each be given your dropping point and your route back here from Bombay before you start. Any questions so far?'

'Ten trips is too much, Tumba,' somebody said. 'The cops get to know your face.'

The Smiling One shook his head gently. 'No, son. There are five different routes—' He counted on his fingers, 'Train from Manmad, bus from Deolali, train from Secundurabad, bus from Sholapur—car to Ahmednagar and bus from there through Poona. You never use the same route more than twice —and that'll be spaced out. You never come back the way you went.'

'What about spot searches on the train?'

'There are no spot searches south of Manmad or west of Nagpur,' the Smiling One explained patiently, and again there was a murmur.

The smile faded for just an instant, and it had the effect of the sun going behind a cloud. 'What do you think Les and I have been doing for the last six months, ever since Istanbul was finally blown, eh?' The voice was cold and very convincing. This was pure, reasoned logic. 'Every inch of the way has been reckied. Listen to me. Junk comes in only from the east—over the hills from China and Burma. It used to go back to Europe overland—north. It can't go that way any more. It goes an entirely different route——'

'Which way *does* it go?' a girl asked, and there was a general laugh.

'A trade secret, lovey,' the Smiling One told her gently. 'Anyhow, I've talked enough. The point is, the cops expect a certain amount of locally produced stuff to go north *from* Bombay—but never to go south *into* Bombay. What would be the point? Bombay's a dead end on the junk line—or so they think. Going to Bombay, carrying, you're safe, because they won't suspect you. Coming back you're still safe, because you *won't* be carrying. You've got nothing to worry about— just so long as you stick to the drill. Any further questions?'

'When do we start the next run?'

'Les and I are going down to Bombay tomorrow to make certain everything's ready at the pick-up points. We'll send word up when we want the first five pairs to start out. Maybe in about ten days. Right? Any more?'

'Where's Driff?' a girl asked.

'He's gone back to Calcutta—special job,' the Smiling One told her.

'How did he go? Your car is still here.'

The Smiling One took a deep breath and appeared to be praying inwardly for patience. 'A second car following us, lovey,' he explained. 'It waited by the turn-off because I didn't want too much traffic coming up this way at night. Why the interest? He your boy friend?'

'Yes,' the girl said simply.

'Aw,' said the Smiling One sympathetically. 'Why the hell didn't he say so? No objection to you going with him.'

'He did mention it to *me*,' Horton said. 'I said I'd tell you, but he said not to. You know Driff. It's duty, duty all the time.'

'Okay, lovey,' the Smiling One said, like an indulgent uncle. 'When we go back to Cal we'll take you with us. All right?' And the girl smiled back at him and nodded eagerly.

The meeting broke up then. They seemed to have picked up eastern ideas very rapidly. The girls did all the chores— carrying water, gathering firewood, washing clothes in the stream and, later, as the sun rose over the trees, I saw several young children being attended to. The men just bummed around—some played cards, some sat in groups and talked, some just sat, then, inevitably, somebody brought out a guitar and they had a folk song fest. A good time was being had by all—if they happened to be built that way. The Hari Krishnas came out again and solemnly circumnavigated the courtyard, thumping their drums and yowling. The folk singers took exception to this and some of them started throwing cow pats, but the Smiling One came out and just looked at them, and they stopped very quickly indeed.

These weirdos really puzzled me. They took themselves so solemnly, yet they must have realized that they were only being used as a front. Perhaps it was a case of pure symbiosis —the hippies providing the substance and the weirdos the illusion. Both made me feel rather ill.

I withdrew into the resthouse garden again. They were here until tomorrow, which gave me some small breathing space, so I set off for where I'd left Safaraz, keeping well away from the road and walking through the jungle parallel to it. I found him in a foul temper, but he did have the car well hidden. Too well hidden, because he had managed to bog it down solidly in soft ground beside a stream, and it took an hour's digging, hauling and shoving brushwood under the wheels before we managed to get it on to the road again.

We went on to Aurungabad then and got rooms at a quite decent though modest Muslim hotel where they had primitive but efficient bathrooms and plenty of hot water. A meal and a couple of hours' sleep and I was more or less back on form. I examined Safaraz's leg again and found that he had been beguiling the time away in my absence by taking the stitches out. However, it looked all right, so I put another dressing on and trusted to luck. As they say throughout the sub-continent, the only thing tougher than a Pathan's hide is a Gurkha's head.

I lay on my charpoy and thought things out fully. They were going on to Bombay tomorrow, but I didn't know whether they would be doing the whole trip by car, or switching to the railway, so I decided to be prepared for both. We would go back after dark and get under cover near the turn-off and wait until they came out. Using the same technique as before, we would get on their tail and hang back except when we were near a station, when we would close up. If any of them got out, Safaraz would get out also and follow them. I would continue to shadow their car until I was certain of its destination. If it appeared to be returning to the ashram or back to Nagpur, I would abandon the chase and head for Bombay. Safaraz, on arrival in Bombay, if they had gone by train, would shadow them from Victoria Terminus to wherever they went, returning to the station the following morning at eight o'clock, by which time I should be there to meet him, whether I had come by road or by a later train.

Safaraz, delighted to be back in business again, took some money and went out into the bazar and bought us a complete new outfit apiece, Mahratta this time as it occurred to me that some of the dropping points the Smiling One had referred to might well be in or near a real or phony Hindu temple where Punjabi Mussulmans would stand out like longshoremen at the Drag Queens' Ball. On the other hand the Mahratta is a pretty tough sort of cooky in his own right, and he wears pantaloons in place of the Hindu dhoti, so it would only be a matter of retying our turbans if we had to switch back in a predominantly Muslim quarter.

We had another hefty meal and took the precaution of carrying some cold chapattis with us when we set out that night. We got into position right opposite the turn-off and went to ground behind a bamboo clump that completely hid the car from view at a distance of three yards.

They came just after dawn and turned right for Manmad again, so we gave them half an hour before following. We caught up with them in the bazar, but there was a lot of traffic and I was pretty certain that we wouldn't have been noticed by them even if they had been keeping a strict lookout.

On they went through the bazar towards Deolali, and then Nasik and the sharp descent of the Western Ghats to the coastal plain, with the smudge in the distant sky ahead of us that was Bombay. They stopped in Kalyan to eat, and here I took a calculated risk and drove on without halting until we came to the outer suburbs of Bombay, and I hired a taxi and put Safaraz in it with instructions to follow their car when it came through, while I, in turn, shadowed the taxi. We waited a good two hours and I was in a sweat in case they had turned off somewhere, but eventually they came through, and Safaraz gave a thumbs-up sign and off he went, the Gujerati driver following intelligently and waiting for me at all turnings and intersections where I might have gone wrong.

They went right on into Worli Bunder which faces on to the sea. There is a large sprawling area of reclaimed land there behind a retaining wall, and a shanty town has sprung up on vacant lots between tumbledown factories, fish-curing dumps and native hotels.

It was evening now, and the sun was dipping below the rim of Malabar Hill, and the roads were filled with honking trucks, buses, bullock carts and the teeming pedestrians of Bombay who exercise their inalienable right to walk where the hell they please, on the sidewalk or bang in the middle of the traffic, with carefree impartiality. So naturally I lost the taxi —and when I found it again it was halted at the side of the road and the driver was arguing with a yellow-turbaned cop, but there was no sign of Safaraz. I parked a little way up from the taxi, which drew the cop's attention to me, and he advanced upon me, pencil and ticket book at the ready, just as Safaraz reappeared. He came up and told the cop that his modesty had been affronted by two naked women who were fighting in the next street, and he wished to make a complaint.

The cop put his book away and disappeared round the corner.

'All policemen are persons of unclean mind and dissolute habits,' Safaraz said severely. 'We had better leave, sahib, before that one discovers that the fighters existed only in my imagination.'

'So you lost them?' I said sourly.

'No sahib,' he said happily. 'The Smiling One got out and went into a Goanese hotel called the Pearl of the West—two hundred yards round the next corner, and the other two went on and garaged the car—bend down and attend to something on the floor, quickly. Here is one coming back.'

'Follow him,' I said as I took a dive floorwards. 'I shall drive round this block for the next half hour. After that I shall go to O'Farrell Sahib's house.'

Horton came past, shouldering through the crowd without a glance at the car. I saw Safaraz slip on to his tail then I risked life and limb by driving out into the maelstrom and circling the block for thirty minutes, but Safaraz didn't show up again. I went off to Marine Drive then, where Red O'Farrell had the last of the lovely old merchants' houses to survive the rash of high-rise apartment blocks foreign business interests were erecting out that way. I drove into his garage and went round to the back of the house and called for a servant. Like me Red employs Pathans, and, as a Mahratta, I was told to go to hell and peddle my filthy pictures, pox cure or advertising matter for the local brothels there. There was nothing for it but to go round the front and try to make direct contact with Red. I wasn't successful because he saw me hanging around and didn't recognize me, so he set his damned great Afghan wolfhound on to me. I ran like hell and tried to call him from a phone booth, but it had suffered at the hands of vandals who had no doubt picked up the pleasant little habit from London-bred hippies.

I was pretty fed up when I returned to Red's place, but

I cheered up a little when I saw Safaraz as bereft of his dignity as I had been, being chased by that bloody dog. Fortunately Red himself came out on to the verandah and I swore at him in the Dublin dialect.

'Come in, you foul-mouthed bastard,' he invited. 'I hate stage Irishmen, but I'll give you a drink.'

He whistled the hound back and Safaraz came slinking sheepishly after it.

'Where the hell have you been?' I asked the latter peevishly.

'Following the Smiling One and Horton,' he growled, equally peevishly. 'They came out of that Goan cesspit dressed like half-pay Colonel Sahibs in English clothes. The other man did not appear. They bought suitcases in the Crawford Market, and many other things—and finally they took a taxi and went to the Taj Mahal Hotel where they were received as honoured guests.'

'How do you know that?' I asked.

'Because I followed them in, posing as a baggage coolie, and was despitefully used and thrown out again by the hall porter and five of his minions.' He sighed gustily. 'Well, four anyway —and at least they were Pathans, so the disgrace is not too overwhelming. Has O'Farrell Sahib invited us to stay here?'

'Not yet, but he will,' I said, and staggered blindly towards where Red was pouring drinks.

Chapter Sixteen

O'FARRELL is neither a Communist or ginger, the 'Red' being merely a diminutive of his Christian name of Redmond. He is of the last of a vanishing breed—an Irish lawyer practising at the Bombay Bar—note the capital B. To his often lachrymose regret there are no more bars of the other sort in Bombay in these piping days of Prohibition, but when there were he practised more in them than in court. He knows the underworld of the western seaboard of India as nobody else of my acquaintance. He is a natural linguist and has a penchant for sticking his nose into things that don't concern him. These two characteristics make him invaluable on occasion, and we have often used him in the past. He says he hates the guts of the British, has only worked for us out of his deep regard for myself and that, anyhow, he always pays our not inconsiderable honoraria straight into the funds of the IRA. I don't believe any of it. He talks about a shadowy 'Mrs O'Farrell' as if she were in the next room and would be joining us shortly, but nobody has ever seen her. Malicious people say that he is as queer as a square tomato and that he invented her to keep designing females at bay. Actually I happen to know that she lives in Cork, has seen him four times since they were married in nineteen-thirty-eight but still writes to him twice a month and knits him, for some reason quite beyond my comprehension, heavy socks in fisherman's yarn, and balaclava helmets. Their three sons and one daughter are all graduates of Trinity College, Dublin, so if he *is* queer he must drop it while on leave.

He handed me a huge amber-coloured drink in a beautiful Waterford glass. I reached for the soda syphon but he snarled at me and said, 'That's whiskey not whisky. Don't castrate it with carbon dioxide, you ignorant Welsh peasant.' Few people outside the British Isles realize that 'whiskey' is Irish and 'whisky' Scotch. Both are pronounced the same, the difference being detectable only by the look of reverence on the Mick's face and that of revulsion on the Jock's when the former is being discussed, and, of course, the reverse in the latter case. I lay back in a long Roorkhee chair and sipped my drink appreciatively. 'Glorious,' I murmured.

'It's straight panther pee, you bloody fool,' he said, taking the glass back and throwing the contents through the window. 'Look at those poor damned roses in the morning if you don't believe me.' He gave me another drink—whisky this time, and shuddered slightly as he watched me put ice and soda in it. I'm sorry if I make him sound either a bore or a boor. He is neither. Just an aficionado of all types of whisky, with or without an 'e', from liqueur Scotch to Kentucky moonshine —and he also likes to shake the credibility early in the conversation, of those he suspects he will soon be arguing with.

'What's the trouble this time?' he asked.

'Who said there was any?'

'Don't try to kid the troops, Rees. You turn up dressed like a bikriwala, sweating and panting, and try to tell me that there's no trouble——?'

'I didn't say that at all.'

'You implied it.'

'Balls.'

'Nice fella. I'm not taking on any jobs—that's for sure.'

'Wait until you're asked—and give me another drink.'

'If I wasn't the descendant of Irish kings I, also, might say wait until you're asked.' He took my glass and poured another straight four fingers. 'All right, you've played the inscrutable Oriental long enough. What's it all about?'

'When I came here I was only using your place as a rendezvous,' I said, 'but Safaraz has just told me something which alters things a bit. Can I borrow a European suit from you?'

'Sure.'

'Two fellows I've been following from Calcutta, dressed in Bengali clothes, have just switched back to gent's natty suiting and booked into the Taj.'

'Two Europeans?'

'More or less. One's an Australian.'

'Hippies?'

'How did you guess?' I asked.

'Europeans wearing Bengali clothes? What else could they be? What have they done that offends the Great White Queen?'

'It's not political,' I told him, and he grinned unbelievingly. 'Pot and horse,' I went on. 'That means——'

'You don't have to translate. You're talking to a luminary of the Criminal Bar. Bhang and heroin. Since when have you been on straight police work—if you'll pardon what may sound like a paradox?'

'All grist to the mill—and this happens to be something I feel strongly about.'

He nodded. 'I'm with you—but I can't understand why you're here. Calcutta is the start of the pipeline.'

'It's coming over this side now,' I said.

'Where does it go from here?'

'I wonder. These two at the Taj may have the answer.'

He pursed his lips and regarded me speculatively for some moments, then he said, 'Do you want my help?'

'I'd appreciate it.'

'Then suppose you cut out the bullshit and come to the point?'

'Fair enough,' I agreed. 'As far as my brief goes it *is* straight police work. Two Scotland Yard men are over here looking for the entrance to the underground rat-run that surfaces in London. I've been told to help them do that and no more, but my sense tells me that there's a political angle to it as well— or the Gaffer wouldn't be interested.'

'What would that angle be?'

'Not my job even to hazard a guess, but it's been common talk for some time that dope has been used to finance espionage, by both the Chinese and the Russians.'

He nodded again.

'More than common talk. Common knowledge. You all do it—yes, you people as well.'

'We don't deal in it commercially,' I bridled.

'You use it to suborn addicts in the Iron and Bamboo Curtain countries,' he accused. 'Don't come the Simon Pure with me, Rees. I *know*—so do you.'

'You just offered your help,' I said, standing up. 'I didn't ask for it. Okay, forget it.'

'Sit down, you damn fool,' he said. 'Of course I'll help—but I always like to clear the ground first. What do you want to do? Put the ferrets in on these two at the Taj? I can arrange that for you—an Indian private eye who looks and talks more English than Burlington Bertie.'

'No,' I told him. 'I'd rather do it myself.'

'I take it they don't know you by sight?'

'One of them has seen me once for a few moments in fairly dim light—when I was wearing Indian clothes. I think I can risk it in a European suit—and sunglasses.'

'Up to you. Can I come?'

'I'd like you to.'

So he bellowed for Sher Mohammed, his bearer, and between them they got me fitted into a Belgian linen suit that was not so tight on me as to be noticeable.

Bombay is a vastly different proposition to Calcutta. It is a pleasanter place geographically—distant mountains to the east, and the Indian Ocean at its front door—and the city itself has retained a lot of its pre-war sparkle. There are pockets of appalling poverty there, of course—that is inseparable from any Indian city—but there is fresh paint on some of its buildings, the streets are cleaner, the many parks and public gardens are better tended—and it has the best hotel in the world, albeit a dry one. The Taj Mahal.

This fabulous pub stretches for the length of two full blocks along the waterfront, and I've heard it described as the epitome of bad architectural taste—bastard Moghul on Battersea Fun Fair rococo—Miami with elephants and curry —Abdul the Damned in Disneyland etc—but to me it has always been sheer delight. In front of it stands The Gateway of India, a triumphal arch somewhat bigger than that of Paris, with a good quarter-acre of cool marble paving beneath it, shaded from the sun and open to the sea breezes, but, alas, nowadays stinking of human urine because it has become a favourite dormitory for hippies, most of whom seem to be too bone idle to walk a few yards to the water's edge to void their bladders. Time was, when I had an office in Bombay, when I would come and sit under the Gateway on sweltering evenings, but that is impossible now.

It was a fine night and there was a steady onshore breeze that made walking a sheer joy, marred only in its latter stages by the black market currency touts that infest the down-town area, peddling depreciated rupees for foreign bills and travellers' cheques at twice the official rate.

We went upstairs to the Harbour Bar and Red conjured an empty table out of thin air with a snap of his fingers. He ordered a bucket of ice and a dozen seltzers which we laced under the table from his specially tailored, form-fitting pint-and-a-half flask. A worried Parsee house dick watched us from under an arch, and Red winked at him. The dick shrugged resignedly and went away and I felt sorry for him because Parsees are men of integrity and really try to enforce the law—but at the same time they adore good scotch. The place was jampacked—Indians mostly, in both European and national dress, but with a liberal sprinkling of British and Americans and, of course, the ubiquitous Japanese.

'Now what?' Red asked.

'I'd like to check the register,' I told him. 'Their names are Hesseltine and Horton, but they may be travelling on false passports.'

'I'll go down to the office later,' he said. 'What do you want done? Their rooms searched? I know a feller who's an artist at the creep. I just saved him from a ten year preventive detention jolt.'

'Maybe later. At the moment I just want to be certain that they are staying here. I only have Safaraz's word for it, and he may have been making a genuine mistake——' And at that moment they came in.

There were four of them—the Smiling One, Horton, a dark, tubby, blue-jowled man and a rather bottle-scarred travesty of the Pukkha Sahib of yesteryear, when Britannia ruled the waves, God was in His heaven and Scotch was four pounds a case. They filed past without a glance at us and took over a reserved table some distance along the balcony.

'That's them,' I told Red. 'The two with their backs towards us. I don't know the others.'

'I do,' he said. 'Pellegrino and Major Miles Dunstable-Waygood. Want a rundown?'

'Please.'

'Pellegrino—lapsed Mafioso—chased out of Milwaukee by a rival family—started a casino in Havana—chased out by Castro—started another in the Bahamas but got on the wrong side of the law and the Bay Street Boys simultaneously. He could have handled the law, but the BSB were a different kettle of fish. His joint was busted up one night, and next morning his own left ear was delivered to him in hospital through the mail. The one he's wearing now is plastic. Well, he could take a hint with the next man, so he left. Somebody must have told him about there being Prohibition in Bombay, so he gave us the once-over in person.'

'With what in view?'

'I don't suppose he knew himself when he landed, but

within a couple of weeks he had it all doped out. Something for the tired Indian businessman—not to mention his British, American and European contemporaries. A Palace of Beautiful Sin—roulette, chemmy, blackjack and craps on the ground floor, and les girls, specially imported, upstairs—and lots of beautifully appointed bars with liquor absolutely true to label.'

'Where would he have got that from?'

'Goa. Portuguese and wide open then, and a handy two hundred miles or so down the coast. He was going to run it in by fast motor cruiser.' Red sighed gustily. 'He'd have rated a niche for his statue in front of the Gateway of India if it'd come off. But as you know, India annexed Goa about then, so Pellegrino was out on a limb again, and he'd sunk an awful lot of money into the preliminary build-up. He started a couple of hotels, one here and one in Poona, but he was being watched too closely for him to make them real boys' playgrounds, so he sold up and drifted off. I heard he'd gone to Kenya—then to the Seychelles. He turned up here again a couple of weeks ago. What he's on at the moment is anybody's guess. Okay?'

'Thanks. And the gent with the face like a sorrowful mule?'

'Not to mention the monocle. The Galloping Major, eh? He was a broadsman—you know, a cardsharper—working the P and O liners between here and Tilbury. The poor bastard is a casualty of progress. There's no regular seaborne passenger traffic out of India any more—and whoever heard of anybody handling five hot aces on a Boeing! The old maestros needed a week for the approach and build-up, a further week in which they steadily lost money to the selected pigeons, then a sudden death, double-or-quits blitzkrieg right through the last forty-eight hours of the trip, during which they skinned the clientele to their socks. Psychologists to a man. Old Dung-stable, known to his colleagues as Horseshit, was the best of the lot. He must have made fifty thousand pounds a year at his peak—with no income tax. And a maharajah

once had the gall to call him a cheat. Dung-stable slapped a
writ for slander across his bracket. We got a hundred thousand
rupees damages, *and* costs—'

'*We?*'

'Well, naturally he had the savvee to engage the best lawyer
in Bombay—but unfortunately the resultant publicity ruined
the business. He came ashore here and drank himself stiff for
a time, then the Indian authorities hinted that his room would
be preferable to his company, and he drifted on to East Africa
—Kenya, I think. That's where he must have met Pellegrino,
because they came back together. Dung-stable was wearing a
bush hat with a bit of nylon simulated leopardskin round it
when they landed.'

'White hunter?'

'Yes—that's their label, but the vast majority of them never
see the sun outside the Nairobi bars. Dung-stable, I'm damned
certain, wouldn't know which end of a gun made a rude noise.'

'But you said he was a major?'

'*He* said he was a major. The Tenth Hussars, he claims
—but I don't think he'd know which end of a *horse* made a
rude noise either. There are more phony majors in Bombay
than there are colonels in Kentucky.' He rose. 'All right,
I'll go down and see what I can fossick out at the office. The
flask is under the table. Don't wander off to the gents' and
leave it there, for God's sake.'

I sat watching them. I'd have given a lot to have overheard
what they were saying. It was obviously a conference because
the four heads were together the whole time. The Smiling
One was grinning wider than ever, and Horton appeared to
be either selling or persuading, because I could see his clenched
fist coming down on the table in emphasis from time to
time. The two newcomers were completely poker-faced. They
just listened.

Red came back after a time. 'Hesseltine and Horton, like
you said,' he told me. 'Booked in this afternoon and said

they'd be staying about a week. Both of London—Hesseltine calls himself a consulting engineer and the other's an archæologist. Pellegrino and the Major have been here since last Thursday. They got in on the Karanja, from Mombasa. They're going to be here about a week also. Developer and Gentleman of Independent Means, respectively, the cheeky old bastard. Now, do you want that looksee into their rooms?'

'Tempting,' I said, 'but I don't know that I'd be able to brief your creeper on what to look for. Can I take a raincheck on that?'

'Certainly. Anything else I can do?'

'Nothing I can think of at the moment—unless your offer includes making myself your guest for the time being?'

'Naturally. Are you putting a tail on them at all?'

'No. I'll just drift around from time to time with Safaraz, to get a general idea of their movements and contacts. Would your influence with the office extend to being able to get advance notice of a move by them?'

He winked and tapped the side of his nose. Red had been dealing with crooks of all colours for so long that he reacted like them.

'Fine,' I said. 'I'd appreciate that. You'll let me know if you're out of pocket over it, of course.'

'You insult me,' he said. 'I'll give you a bill when it's all over.'

'It wouldn't be possible to bug their rooms, I suppose?'

'You insult me still further,' he said, and started to do sums. 'Four rooms at two hundred and fifty rupees each —total one thousand smackers. Tape of all conversations, straight or phone, twenty-five rupees per running minute. That's what this private eye bloke will be charging, and it includes a small commission for myself, so you won't be getting stung for anything more. Call it fifteen hundred altogether. And for another five hundred the creep will do their rooms. Two thousand—how does that strike you?'

'Very generous.'

'On the other hand, if that miserable old son-of-a-bitch, the Gaffer, cares to stick a couple of cases of whiskey, with an "e", in the diplomatic bag, we'd call it square.'

'Couldn't be fairer.'

'Plus one of scotch, and I'll have 'em expertly tailed for you for their entire stay here.'

'Better and better.'

Then began five nerve-racking days because the coverage Red laid on was good—really good—probably too good. I would be wakened at three a.m. by a skinny black claw gently shaking my shoulder through the mosquito net—because Red's house wasn't air-conditioned—and a voice would come through the darkness, softly. 'Sahib, the Smiling One visits a house of joy in Grant Road. His friend goes there also, but only to sit in the room below to drink coffee. Earlier they went to the beach at Juhu, there to swim in the ocean.' Or, 'Sahib, they both visited the Buddhist ashram at Apollo Bundar, where they talked with long-haired white gora-log.' And tapes used to come in at all hours of the day and night —the Smiling One inquiring after his laundry—Horton ordering nimbo-pani, which is the juice of fresh limes squeezed on to cracked ice and sugar, or Pellegrino wanting to know, querulously, when the Goddam hell thatta bootalegga going to come back widda da whisk'. Major Dunstable-Waygood maintained an aloof silence throughout. Their general conversation, when they were all together in one room, never yielded anything but such aphorisms as, 'I'll buy', 'Twist, twist, *Stuff it*,' and 'Horseshit, you bastard, pull another one like that and I'll cut your Goddamned throat,' from which I gathered that a practically non-stop game of pontoon was in progress. Either they were very well trained indeed, or they suspected that Big Brother was bugging them—which really is saying the same thing.

To save Safaraz from extreme boredom and the resultant

mischief he would be bound to get into, I set him on tailing the Smiling One, withdrawing Red's man. Since I didn't want him to climb the front elevation of the Taj in order to snoop into windows—which he would have done with the greatest of pleasure, given the opportunity, I told him merely to follow the Smiling One one afternoon, should he leave the hotel. And, surprisingly, it paid off. He came in that evening very pleased with himself.

'He went to the Goanese hotel they called at the first day, sahib. The Smiling One went inside, then came out with the other gora in the Bengali khamis——'

'You mean Ahrlberg?'

'That is what I have heard you call him, though I, myself, cannot pronounce such an outlandish name. They went together to a big building near the waterfront. See—I have written the words that were painted on the front of it in large etters——'

He had too—stroke by painful stroke he had copied on to the inside of a cigarette packet with a pencil—'MACKINNON, MACKENZIE & CO. LTD. Passenger & Forwarding Agents.'

'That was on the front of the building, sahib. On the side was this——' And on another piece of cardboard he had carefully inscribed 'Commit No Nuisance' and 'Peshab man'a kata hai' which meant the same thing, rather more forcibly. Both, with advantage, could have been inscribed on the Gateway of India.

'You have done very well,' I said, and if he hadn't had a face like the business end of a battering ram he might have succeeded in looking modest.

'The sahib is fortunate in having a man of resource and education in his employ,' he admitted, 'but I did even better than that. While the Smiling One waited in the taxi outside, this—this—Hillpig?——'

'Ahrlberg.'

'—went inside to a place where many babus and others of

low caste sat writing and talking on telephones—and he went to a grating over a counter that was marked thus——' He proudly proffered yet another cigarette packet with the words, 'Deck Passengers' on it.

'Wah! Wah! Ajib!' I said in tones of deepest admiration—and I really meant it.

'A babu came and they started to talk, and I moved nearer to hear what was said——' He looked downcast 'but they spoke in English, and there they lost me. I'm sorry, sahib.'

I thumped him on the shoulder. 'Is it your fault that you had to deal with ignorant men that cannot speak the beautiful languages of the East? Let there be no sorrow, Safaraz. You have acquitted yourself magnificently. Here are ten rupees which you may take as an offering to the mosque.'

'May the sahib have seven sons,' he said solemnly, which, I suppose, would be as likely to happen as would be the mosque to receive the tenspot.

I went and found Red. 'An American hippy may be travelling somewhere as a deck passenger,' I told him. 'Name of Ahrlberg—but there again he might have another passport.'

'How do you know he's shipping out?'

'He was seen talking at the deck passenger window at Mac and Mac's.'

Red was a wonderful guy for action. He did some telephoning and was back with the answer in less than five minutes. 'He's going out on the *Karanja*,' he said. 'Sailing tomorrow.'

'Where does she go?'

'Durban—calling at the Seychelles, Mombasa, Zanzibar, Lourenco Marques and a fistful of other East African ports. Your friend is booked for Beira actually, but he's got stop-over facilities, and he is thinking of dropping off in the Seychelles and getting a later boat onwards.'

'What are the air routes like?'

'Up to the present moment there aren't any, other than a twice weekly hop to Nairobi. Next week it will be different.'

'Why?'

'Christ, you *are* isolated over in Calcutta, aren't you? It's worldwide news. The jet airport opens for business on Mahé —that's the biggest and most important of the Seychelles group of islands.'

I remembered reading various bits of travel blurb then. 'The Bermuda of the Indian Ocean', they were calling it.

'Bloody shame,' Red went on. 'The last paradise. The most beautiful islands you ever saw—and the laziest, friendliest people—all given over now to highrise hotels, casinos, golf courses and fat-arsed near-millionaires in Bermuda shorts and Hawaian shirts. Bacardis'n'cokes, suntan lotion, wrap-around shades, gambling and fornication.' He spat. 'You're not listening to a word I say, are you?'

'Actually I wasn't. I wanted information, not gripes.'

'How long is the sea trip?'

'A week.'

'And by air, when it's eventually running?'

'About two-and-a-half hours, I believe—but the main line will be from that side—London, Cairo, Nairobi, Mahé—and return. There'll only be the odd one from here.'

That settled it. 'I'll send Safaraz on the boat to keep an eye on this type, while I stay on and cover the other two,' I said.

'But they're all going,' Red said. 'Sorry—I forgot to mention that Hesseltine, Horton, Pellegrino and Old Dung-stable are booked on her too—the swell end—first class.'

Chapter Seventeen

WELL, THAT CERTAINLY tidied things up a bit. All the crows under the one net. But it presented me with a very tricky problem. Obviously I would have to travel on the ship now —but on which part of her? With the four of them up the 'swell end'?—or, with Safaraz, as a deck passenger? Both had obvious disadvantages—with a slight bias towards the latter alternative. As deck passengers, we could pass as anything at all, in clothes that could well constitute a disguise in themselves. In the first class, however, I could only be Mr Idwal Rees, a respectably dressed gent of Welsh extraction —bumping into them on the promenade deck, the smoke-room, bar and dining saloon. Even if Horton didn't remember me from our brief Calcutta encounter, I would certainly be fixed in his and the others' memories in the future.

No—it would have to be the deck. I sighed inwardly. I never seemed to be able to carve myself off a hunk of dolce vita on my expense account.

'What sort of people travel on these boats?' I asked Red.

'Saloon or deck?'

'Both.'

'Topside—about one-third European to two of Asiatic with a very small sprinkling of East Africans. The Europeans are about fifty-fifty business men, with or without their wives, and tourists, usually *with* wives. Most go right through to the East and South African ports, though a few drop off at the Seychelles. The Asiatics are usually moneyed people—merchants, doctors, lawyers—returning to Africa after family or business trips to the homeland. Few, if any, ever get off in the Seychelles.'

'Assuming that our people get off there, would I be conspicuous as an Asiatic if I got off too?' I asked him.

'You wouldn't make it. The British Colonial Administration in the Seychelles is traditionally hospitable and easygoing, but since East and South Africa have closed their doors to Indian immigrants there has been a tendency for them to try the shorter jump to Mauritius and the Seychelles, so now they're barred—on the principle of the inability of holding a quart in a pint pot.' He looked at me aghast, as a thought struck him. 'Christ! You're not thinking of going as a deck passenger, are you?'

'Yes—there will be fewer problems that way,' I said.

'You're mad. Go as an Asiatic if you like, but why not first class?'

'It would be much safer to merge into the background—a really crowded background.'

He shrugged, then shuddered. 'Sooner you than me, cocker,' he said.

'Oh, it won't be too bad,' I said, more to reassure myself than him. 'It's only for a few days after all.'

'I had to go to Jiddah once. That's the port for Mecca. There was no airport there in those days and the only way in was by pilgrim boat.' He shuddered again. 'My God! I spent the last three days permanently in the delousing bin. And to make matters worse it was a dry ship. What will you front as?'

'It will have to be as a Muslim,' I told him. 'I've got a phony passport in the name of Mohammed Ishaq.'

'Better be an Ismaili then,' he suggested. 'Not all of them wear whiskers.'

He was absolutely right. The Ismailis, that powerful if unorthodox Islamic sect which is headed by the Aga Khan, are congregated for the most part in Bombay and the East African ports. They are shopkeepers and merchants—light complexioned and finely featured—and they dress in a distinctive style—jodhpurs, silk frockcoats and small embroidered skull-caps. Most of the older ones grow a fringe of chin-whiskers, but there are many who don't.

I told Safaraz to go out and buy two complete sets of Ismaili clothes for each of us, and, as I fully expected, I got a reaction of pure horror.

'Ismailis, sahib?' he gasped. 'We men of action to dress as boxwallahs? Oh, *no*, sahib——'

'You're quite right,' I told him. 'Make it two sets for me alone—and buy yourself a rail ticket back to Calcutta at the same time. Whoever heard of a Pathan trying to pass himself off as an Ismaili? He would be recognized for what he was immediately. The Ismailis are a fine intelligent race with the manners of kings and chiefs—not belching, swearing, fornicating, boastful rascals who——' But the last words fell on empty air as he was already on his way to the bazar.

I had less difficulty than I expected in booking passages on the *Karanja*. I always carry three passports when on a job —my own, one in the name of Mohammed Ishaq, and Safaraz's. It was ironic to think that only my own was suspect, and that if I slipped up on this mission or in any other way incurred my master's displeasure I'd find myself a stateless person. The prospect wasn't quite as bad as I thought it would be at first because I found that there were degrees even in the third class section, and 'deck passenger' was a misnomer. One could sleep in open section standees, which were berths something like the couchettes on Continental trains, or, for the expenditure of a few more rupees, even book a small, plain but quite adequate cabin. The most expensive ones were four-berthers and I pondered long over this. Being cooped up with two strangers, quite possibly real Ismailis, would probably prove to be an insupportable strain. One word out of place—one northern phrase in the normal southern idiom of these people, and suspicions would inevitably be aroused.

But Red not only fixed it so that the two of us would get a four-berth cabin to ourselves ('I got the chief booking clerk's brother off a nasty one a couple of years ago.')—he also obtained a promise of assistance from the First Mate should we need it. ('He was being jacked out of a legacy back home in Swansea, but I got a judgement in absentia in his favour.') All I had to do, apparently, was to mutter in English, 'I bet it's raining like hell in Cardiff,' to secure the wholehearted co-operation of all hands and the cook, if anything went wrong on board.

Ballard Quay the day we sailed was like the anteroom to hell itself. Passengers, cargo, emigration officials, police, medical, currency control and just plain hustlers, con men and peddlers jammed a couple of hundred square yards of wharf space under a tin roof on which the sun beat down with implacable ferocity. The din and the stench had to be heard and smelt to be believed—and yet, in some peculiar way, the whole scene had a fascination of its own. I suppose every race in India was represented there, and not a few from other parts, because a group of about thirty hippies of both sexes were sprawled on the ground with their sleeping bags and odds and ends of miscellaneous junk. They had a Persian huqa, the big ornate tobacco pipe that is watercooled and stands on the floor, and they were passing its flexible stem round the assembled party. This mob had pot mixed with the tobacco, and the stink of it transcended that of the packed mass of bodies and even some baled hides nearby.

Safaraz and I tailed on to the end of the queue that led up the third class gangway, and inched forward at an overall rate of one yard in ten minutes, which suited me because it enabled me to study the people going up the first class gangway farther along the wharf. Red had checked for me that morning that the four were still booked on her in the first class section and that Ahrlberg was riding with us, but I knew that I'd be happier when I actually saw them embark.

Ahrlberg arrived some time after us and I saw him join the gang of hippies. He knew some of them because there were a few perfunctory 'Hi-s' and a peace sign or two, and somebody offered him the mouthpiece of the huqa, but he shook his head.

The queue crawled on, and just as we got to the foot of the gangway, Safaraz nudged me and gestured towards the other one, and I saw the four of them filing up and disappearing into a doorway on deck. I heaved a sigh of relief. A bell was ringing somewhere and there was an impatient toot on the ship's siren which seemed to galvanize the officials at the foot of the gangway, because they started to round up the hippies and hustle them aboard at the tail of our queue.

I was pleasantly surprised at the state of the ship. She was an amiable old lady of pre-war vintage, but was as clean as a hound's tooth and meticulously maintained. We followed a Goanese steward down a series of companionways to a minuscule cabin with four bunks and a wash basin in it—and Safaraz threatened to emasculate him when he demanded a tip, which was out of character for an Ismaili, who are a gentle people. The Goan departed hurriedly, and I turned on Safaraz and rended him, then I saw that he was green about the gills, so I relented. That was his weakness. He had travelled with me by sea before—and he was always as sick as a dog even before we got out of harbour. I told him that he could go ashore if he wished, and return to Calcutta, knowing full well that he'd have faced a firing squad rather than that.

And so eventually we got under way, and I watched the skyline of Bombay receding in the distance—a skyline where once the Gateway of India, the Taj Mahal Hotel and the palm trees round Government House on Malabar Hill were the highest features, but now it is coming into uniformity with every other dreary seaport in the world and is being poxed and polluted by the highrise developers. But the dhows are still there—the magnificent lateen-sailed vessels that ghost their way on the huge triangle formed by Basra, at the head of the Persian Gulf, Bombay and Mombasa. A group of them was leaving harbour with us, their crews of Aden Arabs and chattering Somalis holding their courses even when the scant and erratic shore breezes took them across our bows, knowing that, with the exquisite courtesy of the sea, power would give way to sail if it came to a tight pinch.

I walked round our crowded section of deck looking for a vacant patch where I could place my prayer mat and ostensibly study the green covered Koran I had furnished myself with. No Indian of any religion whatsoever will attempt to get into conversation with a man studying an obvious devotional book. I found a place at the foot of the after mast, on a platform that supported a battery of cargo winches and which raised me to the level of the promenade deck so that I could see right along the port side of the ship, and I told Safaraz to find himself a similar position on the starboard side—not that any useful purpose would be served by watching these types, but because, as I have explained already, a job, any sort of job, tends to keep him out of mischief—and there were some very sonsy wenches on board, African and forthcoming, not meek and modest like Asiatic women. But I needn't have worried—all the houris of Paradise wouldn't have interested him at that juncture. All he could do was to lie on his back and moan, 'A-ree! Bahud taklif hamara pait men hai' (There is great sadness and trouble in my belly). I was very sorry for him—but very relieved also.

I sat on my mat, sandals off, bare feet tucked beneath me, my nose a few inches from the dog-eared pages of the book, gently rocking to and fro and mumbling reverently. Ahrlberg passed close to me. He gave me a casual glance and walked by, and I studied him obliquely to see if there was a double take, but I needn't have worried. If I were recognized for something other than I purported to be, it would be by another Ismaili not a Minnesota farm boy to whom, no doubt, all Asiatics, real, or pretended, would seem alike.

I moved from my perch before the hour of the sunset

prayer. I know the routine of it—the standing, the bowing, the kneeling and finally the prostration—and I have memorised the sonorous Arabic phrases that go with it—but I've always had a strange reluctance to go through with it merely for my own ends—to sustain a role. I stirred Safaraz as I passed and warned him that as a genuine Muslim he would have to start thinking about his devotions in a few minutes, unless he wished to be looked askance upon by his co-religionists. He moaned that Allah and his Prophet Mohammed knew what tortures he was going through and would therefore forgive him missing prayers this once.

'Get up you bum,' I said. 'The ship is as steady as a rock.'

'The devils in my belly aren't,' he snuffled. 'Let me die here in peace, sahib.'

I hoisted him to his feet and got him down to the cabin, deck by deck, and dumped him into his bunk. The steward —Goanese and therefore Christian—was watching us balefully from the end of the alleyway. He came along and said to me, loudly and with malice aforethought, 'Are the Ismaili gentlemen taking the evening meal? Tonight it is a very good mutton curry—nice and fat and cooked in ghee, which as Your Excellencies know, is clarified butter——'

I managed to jump clear just as Safaraz unburdened himself, but it put paid to the cabin as a sleeping place as far as I was concerned, so I grabbed a pillow and a blanket and, as the Imam intoned his last call, I found myself a space away up in the bows, and after finishing a large bowl of curry I settled down to sleep, lulled by the gloriously cool breeze that blows constantly across the Indian Ocean at the end of the monsoon.

Safaraz was marginally better next morning when I went down to see him. 'Last night I wished to die, sahib,' he said faintly, 'but today I wish to live—just long enough to cut that damned Goan's throat when a little of my strength has returned.'

The ship was magnificently run and there was no herding of third class passengers into the well decks—first and second class passengers had the upper promenade and part of the boat deck roped and railed off for their exclusive use, but we humbler folk had the run of the rest of the ship. Solemnly circulating round the lower promenade deck, from time to time reading aloud to myself from the Koran, I saw the quarry on several occasions—sometimes singly, sometimes together, but naturally I wasn't able to get near enough to them to eavesdrop. Where were they headed for, I wondered? Their tickets were for the whole trip, but they were tourists' 'stopovers', which meant they could get off anywhere, and join a later boat.

The next few days passed pleasantly enough, each exactly like the one before it. There was a cinema show every night, Indian films alternating with American and British ones. With the south-east monsoon now over, the sea was as calm as a millpond, so much so that even Safaraz surfaced once more, swearing that an amulet which he had bought from a mullah in Waziristan many years ago, and which he wore round his neck on a thin silver chain, had finally overcome the devils which battled in his belly. He now ate like a starving horse, slept, lounged, got bored and, in normal sequence, went looking for trouble—and found it.

It started small, as these things always do. Two young Englishmen strolled along the first class promenade deck and leaned on the rail and looked down into the well deck. I'd seen them before and had categorized them as soldiers because their hair was cut short back and sides and there was a drilled set to their shoulders. I was sitting in my usual place by the winches, which brought me level with them. They must have noticed the green-covered Koran on my knees, because they inclined their heads civilly and intoned, 'Salaam a'leikoum,' (Peace be unto you) and I gave the formal answer of 'Wah a'leikoum salaam' (And to you also be peace). Then, obviously to practise their quite good but very stilted Arabic, they told me that they were 'soldiers of price' (mercenaries), Sandhurst-trained youngsters who had found present day service in the British Army rather claustrophobic, and had volunteered for service in the army of one of the small but incredibly rich oil sheikhdoms on the Persian Gulf. They were now on end-of-contract leave and were taking a vacation to the Seychelles before going back for another three years. Safaraz listened entranced. These were pukkha officer sahibs of a type whose passing he was constantly bemoaning. All Englishmen in India nowadays, with the graciously conceded exception of myself, were box-wallahs—a term of opprobrium for businessmen. I had to kick him furtively once or twice to forestall attempts to butt into the conversation. Ismailis are never soldiers, and since most of Safaraz's anecdotes concerned his army days, they would have been right out of character.

They went off as the saloon luncheon gong sounded, but they came back at the same time the following day. We had been conversing for some minutes when a hippy, stoned out of his skull, climbed the ladder from the well-deck and called these two 'cossacks of capitalism', 'janissaries' and finally 'boss's bully boys'. It was obviously a resumption of a previous rumpus, and the two boys took it very well indeed until the hippy was ill-advised enough to take a swing at one of them. The mercenary had evidently been taught in a very rough school indeed. He brushed the clumsy swing off with his left and countered with his right—fist up and elbow down, a nasty combination when one's nose happens to be the point of impact for both blows. The hippy shrieked and did a back somersault down the ladder. It acted like a match to a powder keg, and the rest of the hippies who had been watching and listening to the verbal exchange and egging their pal on, now came surging up the ladder—and before I could stop him, Safaraz was into the mêlée with a howl of pure joy.

Odds of some thirty to three sound pretty formidable, but

when the three have the higher ground, their backs to a steel bulkhead and really know their rough-housing tactics as these did, it evens things out considerably.

I sat there sweating and at the same time thanking my lucky stars that I'd had the foresight to take the Khyber knife Safaraz always carried under his shirt away from him on embarkation.

It didn't last for long but there were some twenty of them out cold in the well deck, having fought their way up the ladder only to describe a series of parabolas through the air back to their starting point, when the three mates, a couple of large engineers and the serang with the deck-cleaning hose arrived at the double, and the whole thing was sorted out in a matter of minutes. But unfortunately, with true British impartiality, they pinched the mercenaries, six hippies who were on their feet at the top of the ladder—and Safaraz. They had their work cut out with him and I was thankful when the serang crowned him with the heavy brass nozzle of the hose, because he was bellowing the only four words of English he knows, extremely dirty ones, at the top of his lungs, and attracting a lot of unwelcome attention to himself thereby, because by this time the first class passengers had turned out to a man, plus quite a high proportion of the distaff side, to see the fun.

The combatants were frogmarched down to the ship's brig in jig time, and I sat on in my place by the winch and listened to the babble of excitement on the well deck.

'Ah, my brothers,' one old greybeard was saying, 'I had my doubts of that tall one. He was no Ismaili. Didn't I say that to my son Ali only yesterday? Tell them, Ali.' And other inspired liars were joining in the denunciation. I buried my nose in the Koran and tried to look as if I wasn't there. What the devil happened now, I wondered? We were due into the Seychelles tomorrow. Suppose the quarry disembarked here —what then? I'd naturally follow—but what would happen to that fool Safaraz if he were still in the brig? The ship stayed only a matter of some hours I had been told.

I sighed. There would be nothing for it but to contact the First Mate. I hate disclosing my identity once I've embarked on a job. It would probably be all round the ship by this time tomorrow—an Englishman and a Pathan—both always suspect in the East—on board in disguise. That would make a juicy little bit of shipboard chitchat, and blow the whole thing to the opposition. I resolved for the fortieth time to fire Safaraz when we got back, once and for all.

I sat on cogitating until late in the evening, to that magic hour at sea—if you are lucky enough to be travelling with the upper crust—when the world stands still between daylight and darkness, and the women are all below dollying up and the men are gravitating to the bar to load up on cut-price, duty-free drinks before dinner. I had noticed the First Mate on previous days. He was obviously a man of set habits. He always came down from the officers' quarters on the boat deck, immaculate in tropical mess kit, and he would pause for some minutes leaning on the rail and finishing a cigarette before going in to the smoke-room bar.

He did the same this evening, just as the bridge bell struck seven times. I ghosted along the promenade deck towards him. It was deserted except for an Indian ayah playing with a couple of small white children. I came up beside the big man, checking that he had three gold bars on his blue epaulettes, and said, 'I bet it's raining like hell in Cardiff.'

Chapter Eighteen

HE SAID, without looking at me, 'If you go up the companion-way at the after end of this deck, you'll see a recess along-side the last lifeboat. Wait for me there.'

I found my way past a multi-language notice barring this part to passengers and climbed to the boatdeck, and a few minutes later he joined me.

He said, 'What's the trouble?' and I thought I detected a note of irritation in his voice, like that of a man who had promised a favour that he never thought he'd be called upon to honour.

'That fracas on the after well deck,' I said, 'one of the people you ran in happened to be my assistant.'

'Which one?'

'The Ismaili——'

He scowled. 'It would be. He's the only one who has given trouble. They all came up in front of the Old Man half an hour ago. The hippies and the tin soldiers apologized and gave an undertaking to behave, but your chap didn't under-stand—or *said* he didn't understand English——'

'He doesn't.'

'We got the serang—that's the Lascar bosun—in to inter-pret, and your man called him a fat-gutted, lying son of a whore. The serang lost his head and the next moment they're having a set to in the Old Man's day-room.'

'I'm sorry about that,' I said.

The mate grinned grudgingly. 'So's the Old Man. He was about to give a drink party to some of the saloon passengers, and his cabin is ankledeep in peanuts, olives and gin. He's let the others out, but the serang is in the sick bay and your bloke is back in the rattle.'

'How long is the Captain keeping him in?' I asked.

'Until he disembarks. Which *is* your port, by the way?'

'That depends on where certain other people get off.'

'Who are they?'

'A party of four—an Australian, two Englishmen and an Italian——'

'Oh, *that* crowd? They're getting off tomorrow at Mahé—but you two won't be able to—not unless you've got special authority.'

'We haven't.'

'It'll have to be Mombasa then—and even there it will be a bit sticky for Asiatics.' He peered at me closer. 'You *are* an Asiatic, aren't you? Although Mr O'Farrell said you were British.'

'All things to all men,' I parried. 'I'm afraid Mombasa won't suit me at all—not if these others get off in the Seychelles. Can you help us slip ashore?'

'I'm afraid not. I take it you've never been there before? You'd understand if you had. Ships have to anchor a mile and a half off-shore—and passengers and cargo are lightered in to the Long Pier where the Customs, Police and Medical people are stationed. You'd have to run the gauntlet of the lot.'

'No chance of slipping off in a hired boat?'

'Not with this Old Man. He hates bumboats hanging around and the harbour police have orders to keep them away.'

'What sort of swim would it be?'

'Not one I'd care to risk. There's a hell of a tide-rip there and possibly the odd shark or two.'

'Forget the swim,' I said hurriedly. 'Damn. That means that I'll have to radio for special facilities. How long do we stay there?'

'Twenty-four hours—a bit longer than usual—because we're taking on water. The Old Man hates Bombay water so he only quarter fills the tanks there.' He broke off and thought for a moment. 'There's a possibility there—but only a faint one.'

'Of what?'

'The water lighter. There's always a crowd of Seychellois longshoremen aboard it. If you could slip on to it and lay low until it returns to the shore——'

'Fine,' I said. 'So it will only be a matter of getting my man out of hock first——'

'We'll have to play that as it comes——' And then we heard footsteps approaching and in the darkness a match flared as someone lit a cigarette, so I gumshoed off to the companion-way.

The clangour of the anchor being dropped woke me before dawn next morning. I went up on deck and found it deserted except for a couple of Lascars getting ready to lower a boat ladder from the promenade deck, and others about their quiet and well-ordered business on the fo'c'sle and poop. The sky was lightening to the east, and even as I watched, the first rays of the sun came up over the horizon and caught a huge white sphere perching on top of the highest peak of the island like a gigantic golf ball on a tee. This, I remembered reading somewhere, was the aerial of the American Satellite Tracking Station that had recently been set up here. The town of Victoria was right abeam of us, a cluster of lights that were paling in the rising sun. Away to the south I could see the winking light of a plane taking off from the new airfield.

Motor launches were puttering out over the glass-smooth blue-black of the lagoon on which a string of smaller islands floated like dark jewels, and soon two or three of the boats were within the light cast by electric clusters round the boat ladder, and the first of the shore people came aboard—a keen young British type in the uniform of the Colonial Police—too bloody keen by far, I thought—two portly Seychellois Customs Officials conversing in something I only partially recognized as French, which is the basis of the lingua franca they call Creole. The port doctor came alongside then, but couldn't get close enough to the foot of the boat ladder to jump, and he was yelling, 'Vit' vit' vit', salaud!' and a couple of large black boatmen in an oil company launch hanging on to their vantage point with a boathook, gave him a V sign, rudely. Then the police launch came back out of the darkness and swooped to the assistance of the medico, and there was a certain amount of not too rancorous bellowing and shoving— and the first of the boats, having deposited their men on board, were making back for the shore. I looked longingly at them. If only that fool Safaraz had been with me instead of being locked up in the brig, we could have got aboard one of them in the momentary confusion, because now there was a two-way stream jostling each other up and down the ladder.

The loudspeakers were clearing their throats for the first of many announcements in English, Gujarati and a couple of African dialects I didn't understand. The gist of them was:

'Passengers disembarking at Mahé will please assemble in the second class saloon with their passports, vaccination, yellow fever and cholera immunization certificates, when landing permits will be issued. *Through* passengers wishing to go ashore for shopping or sightseeing will go to the second class smoke-room with the same documents, for the issue of temporary landing cards.'

I was standing near the windows of the smoke-room, which opened on to the lower promenade deck, and I could see a Seychellois police sergeant and a couple of civilian clerks arranging a pile of yellow cards at the end of a table. The first of the sightseers arrived—an African with his wife, and I watched as their documents were scrutinized and then retained in place of one of the yellow cards. 'You get them back when you return the card,' the sergeant explained. Several Africans and a dozen or so hippies went through without a hitch, then a Sikh came in. I saw a quick glance dart between the sergeant and his assistants, and even out on the deck I could feel the change in atmosphere.

'Name please, sir?' the sergeant asked politely.

'Kushipal Singh.'

'Domicile?'

'Look at damn passport, man,' the Sikh grated. 'I am only wanting to go ashore for short period.'

The sergeant took the passport, studied it, then returned it. 'I'm sorry, sir. Regulations——'

'What damn regulations?'

'I think you know already, sir. Asiatics of East African domicile are not permitted to land.'

'Why not?'

The sergeant sighed. 'Because, sir, if you did not return to the ship before it sailed you would have to remain here for thirty days until the next ship, thereby establishing temporary residence, then both Indian and East African authorities can refuse you entrance—and we have got you for all time. Now move along, please.'

The Sikh yelled, 'If I give you bakshees I can go—That is it, no?'

The sergeant's face hardened, and the careful English started to slip. 'Attention, m'sieur——' he began, then corrected it to, 'Watch it, sir. You are committing a breach of the peace.'

The Sikh hammered the table, snarling with fury. The sergeant stood up. He was a big man, café au lait in colour but with Negroid features. The Sikh stopped his hammering, shrugged hopelessly and went out through the end door, and by this time I was hard on his heels. I was genuinely sorry for him and for all other Asiatics of African domicile. Many of them have been in Kenya, and Uganda particularly, for generations. They hold British passports dating from the old Colonial days, but these will not take them into England*— and India no longer acknowledges them as nationals—and

---

* Written before September 1st 1972, when such passports were, in fact, honoured by the British Government for humanitarian reasons.

the new African rulers want to get rid of them because they control most of the business in East Africa, and are the doctors, lawyers and bankers. The sergeant, thoroughly put out, merely looked at me and shook his head, so I filed meekly past and out the other end, and the chance of pinching two of the yellow slips in passing perished stillborn.

I sat in my accustomed place looking wistfully shoreward. It was a magnificent sight now the sun was up, not unlike Hong Kong—soaring peak over narrow foreshore, with winding mountain roads and attractive bungalows tucked away on shelves. But it was, as yet, not as cluttered as Hong Kong, although ominously rising above the green of coconut palms, mangoes, breadfruit trees and casuarinas were the incipient steel skeletons that all too soon would be highrise hotels. Looking the other way I could see St Anne, Moyenne and Cerf Islands, with a dozen smaller ones strung out between them forming the reef which encloses the huge lagoon of Victoria Harbour, while far on the eastern horizon were the twin blue blurs that were Praslin and Frigate Islands.

I like to orientate myself in a new place, and I was very grateful to the thoughtful type who had put a large chart up on the third class notice board which I had memorized over the last few days.

Someone said in careful Arabic, 'Salaam a'leikoum, effendi,' and I turned to see the two young mercenaries. I returned the greeting, and the shorter of the two said, 'We regret that your companion is in trouble through us, particularly since he fought so valiantly by our side.'

'Allah b'ismillah—It is the will of God,' I intoned philosophically.

'Can we help by going to the Captain Effendi and asking for his release on the grounds that he merely assisted us when we fought against vast odds?' the other asked, but I shook my head.

'It is not for that that he is in prison,' I explained, 'but for assaulting the serang in the august presence of the Great One. Wah! wah! young men—a great sorrow is upon me.'

They looked really concerned, so I piled on the agony, moaning about the flinty-heartedness of authority and the unkindness of Kismet, because an idea was forming even as I talked.

'We have come a long way,' I wailed. 'A kinsman has died in this place and we have to look to the interests of his family back in India—and now they will not allow Asiatics to land here.'

'Would that we could help,' one of them said, and I pounced.

'You could, young sirs,' I said earnestly, 'but I would hesitate to ask such a favour—particularly since it would involve a certain danger to yourselves——'

It reacted on them like the smell of blood to a tiger, and all I had to do thereafter was steadfastly to refuse their offers of assistance, and let them make the running.

I shook my head firmly. 'I would not do it,' I assured them. 'It would be a grave abuse of friendship to ask you to hazard a fine—or even imprisonment on our behalf.'

'What the hell is he talking about?' the taller asked the other in English. 'Come on, Charles—your Arabic is better than mine.'

'Something about taking a risk and landing in jug,' Charles said. 'The whole point is that he wants to get ashore, and these mean buggers won't let him.' He turned back to me and said in his slow, schoolboy phrases. 'But even if you managed to get ashore, how would you return without detection?'

'I would not be troubled by detection,' I told him. 'I would return quite openly. They would no doubt be angry, but there is little they could do, and by then my business would be completed.'

'He said he'd give them the two-fingered salute when he came back,' Charles explained. 'No—the problem is getting there. Shut up, Toby—I'm thinking.' He turned back to me and switched to Arabic again. 'How long would your business take, effendi?'

'One hour—two, who knows?' I shrugged. 'But it is useless —I cannot leave this ship——'

Charles halted me in mid-wail with an upraised palm and said to Toby, 'What's to stop us going ashore and hiring a boat and coming out for them after dark?' Which was exactly what I had been thinking of myself.

Toby said, 'But we'd be spotted. Anyhow the other bloke is still in the nick.'

'That can't be helped. At least we could get this one off— and there's no need for us to be spotted if we're careful. Of course, if you're scared——'

'Do you want a thump under the ear, old boy?'

'No, old boy. What I meant to say was that I could do it on my own if you'd rather not be involved——'

'That's the same as saying I'm scared, old boy—so bloody well watch it——'

'Certainly, old boy—now suppose you belt up for a moment while I get it all over to old Ali ben Bughouse here.' He took a deep breath and carefully translated to me, 'If my friend and I went ashore and brought back a boat after darkness has fallen, could you climb down a rope from the after part?'

'Wah! Wah!' I said in tones of deepest admiration. 'It would be child's play to me—but I cannot allow——'

'Peace, my friend. I observed before dawn this morning that there were lights at the gangway, but the rest of the ship was in darkness. Now, if we came some time before midnight and flashed a torch three times, and then paddled quietly to a spot right under the stern——'

'I could already be waiting with a rope secured to the rail, and I could lower myself to the boat,' I began, and then broke off and shook my head sorrowfully. 'But I couldn't allow you to take the risk——'

'Balls,' said Charles, then translated it to, 'Nonsense. Watch

for us at the ship's extremity from eleven o'clock onwards—
but remember that you sail again at five-thirty tomorrow
morning, so be back at the pier in good time.'

I touched my forehead, lips and heart in the approved
Hollywood-Arabian gesture and poured out my thanks
brokenly, and they winked and went off.

I spent the rest of the morning watching the coming and
going of people from the shore. They were of every colour from
jet black to Nordic fairness and there seemed to be a high
proportion of Indian descent amongst them, dating back to the
days of unrestricted immigration, no doubt. Dress appeared
to be almost uniform—white shorts or slacks and bushshirts
for officials, clerks and other solid citizens, with anything from
ragged khaki pants to loincloths for the longshoremen who
now swarmed over the decks from bow to stern. Dress, at least,
would present no difficulties because I had a couple of pairs
of slacks and some shirts in my luggage. Yes, I decided, once
ashore we could merge perfectly into the background.
Language seemed to be the native Creole and pidgin English,
but I also heard bits of Urdu and Hindi from time to time, so
even Safaraz would be able to get by—And there I pulled up
short. What the hell was I going to do about *him*? If I left
him aboard, the worst they could do would be to take him
on to another port—East or South African—or on the round
trip back to Bombay—and then——

And then I abandoned the whole thing—because I knew
damned well that I couldn't leave the fool to fend for himself.

So I went down to the cabin sadly—and there he was. I
don't think I was ever gladder to see him.

I said, 'You camel-faced son of a noseless mother! Why was
I ever cursed with your presence?'

'Because Kismet was kind to the sahib,' he grinned, completely unregenerate. 'How would you ever have survived
without my bravery and intelligence to support you?' They're
a modest race, the Pathans. The Captain had released him

with a solemn warning of what would happen to him if he came before him again apparently, so I left him in the cabin with strict orders not to put his nose outside without my express permission, and went back on deck.

The water lighter was alongside now and I realized that it would have been hopeless even at night to try and find cover on her long open deck which would have been right under the midship lights. I went down to the stern and looked over the rail. This was distinctly more promising. The poop superstructure blocked the view from the bridge and the promenade decks, and there seemed to be no living accommodation down here—only a steel housing for the steam steering gear and a couple of locked doors with 'Isolation Hospital' and 'Chief Officer's Stores' over them respectively. So unless we were struck with a cholera epidemic or the mate suddenly felt an ungovernable urge to have the ship painted overnight, this end should be deserted after dark. There were two decklights behind curved, salt-encrusted glass covers, with knurled butterfly nuts securing them, and I took the precaution of unscrewing them and removing the electric bulbs. I judged the drop from the rail to the water to be about twenty feet, so I cast around for a rope, and one devil of a job it was to find one that wasn't doing some essential job and which would accordingly be missed if I stole it. But eventually I found a piece attached to a plank that was evidently used for painting over the side. I went down and got Safaraz's knife and cut off a generous twenty feet and smuggled it down to the cabin wrapped in my prayer rug.

After all this it was just a matter of waiting. About thirty hippies seemed to be disembarking here, with a similar number going on, yellow and white permits indicating the sheep from the goats.

We had a large evening meal and then, well after dark, we went up on deck and slipped unobtrusively along to the stern, carrying our change of clothes in a bundle, with money, passports and my gun in an air travel bag. All was quiet here, and completely dark. At ten o'clock two large launches came out from the shore with returning sightseers, then various local people who had been dining on board as guests of the Captain went off, and the stillness was broken only by the sound of the pumps on the water lighter.

Five bells sounded from the bridge—half-past-ten—six bells —eleven o'clock. I was sweating a little now. What if these two lads were talkers rather than doers? What if they were drunk or shacked up with a couple of nubile Seychelloise? It was too late to do anything more now if they let us down. The quarry was ashore, all five of them. I'd watched them go. We'd just tamely have to go on with the ship to Mombasa and then, eventually, return to India—the whole thing an abortive sortie. The very thought of it brought a sour taste to the back of my throat.

And then, when I'd worked myself into a state of lathered anxiety, the three flashes came from right under her stern and I was nearly sick with sheer relief. I flashed back with my pocket torch and then sent Safaraz down the rope. Another flash came from below so I went down myself, hand over hand, until I felt my ankle grasped and guided on to the gunwale of an exceedingly unstable craft. I sat down on the bottom boards and realized from the narrowness of the thing that we were in one of the graceful but skittish canoes I had been admiring earlier from the firmness of the deck. I wasn't admiring it at the moment though, because it threatened to capsize if one blinked too hard—and these two lads weren't experts by any means.

They started to paddle away from the shadow cast by the hull, erratically and out of unison, and watching the lights on the ship's gangway I saw that we were going in a circle, so I took a calculated risk, and said in English, 'You've both got your paddles over the same side, gentlemen. I suggest that one of you changes to the other.'

The start of astonishment they gave nearly tipped us over, and Safaraz yelped with terror.

Charles stopped paddling and said quietly, 'So the joke's on us, eh? Very funny man, Mister Ali Boop, or whatever your name might be. What's the little game?' While Toby contented himself with calling me a bloody bastard.

'I'd start paddling if I were you,' I said as the shore lights started to slide past rapidly. 'We're being swept sideways by the tide.'

'You haven't answered my question,' Charles said.

'I can't at the moment,' I told him. 'I'm sorry if you think I've been pulling your leg just for the hell of it. Actually we're in the same line of business, although we have different bosses.'

'Who's yours?' Toby demanded belligerently.

'The British Government. Look—hadn't you better start paddling? We'll be on the reef in a minute.'

'How do we know that's the truth?' Charles asked, but I was relieved when I saw him start to paddle, and to hear Toby doing the same behind me.

'I haven't a badge or a piece of paper, if that's what you mean,' I said. 'You'll just have to take my word for it.'

'Why should we?'

'Why not?'

'This is a British Colony. If you were working for the British Government you wouldn't have to come here in disguise and sneak in by the back door,' Charles said.

'You're talking like a twit,' I said impatiently. 'Have you never heard of undercover work?'

'Yes, sure. I've read all about it in paperbacks and I've seen it on TV—as no doubt you have too,' Toby said nastily. 'What are you supposed to be working on, anyway?'

'On who pinched Little Red Riding Hood's basket,' I snapped. 'Look—put me back on board or hand me over to the police ashore if you're feeling public-spirited—but for Pete's sake don't ask bloody fool questions.'

And surprisingly, that clinched matters, because Charles said simply, 'I believe you.'

'Why?' I asked, genuinely curious at this *volte face*.

'Because you gave that stupid clot the correct answer. If you'd invented a convincing story I think I'd have known,' he said.

'I'm damned certain you would,' I told him. 'Nobody can work up a good cover story on the spur of the moment. It takes time.'

'So we'll put you ashore as arranged. We owe you that much for the help this other chap gave us with the long-hairs. Does he come from Wigan too?'

'No—he's genuine,' I said. 'And he doesn't speak English.'

'Where did he learn to fight?'

'He didn't need to, any more than a duck learns to swim. It comes naturally to a Pathan.'

Then Toby, who had apparently been mulling over things, said wrathfully, 'Who's a stupid clot?'

'You, you thick-headed sod,' Charles told him succinctly. 'Are introductions in order?'

'You're Charles I understand,' I said. 'And the gentleman behind me is Toby. My name is Idwal Rees and this is Safaraz Khan.'

'You call me a thick-headed sod again, you bastard, and I'll——' Toby roared, and a powerful beam of light hit us from the end of the Long Pier and someone called:

'Ahoy, pirogue! Qui vive?'

'Paddle, gentlemen, paddle,' I pleaded, 'or we'll be up a certain creek without an anchor.'

Chapter Nineteen

IT WAS A POLICE LAUNCH, but fortunately for us it was moored the other side of the Long Pier, and by the time it had got its diesel going and had rounded the end of the mile-long structure we had reached some slippery steps where other pirogues were moored. We jumped out and scuttled up to the top and laid low among some bales of coconut fibre. The launch cruised up and down for some minutes, its searchlight stabbing suspiciously along the pier and sweeping the surface of the bay, then it appeared to give it up and it returned to its moorings.

Charles said, 'What are you going to do now?'

'Immediately, get out of these Indian clothes,' I said, and started to change.

'And after that?'

'You don't have to worry,' I told him. 'We're very grateful for what you've done.'

'Come on,' he said decisively. 'We can at least give you a doss down for the rest of the night.'

'Where?'

'The place where we're staying—all home comforts and no questions asked.'

'That sounds mighty like a brothel to me.'

'You must be psychic,' Toby growled. 'The ugliest bints south of the equator—but at least the beer's cold.'

We walked along to the shoreward end of the pier where Charles left us for a few minutes, and came back in a Mini. He sensed my surprise and chuckled, 'All mod cons as well as home comforts. Hop in—there's a cop wandering about near the Club.'

We drove a hundred yards or so along the road which is the continuation of the Long Pier, and turned left at a clock tower that stands at the crossroads which mark the centre of the tiny town. I'd ceased to wonder at anything by now. I just sat back and enjoyed the ride—and tired though I was, the ride *was* enjoyable. The smell of warm, moist earth mingled with the salt tang the inshore breeze brought from the reef, and there was the heavy scent of cinnamon and vanilla and other spices I couldn't identify. I'd read about the poverty of the native Seychellois, and tomorrow, no doubt, I'd see it—but now it was hidden by the night and there was nothing to break the spell of the place. Or so I thought in that first five miles—then, rounding a bend, the whole hideous thing hit me with the force of a physical blow: 'Welcome to the Garden of Eden—Q.A.N.T.A.S.—B.O.A.C.—PAN-AM—S.A.S.—LUFTHANSA —COCA-COLA—MEET ME AT THE BEACHCOMBERS' BAR CASINO ROYALE—GAMING—CABARET—GRAND OPENING—' miles of multicoloured neon—billboards—men working like ants under floodlights putting in the last of the wiring—smacking on the final coat of hi-gloss paint—smoothing out the wrinkles in wet concrete. I wanted to weep, laugh and puke simultaneously.

Charles said, 'What do you think of it?'

'I'd rather not,' I told him.

'Bloody awful, isn't it? But only that bit—the new airport —is affected so far, although it's spreading. There's a de luxe pub down the road that has plastic coconut palms round its open-air ballroom, because they found in the Bahamas or somewhere that the real thing drops fronds and nuts on the guests—and hotels get sued that way.'

'For somebody who only landed here a few hours ago, you seem to know your way around very well,' I said.

'Actually it's my second visit—and Toby's third,' he answered. 'There are twenty-five of us in our sheikhdom— Army, police, and the oil-well security corps—with anything from two to five of us on leave at any one time, so the boss set this place here up for us—all on the house.'

He slowed down and turned off the road on to a drive that

wound through coconut palms to a clearing on the hillside, and stopped in front of a long, rambling bungalow. We climbed out of the car, and an immensely fat Negress came out on to the verandah.

'Two more gentlemen, Vivienne,' Charles said. 'Can do?'

'Can do rooms, beds, ah oui—but no girls until tomorrow. Why you not tell me before?'

'That's all right. They've each got ten wives back home. They've come here for a rest,' he told her, and she giggled and said, 'Tu blague!'

The rooms they showed us to were large, clean and airy. Charles said, 'Just get down to it. You won't be worried by anybody here.'

'That's very good of you,' I said gratefully. 'But my conscience is pricking me a bit. If we are found here by the police it could mean trouble for you both.'

'Nary a cop,' he said. 'This is a private house so we're not under police supervision. Yes, I know Toby called it a whorehouse, but it's not in the strict sense of the word. So long—I'll see you in the morning.'

He went, and Safaraz, who had been becoming more mystified every moment, took a deep breath and said, 'And now, if the sahib would be good enough to tell me just what this place is and what we are doing here——'

'It is a convent,' I told him. 'The nuns are all away at the moment, saying their prayers, but they are most hospitable and have invited us to stay here. See that you behave yourself and don't bring shame upon me.'

'As a Pathan of noble birth I know how to comport myself, sahib,' he said loftily, and stalked out.

I woke next morning and sat up and looked out on one of those scenes that one knows will remain crystal clear in one's memory over the years. The house was set on a hill which sloped down to the coast road, the other side of which I could see a beach of blinding whiteness between the trunks of the

227

coconut palms—then came the lagoon, as clear and smooth as crystal with, a mile out, the reef on which the surf was pounding, then the blue of the deep water reflecting the completely cloudless sky. Immediately in front of the house was a natural garden of hibiscus, frangipani and passion flowers while the supports and crossbeams of the verandah were clothed in bougainvillaea ranging from blood red through a dozen shades to purple.

By craning my neck out of the window and looking up to the left I could see the underside of the 'golf ball' at the Tracking Station, but mercifully the intervening palms, mango, jacaranda and gul mohur trees hid the airport.

A movement behind me brought me back to the present and I turned to see Safaraz with a tray of tea, croissants and fruit. He was standing rigidly to attention, poker-faced and looking at a spot over my head, just oozing disapproval from every pore.

'I took this tray from a *nun* who was about to enter the sahib's room—almost unclothed,' he said.

'Thank you,' I said gravely. 'You may go and sleep on the beach if your modesty is affronted, but don't be impolite to anybody in this house unless you want the weight of my anger to fall upon you.'

He said, 'As the sahib orders,' miffishly, and went out, looking like a seaside landlady who has just caught her daughter in bed with the star lodger.

I mulled over things as I ate my splendid breakfast, and when Charles came in about an hour later I had a plan sorted out, albeit one that went against my every instinct, because it meant blowing my cover.

I said, 'I am going to require some help here. I can give you my word that it's nothing illegal—and I am authorized to pay the going rate for services rendered.'

He pursed his lips and looked at me for some time speculatively. 'All right,' he said. 'Suppose you spill it? I reserve the right to turn it down if I don't like it—but I'll respect your confidence.'

'Good. I'm on the tail of four men. You know them by sight, two Englishmen, an Australian and——'

'And Tony Pellegrino,' he supplied.

'You know him?'

'I know the bastard—and one of the Englishmen. Old Horseshit Waygood.'

'You sound as if you don't like them.'

'I don't like Pellegrino.'

'Anything specific—or just general principles?'

'Both. He chiselled an old Indian Army pensioner over a land deal here—legal but dirty. The old boy happened to be a pal of my father's. That's the specific one. On general principles I don't like Mafia types—and these bloody islands are getting full of them.'

'And what about the other fellow?'

'Horseshit? Oh, no strong feelings about him, one way or the other. He's just a sleazy old bum out to make a fast buck or two. He's Pellegrino's messenger boy at the moment. He used to run the blackjack game at the Casino Royale, that's Pellegrino's place, but he was too fond of miracles to please the customers. Coo! He can make a pack of cards talk.' He paused and lit a cigarette. 'But *you* were going to spill it—and I'm doing all the talking.'

'We have reason to believe that they are setting up a dope running line.'

'Who's we?'

'The British Authorities.'

'This place is nominally British, admittedly, but the *Authorities* are a hell of a long way from here. Can't *you* be a bit more specific? I mean, are you a cop—or what?'

'I'm not a cop.'

'Then I don't understand. Junk is police business—international police business if you like—but still police business.

Rightly or wrongly I have the impression that you're in some sort of Intelligence racket.'

'I am.'

'Then how come Intelligence is concerned with junk?'

'Simply because today junk finances espionage. It used to be gold, but weight for weight junk is worth ten times more. Work it out for yourself. The official price of gold is thirty-five dollars an ounce—but you try buying it for that. It would cost something nearer to seventy. But an ounce of pure Chinese heroin, cut and cut again with milk sugar, makes up into about seventy-five capsules, which the street pusher in London and New York sells for anything up to ten dollars a time. The Annamese peasant who grows poppies on the Burma-Thai border in the first place, gets about a quarter of a cent per ounce for the raw material.'

'Kee-rist! That's what I call a profit,' he whistled.

'You're right. The most profitable business the world has ever known—and the dirtiest.'

Charles walked to the window and stood looking out for a few moments, then he turned back to me.

'All right,' he said. 'These four——'

'Five,' I corrected. 'There was a hippy with them, travelling third class.'

'These five are running junk. You catch them at it. What then?'

'I hand the evidence over to the police and fade out.'

'Which police?'

'The police of whichever country I catch them out in.'

'Hm, I see. But what I don't understand is why they would be running junk here. I don't think it has touched these islands yet. Would they be setting it up for the tourist trade?'

'Probably they'd siphon a little off here if the demand were big enough—but I think there's more to it than that. They're establishing a line in place of one that has been cut clean through in Turkey—hippies used to carry it in small quantities, then consolidate it at prearranged dropping points. They're doing the same thing this way—but why they're bringing it to a cul-de-sac like the Seychelles, I just can't imagine. There's only one way out from here at the moment —ship to an East African or South African port.'

'And you can wash out South Africa,' Charles said. 'They're mustard there. You couldn't smuggle a grain of wheat let alone an ounce of junk.'

'All right. So that leaves East Africa——'

'They're no slouches there, either. Anyhow, hippies don't usually travel from here to East or South Africa. They come here on return tickets from Bombay—lotus eat for a month until the ship goes back the other way, and off they go.'

'So where and how does it go from here?'

'The jets will be coming and going in a matter of days——'

I shook my head firmly. 'Junk is never shipped commercially by air. A plane is too easily turned over.' I stood up. 'Well, I certainly won't find out sitting on my backside here. Tell me— do they want papers, passports, landing permits and all that sort of thing when one books into a hotel?'

'Not usually. The assumption would be that you were a tourist who had just arrived in on the boat. But there's no need for you to go to a pub. Why not stay here?'

'For the simple reason that you'd be for it if the police did start to take an interest——'

'Balls. I'd merely say that you were somebody I had met in Bombay and who I'd invited along—together with your servant. They mightn't believe it, but they couldn't prove anything to the contrary.'

'Well—it's very good of you,' I said. 'I wonder where *they* are staying, by the way?'

'I can tell you that—at Pellegrino's place—the Casino Royale. It's a restaurant, gambling-cum-country club mostly, but he's got chalet accommodation for about twenty. All very lush and in the worst possible taste.'

'What do people wear there?'

'Casual during the day, just as you are now—white safari jacket and slacks at night.'

'Fine. I think I'll drop in there.'

'I'll run you down—and come in myself. The dedicated start drinking about an hour before lunch.'

'I'm carrying a fair amount of money,' I told him, 'in dollars and pounds. Will I have any difficulty in changing it?'

'They'd want to see your passport at Barclays. Give it to me and I'll give you the equivalent in Seychelles rupees.' He went out and I got up and partially shaved. I say partially because I had been letting my moustache and beard grow ever since we had left Bombay, as being more in character for an Ismaili, until now I had quite a respectable crop. I took my beard off but left the moustache which, together with wrap-around sunglasses, made a considerable difference to my appearance.

We drove back into town. It's a charmingly shabby little place of just two streets that bisect each other at the hub of the business quarter—double-storeyed buildings—corrugated iron gradually giving way to more substantial bricks—government offices, post office, Carnegie Library and, inevitably, the Club, a beat-up shack waiting to be demolished when the smart, air-conditioned premises next door are completed, to the undisguised sorrow of the old timers. A few shops—Parsee and Ismaili for the most part—two smallish churches, Anglican and Catholic, exalted to cathedral status—a colourful market and an assortment of agencies, offices and banks, the whole watched over maternally by a stone Queen Victoria.

We went on about a mile towards the north of the island to where, above a beach of breathtaking beauty, Pellegrino's spread was laid out. It was Hollywood's dream of Africa, with touches of the South Seas and a hint of Spanish Mission. With the crystalline lagoon and the whole of the Indian Ocean before it, it still had to have a swimming pool that you knew would come up in a splodge of submerged coloured lighting after sunset. There were chalets masquerading as Zulu kraals scattered around, and a plethora of bars rejoicing in names like the Sundowner, the Safari, and the White Hunter. Gaming rooms, dining-room and offices were housed in a central ranch-house type of building.

'Here you are,' Charles said. 'Disneyland, Forest Lawns and Knott's Berry Farm all in one—*with* lions.'

And there were too—stuffed ones glaring balefully out of a thicket.

We sat at a table under a tree and a pretty coffee-coloured girl brought us a couple of bottles of lager. The bottles were wet and the labels were sloughing off, but the lager itself was lukewarm.

'Is this the best they can do?' I asked Charles.

'Lousy, isn't it?' he agreed. 'But that's the way it's always been. Rottenly cooked food, bad service, warm drinks and thinly veiled impertinence if you complain. He doesn't want local business. He's waiting for the airborne tourist trade. Except for a few of the top families, les grands blancs as they call them, the native Seychellois have no money, while the settlers are mostly Army and civil service pensioners from India and East Africa—and they haven't much to throw around either. He's marginally more gracious to the American personnel from the Satellite Tracking Station.'

'How many of those are there?' I asked.

'A hundred and seventeen, plus their families in some cases.' He stood up and peered down towards the beach. 'Hallo—here's our mob. All four, no five of them.'

A big motor cruiser was nosing into the beach through the gentle lagoon wavelets. Ahrlberg dropped down over the bows and carried a mooring warp up to a ring set in a concrete block near a bathing pavilion. The others dropped down after him —Pellegrino, the Smiling One, Horton and the mournful Major Dunstable-Waygood. They crossed the beach and came up to the restaurant in single file. There was nothing of the lightheartedness about them of men who had been pleasure cruising or fishing—in fact they all looked pretty glum, even the Smiling One was not his usual sunny self, and when Horton muttered something to Pellegrino the latter snarled at him and told him to shut up. They passed us without a glance, then split up, Pellegrino and the Major going to the main building, and the others to one of the chalets. The Major turned and called, 'Right—try again—same tide tomorrow,' and the Smiling One acknowledged with a perfunctory wave.

'Now what did all that add up to?' I mused.

'Twelve o'clock,' Charles said, looking at his watch. 'It's just about high water now—It will be at this height again at eleven tomorrow. Now, if we were hanging about in the bay we might get an idea of what they are doing.'

'Can you arrange a boat?'

'Like I told you—all modern conveniences. There's one in the boathouse in front of our place. Some of the boys are keen on scuba-ing, water ski-ing and fishing. Let's go back and check up.'

The boat was a medium-sized thing with an outboard motor that looked as if it hadn't been serviced since the day it was installed—and acted like it too. But Toby turned out to be a man of parts. He stripped it down, went into town and bought some new bits and pieces from one of the agencies, then spent the rest of the day happily reassembling it again. Then we water-tested it on the lagoon and it ran superbly.

We had an early breakfast next day, and then we took some fishing gear, food and a crate of beer, and stooged up and down the reef a mile or so to the north of the Casino Royale and just waited like men with nothing on their minds but fishing. And at a little after ten we saw the motor cruiser set out from the beach. Through the glasses we saw that today there were six of them—the newcomer being a small man whose face was hidden by a big palmetto hat.

They headed straight for a break in the reef directly opposite the restaurant, and then, when outside in deep water, they set a south-easterly course for the ring of islands round Victoria Bay. We let them establish a long lead, then we ran due south down the lagoon to the next break. We came out into the open near the most southerly of the islands. Charles got a chart out of the locker and pointed out our position.

'Cerf, that one nearest us—then comes Long, Round, Moyenne, Beacon and Ste Anne—that's the biggest of them. We're right—*here*—at the moment.' He pointed to a spot some three miles due south of Cerf.

The cruiser was out of sight now, hidden, I judged, by a rocky islet marked Ile Cachée on the chart, which was separated from the southern tip of Cerf by a strait some two or three hundred yards wide.

'Where do you think they're making for?' I asked.

'It could be any of these islands,' he said. 'They might even be overshooting the whole ring and going on to Praslin, La Digue or Frigate Islands. They're all between twenty and thirty miles away to the east.'

I took up one of the superb game fishing rods the boat was equipped with, and Charles showed me how to tie a brightly coloured feather lure to it, over a three-pronged hook that looked hefty enough to use as an anchor. We cut the engine while he adjusted my harness, then started up again once I was ensconced in the fishing chair on the stern. I trailed about a quarter of a mile of line, and had mug's luck almost immediately. A shock wave that nearly stopped the boat dead travelled up the line and transformed itself into a punch in my belly with the butt of the rod that would have knocked me flat had I not been strapped into the chair. Away in the distance a huge golden fish leapt out of our white wake.

'Dorado!' Charles yelled over the noise of the engine. 'You lucky bastard. Lose it and I'll drown you.'

I played it like the novice I was, using the big complicated reel like a steam winch, and setting Charles's teeth on edge—

then I handed it over to him and took the wheel. He got it alongside after about fifteen minutes' hard fighting, and we gaffed it and lifted it into the boat, and I felt a pang as it died, and the gold, red and purple of it faded.

'Good alibi,' Charles said. 'They were looking at us through the glasses.'

'Where are they now?' I asked.

'They've gone round Cerf, anti-clockwise.' He gunned the engine and we lifted another couple of feet of keel clear of the water. 'If we go round the other way it won't look as if we're following them.'

He was a pleasure to work with. He had all the instincts of the born hunter and tracker, without any of the boring mystique of the keen amateur. Anybody watching us would have seen two fishermen intent only on their sport—but his eyes were sweeping the whole time, like a radar scanner, missing nothing.

'Don't look now,' he said. 'They're anchored close in to Round Island. Some of them seem to be going ashore in the dinghy. Now what the hell goes on? There's damn all on Round—just a few palms and some undergrowth.'

'What about the other islands?' I asked. 'Does anybody live on them?'

'On Ste Anne and Cerf—one or two bungalows on each. The developers have plans for them both, damn them. Expensive pubs, glass-bottomed boats and all that crap, à la Bermuda.' He spat over the side. 'See where we are now?'

I nodded. We were right opposite the town, in the middle of the main harbour, close to the four big red mooring buoys that the deep water ships tied up to.

'Get your line over the stern again,' Charles directed. 'I'm going to stand right on for Ste Anne's, and we'll fade out of their line of sight. We can swing round on to Moyenne then on a throttled-down motor, still out of sight. From the top of the hill we ought to be able to see what they're doing.'

And we did just that, and I caught a small bonito as a bonus just as we rounded Ste Anne. We ran up on to the beach at Moyenne and climbed a low wooded hill. The cruiser had gone out into the harbour and was drifting with its engine stopped, and as we watched through the glasses, we saw the Smiling One stand up and wave to someone on Round who was out of our vision, but who we knew by simple elimination to be Pellegrino and the Major, because the others were in the boat. The Smiling One seemed to receive a signal back, because he waved again, stooped and picked up what looked to be a heavily weighted sack and dropped it over the side. They all watched its descent through the water, then, after an interval of some minutes, the new man stood up and took off his palmetto hat. Charles reached out and took the glasses from me and studied the boat intently.

'Yes, I thought so,' he said. 'The bloke in the straw hat is Langlois—Mochi Langlois, the skin diver—he's a Mauritian —vicious little bastard——'

And as if to confirm this, Langlois shrugged into a two-bottle harness, adjusted a mask, tested his hose, bent and slipped on flippers, then dropped over the side.

He was down for about twenty minutes, then he broke the surface a hundred yards from the boat. The Smiling One started up and steered across to him and he climbed aboard awkwardly over the stern ladder. He had the end of a line secured to one wrist. He untied it and passed it to Ahrlberg who began to pull it inboard. It was a long job and there was obviously something heavy on the end of it because Ahrlberg was feeling the strain by the time the thing broke the surface. It looked like an exaggerated soccer ball—leather, rubber or some composition—about three feet in diameter I should have estimated. The diver took a brief rest, then shed his gear and stood up on a seat, steadying himself against the slight roll by the awning strakes. The Smiling One passed him a small object —too small for me to make anything of until he started to use it, then the penny dropped. It was a Service prismatic compass, and he was doing a resection with it, obviously calling out his angles to the Smiling One who was making notes on a surveyor's board. For the uninitiated, a resection is drawn by taking a compass bearing to three or more, preferably many more, prominent objects—a mountain top, a distant building, a lone tree on the skyline, etc., etc. With a protractor and an instrument called an alidade these bearings are then drawn on the board in the form of rays converging on the centre. Where the rays cross is the spot where the operator is standing. Should he ever wish to come back to that exact spot again at any time in the future, all he has to do is come as near as he can judge to the approximate spot, then move about taking the same bearings with the same compass, until he has them once more in the same juxtaposition.

It is a long and cumbersome operation, and one which would only be done by surveyors or engineers in peacetime—and artillerymen in war. Someone, in fact, who requires absolute exactitude in fixing a spot, when it is impracticable to drive in a peg or plant a stone—as here, on water.

They took some time on this job, then they dumped another weighted sack, like the first, and followed it immediately with the big ball, after which they started up again and came into the beach on Round Island slowly. They were out of sight now, but after some minutes we heard the engine open up, and the boat came into view again, streaking for the shore.

Charles said, 'What the hell are they doing? Chucking stuff into the water, diving for it, then chucking it back again.'

'And doing it right on the minute of high water,' I said, checking my watch. 'And then making a resection—which means they want to do it again, from the same spot.'

'When, I wonder?' mused Charles.

'At the next high water presumably—or rather the next daylight high water. He couldn't check bearings at night,' I said.

'So we follow him out again?'

I shook my head. 'I don't think we could risk it a second time. Anyhow, what good would it be? We'd only be guessing again. Let's have a look at the island.'

We went across and landed on the blind side, shielded from anybody who might have had a glass on us from the mainland. We walked round to where they had landed. The spot was plainly marked by empty beer bottles and a few recently opened cans which were attracting a swarm of flies. They were that sort of people.

The island was minuscule, just three or four hundred yards in circumference, but it was rocky and thickly covered with undergrowth.

I said, 'I'm going to follow a wild hunch.'

'What?'

'I feel they may be back tomorrow, to check the stuff they dumped out there.'

'That's what I said. We follow them out again.'

'No,' I said. 'I'm going to stay out here and go under cover.'

'You mean we park here for twenty-four hours?' He didn't seem to like the idea at all.

'No, not you—just me on my own. There's food and drink on the boat—leave it with me and go on back, then watch tomorrow and come out when they've gone—or two hours after high water if they don't come.'

He shrugged. 'As you wish. Sooner you than me though. What if they find you?'

'They won't. Anyhow, I'm carrying a gun, though I'm certain it won't come to that.'

He stayed on for an hour or so while we concocted theories then knocked them down again. He left as the shadows lengthened on the slopes of Mahé opposite us, and I had a swim in that wonderfully clear water in which myriads of coloured fish darted in and out of the rocks. Then I had a supper of sandwiches and beer, after which I sat and went over the train of events of the last month or so, and got nowhere. The night

239

was comfortably warm, a soft breeze was blowing in from the sea and I hadn't the slightest difficulty in going off to sleep. One minute I was trying to pick out the Southern Cross, and the next, seemingly, I was waking as the sun came up over the horizon and gilded the 'golf ball'.

I had some more sandwiches and half a flask of lukewarm coffee, then I started to look for a hiding place, and found a very good one almost immediately. It was a cleft in the solid granite that formed the miniature cliff fronting on to the beach where they had landed, running like a knife slash back for some twenty yards or so, just about eighteen inches wide at the mouth, but opening out a little farther back—and it was overgrown with a prickly type of lantana creeper that would discourage anybody from exploring it further. I carefully parted the stems and eased myself in gingerly until I came to the bottom of the cleft which was floored with clean white sand, and I crawled along it until I came to the seaward end of it, pulling my air travel bag with my gun and a bottle of water in it, behind me. I was now within five yards of their landing place and I could see the broad expanse of the deep anchorage quite plainly. If today was to be a repetition of yesterday, I couldn't be better placed.

But the waiting was hell, because now I was in position I couldn't risk worming my way out backwards in case they arrived while I was still in the pipeline, so I was a fixture until they came, or, if they didn't come, until an hour after high tide—and according to my calculations that was still two hours away. My God—three hours at least, in what was fast becoming an oven. Thirst was bothering me, but I sternly denied myself a drink, because there was barely a pint in my bottle. Then those damned great bloated flies, which had laid up somewhere during the night, came out in squadrons and attacked the stinking remains of the filthy bastards' picnic, and when they had exhausted all possibilities there, they turned their attention to me, sneaking in through the undergrowth with diabolical cunning and stinging me in spots which I couldn't scratch without creating an upheaval in the foliage.

And then, when I knew I couldn't stand another minute of it, and was about to mole my way out of it backwards, I heard the beat of an engine, and the motor-cruiser came sweeping into sight.

Chapter Twenty

PELLEGRINO was at the wheel, and he brought her in close and threw her into reverse and stopped flashily in a smother of foam. The same six were aboard, and Pellegrino, the Smiling One and Ahrlberg jumped over the side into waist-deep water and carried a wickerwork basket ashore. The Major called out forlornly, 'What about the dinghy?' and the Smiling One blew a raspberry and shouted, 'Walk on the water, you silly old bastard.' But the Major stayed aboard with Horton and Langlois and the cruiser moved off at half-throttle to the middle of the anchorage.

The Smiling One opened the hamper and took out what looked like a telescopic camera tripod. He opened it and planted it firmly in the sand, then fixed an instrument on to it that I remembered from my Army days was a 'director', which is a simplified and much smaller version of a theodolite. He levelled it off and zeroed it with a compass. Pellegrino watched him sourly. 'Lotta bullshit,' he retorted. 'You make it troppo complicato. No need.'

'My oath there's a need,' the Smiling One answered. 'Look —same setting as yesterday, 351 degrees. Right? I bet you they recover it dead on that line.'

'Getta a storm—winda blow other way, then goddam packet finish up somewhere else,' Pellegrino said.

'Look, Mr Pellegrino,' Ahrlberg began, but the Italian cut him short. 'I talk to the organgrinder, notta the bloody monk',' he snapped. 'Listen to me——'

'Later,' said the Smiling One bending over the director and squinting through the eyepiece. 'Signal 'em, Swede—left, a hell of a lot left——'

Ahrlberg extended his left arm and somebody acknowledged from the boat and it began to edge over.

'That's the idea,' the Smiling One said, '*Right!* Stop 'em now—They're dead on for line.'

But they were out of my vision now and I could only piece together what they were doing in the boat from the Smiling One's orders and Ahrlberg's signals.

'That's right—that's right——' the Smiling One was saying. 'Let's see how good your resection is—right—right—No you bloody drongo, you've gone too far over. Get him back on to line, Swede—bit to the right. Good! Hold it there—Ah— stupid bastard—too far the other way now. That's better——'

'The nigger's dived now,' Ahrlberg said.

'You letta him hear you say "nigger" and he'll cut your goddam throat,' Pellegrino warned.

The Smiling One straightened from the director. 'Well, let's see now,' he said. 'I reckon that if he picks up the last two containers from the same spot, we've proved it.'

'Proved what?' Pellegrino bit the end from a cigar and spat the piece and the question out simultaneously.

'Oh Gawd!' the Smiling One sighed. 'Real little ray of sunshine, ain't you? Listen, Mario, for the last time. The ship comes in. Right? It can only come in at high water, because it'd rip its bottom out on the reef at any other time. Right? It's got to tie up to one of them big buoys out there. Right? We've proved, we hope, that a container of one metre diameter weighing fifty-five pounds dropped over the side anywhere inside the square made by the buoys will finish up in the same spot—that's dead under where the boat is now—if they've positioned themselves properly. Do you see?'

'No,' Pellegrino said flatly. 'Thatta the point that stick in my neck. *Why* should it always go the same place?'

'Because it's like what Langlois said. The anchorage is a washbowl. When the tide goes out it's like pulling the plug out of a washbowl—the water funnels round and out through the pipe——'

'What pipe?'

243

'Oh, Christ. No pipe, Mario—just *like* a pipe.' He held up his hand. 'Shut up—Langlois has surfaced—and—yes!—he's got the rope. Dead on—the same spot. Now are you satisfied?'

'No.'

'Too bad. But *you* picked Langlois, didn't you?'

'Sure—because he's the best diver in the islands—not like you punks that don't know your arses from your elbows——'

'All right—agreed. He's the best diver in the islands. Will you take his word for it then?' He peered out to the sea. 'Call them in, Swede. I don't think we need drop any more.'

The boat came back, and Horton and Langlois good-naturedly carried the Major ashore. Langlois was in high spirits. He capered like a black frog, slapping his flippers on the sand and kicking the big football-shaped thing that they brought with them.

'C'est exactement!' he crowed. 'She go ever'time same place. Always the tide take her there. We don't need the compass. Any place inside the four mooring buoys all right.'

Pellegrino said, 'Yeah—*one* tide take her there. Suppose we can't get out next tide? Suppose the harbour cops hanging around—two tides—three tides—what then?'

'One tide—twenty tides—même chose—same thing.' Langlois shrugged. 'A ledge, my friend. It go under that—it stay there.'

'And suppose the sea water gets in,' Pellegrino went on. 'What then? Ten, twelve kilos of junk go to hell, eh?'

'No water'll get in,' the Smiling One said positively. 'Look.'

He brushed sand from the wet sphere and detached a long length of thin but apparently very strong nylon rope from it, then he felt under a flap and pulled at a metal zip and the sphere dropped apart into two limp sections, revealing another sphere inside. He picked up one of the sections and shook it. 'Here you are—this is how it comes aboard in Bombay. It's part of a hippy's sleeping bag, see? And so's the inner one——' He unzipped the second sphere '—and the one inside that, too. Three bags, one inside the other—all waterproof—then the kernel inside the nut——' He lifted a small suitcase. 'Just another plastic suitcase to anybody interested enough to look at a hippy's lousy baggage—but with a difference. *It's* waterproof too. Tested to a depth of three hundred feet. All we ask of it is eighty feet. Lovely job.' He opened it and there was a hissing sound as the seal was broken and the pressure equalized. He took out a number of polythene containers and shook some white powder out of one of them. 'And these are waterproof too. This powder is silica-jell—about the most absorbent stuff in the world. Look at it—feel it. Bone dry—and this is the one we dumped the day before yesterday.'

I could see that Pellegrino was becoming convinced in spite of himself, but he wasn't giving in yet.

'And how does the guy fix all this up on a ship when a lot of bums hang about?' he asked.

'Dead simple,' the Smiling One told him. 'Ahrlberg here has made the run on the cattle deck as you know yourself. He reckons there's nothing to worry about. Tell him, Swede.'

'The carriers come and see the collector one by one and hand their body belts over—on deck when there's nobody about, in the john—anywhere. Who's interested? Nobody. The collector puts the stuff into these bags and seals 'em up. He's got to be careful of them then, of course. They stash them in his bunk and he or his sidekick have got to be there on watch the whole time. When the suitcase is packed with the whole consignment, he makes up the three zipped balls. It's quite simple with a bit of practice. He keeps them flat under his bunk until the ship is in harbour, then he packs the lot finally and zips them together. If the ship has come in at night, he drops the thing over the side as soon as she is tied up to a buoy. Plenty of the crew are dumping things then—trash cans are being emptied—dunnage being thrown over—nobody would take any notice. If she comes in during daylight, he waits until it's dark. Nothing to it.'

'Suppose he's had to go ashore before it gets dark?' Pellegrino asked craftily.

'Nothing to that, either,' Ahrlberg answered without hesitation. 'The collector is always booked right through. Only the sidekick disembarks here—so one of 'em's got to be aboard.'

'Any more questions?' the Smiling One asked. He was positively beaming now, like an amiable schoolmaster when a favourite lesson is turning out well and his pupils are right on the ball. 'Come on—let's settle 'em here and now. This is a good place to talk. You never know who the hell is listening ashore.'

'All right,' said Langlois. 'So I go down and get the ball, no? I bring her up to the bateau—right—what then?'

'Mario here takes charge then,' the Smiling One told him. 'It goes into a safe place until the *Jeanne-Marie* is ready to sail, then it's handed over to your brother.'

'That's what he wants to know,' Langlois said. 'How and where is it handed over? Don't forget he is tied up to the Long Pier. All flics are not stupid. They see things being carried aboard, one day one is going to get curious—have a look for himself——'

'Good question,' the Smiling One chuckled. 'I've been waiting for someone to ask that. At night, cobber. Mr Pellegrino chuffs past slowly in his boat, and the ball goes over the side near your brother's schooner—and you go over after it—with the end of the rope—and you swim under water to the blind side of her and hand the rope to him. He pulls it in when it's safe to do so. All right?'

'C'est bon,' approved Langlois.

'Any more?' asked the Smiling One.

'It's still a bit dodgy at my end,' gloomed the Major.

'I don't see why,' the Smiling One said. 'The same thing in reverse. The schooner anchors off Kilindini, like she always does, and the ball is dumped over the side, *immediately*, before customs and the other people come out to her. The end of the rope is tied to her below the waterline. Our friend here does another underwater swim after dark, with the rope. Your people haul in. Dead simple.'

'How long will it be left with me?' the Major asked. 'Those African police are all Kikuyu, don't forget. Nosey as bloody monkeys—always hanging around. Asking your houseboys questions——'

'Not getting windy, are you?' the Smiling One asked.

'Not exactly windy—but a feller can't be too careful nowadays.'

'It will be with you until Shelton picks it up. He runs an animal photographing safari once a fortnight. He carries the stuff up to the national park the other side of Nairobi.'

'What then?'

'It doesn't concern you once you've handed it over, cobber.' The Smiling One wasn't as cordial as he had been up to now. 'I'm asking you again. Are you getting windy?'

'Me? No—no—of course not,' the Major said hastily. 'Only asking—matter of interest——'

'Good,' the Smiling One cooed. 'Windy fellas always make *me* windy. Well, since it's only a matter of interest, I'll tell you. Shelton runs these safaris in a string of station wagons. In the national park he liaises with some more safaris—hippies in Land-Rovers doing the Sahara run—the blokes that used to do the overland scene to India before they were warned off by the Turks. Same people. As one door closes another opens. They carry it all the way to the Algerian coast—then Algerian fishermen take it halfway across the Mediterranean and transfer it to French fishermen who see it into the Marseilles factories, and Bob's your bloody uncle. Happy now?'

'Yes, yes,' the Major wuffled. 'Not windy—like I said— matter of interest——'

'Ah, belt up, you silly old bastard,' the Smiling One said, still smiling. 'All you've got to do is to have one good strong nig—er—boy on the beach when you're told, ready to pull on a rope. You've then got to keep this ball thing in a safe place until Shelton asks for it. Slip up on it just once and—' his voice dropped to a whisper but I could still hear it quite plainly '—I'll cut the goddamned liver out of your skinny, useless bloody carcass. Just hang on to that.'

'Yes—yes—of course—Anything you say, my dear chap——' the Major gibbered.

'Anything more?' the Smiling One asked sweetly.

There were a series of shaken heads.

'Good,' he went on. 'So we wait for the *Kampala*, and our first run with the real stuff—and the best of bloody luck to us all. No more meetings until the day before she gets in, unless I send word round.'

They got up and walked down the beach and waded out to the boat, and in a matter of minutes they were heading back to the mainland, leaving the tiny island to me, and the flies.

Charles came out an hour after that with cold beer and hot rolls, and I gave him the gist of things between mouthfuls and swallows on the run back.

'The *Jeanne-Marie*?' he said. 'Yes, that clicks. She's one of the last of the old island schooners—a freelance—Langlois's brother is her skipper and owner.' He put the wheel over. 'I think she's in port now—Yes, just off the end of the Long Pier.'

We swept past her. She was a very dirty wooden craft with sparse schooner rigging and a blackened swathe up her side from a protruding exhaust pipe which showed clearly that she ran more on her engines than under canvas.

'She's not very big,' I said. 'Yet they were talking about Kilindini. That's on the East African coast, isn't it?'

'Yes, it's near Mombasa. Not very big? She's the usual size. There are about six of them left in private ownership. They pick up a cargo here and there—copra from the Amirantes, Farquhar and Aldabra—stores from here out to the plantations. That sort of thing. They run down to Madagascar and

248

Mauritius regularly, and that's much farther than to the East African coast.'

I spent the rest of the day making out a long report—too long for coding, thank God, which meant that it had to go by mail. The jets weren't arriving for some days yet, but they already had an air mail from here. It was carried by an island-hopping light aircraft usually, and on occasion by the amphibious plane owned by the Tracking Station. I sent it to the Gaffer, and then sat back with an easy mind and just enjoyed life—the sun —that wonderful surf—the fruit—and above all the sheer peace of the place, made all the more precious by the knowledge that it was to be shattered all too soon. The last Eden—the ultimate paradise.

The answer arrived in six days. It came in the form of a cable to me care of Charles, and it said that Uncle Harry would be arriving by the first jet and would be delighted if I could meet him. I did, and stood in the background as the police band played and the inaugural ceremonies dragged on, and then I saw him coming towards me—in a dingy white linen suit that he was always telling me he had made for him in Shanghai in 1937. It looked it. Yes—the Gaffer—the maestro himself. 'Uncle Harry' is merely a direction to meet somebody—it can mean anybody at all—and you can't blame me for hoping against hope that it would be somebody else.

I took him back to the bungalow, and made it clear to Charles that he was under no obligation to be hospitable to this old bum, who would be drawing first class expenses, top rate—but Charles said what the hell—the Sheikh could afford it, and so we were lumbered with him.

'When does the *Kampala* get in?' the Gaffer asked me.

'In ten days' time,' I told him.

'Good, then your Cook's tour is over. We're going to be busy,' he said.

Chapter Twenty-One

SHE CAME IN through the north-east passage while there was still two hours of daylight left, slowly, gracefully, like an Edwardian dowager making a circuit of a beautiful garden, and tied up to the farthest of the red mooring buoys, and launches and lighters from the Long Pier converged upon her.

There were five parties watching her—four from the Seychelles Police on Ste Anne, Moyenne, and two fishing boats ostensibly about their normal business in the harbour—and lastly the Gaffer, Charles, Safaraz and me on Round Island. This post had caused considerable acrimony amongst us. I had laid down that Safaraz and I would be more than sufficient there, but the Gaffer said not bloody likely—it wasn't often nowadays that he got a chance to see any of the fun without danger to his hide, so he wasn't missing this, so reluctantly I had to include him. Then Charles kicked up a fuss. I was adamant at first, but when he started chucking his hospitality in our faces we gave in, albeit with extremely bad grace.

It was sheer hell, because there just wasn't space enough for a proper stake-out, so we all crowded into a saucer shaped hollow in the undergrowth overlooking the tiny beach, and we stewed under the blazing sun for five hours, the Gaffer croaking that he was dying, and I fervently wishing that he was, for once, stating nothing more than the literal truth. I could, of course, have cut it considerably finer than five hours, but this looked like being the final roll-up of the thing—and that is when I invariably start getting over-cautious. But at least I had ameliorated conditions as much as possible by bringing two crates of beer and several thermos flasks of iced water, of which the Gaffer guzzled so much that he brought on a distressing kidney ailment that manifested itself in a peculiarly unpleasant manner.

'You bastard, Rees,' he snuffled. 'There was no need to be here this early.'

'*I* thought there was,' I told him sweetly and quoted one of his own maxims at him. 'Over-insurance of the time factor is always to be recommended—or in other words, getting in position too early is better than bustin' your arse at the last minute.' And he swore weakly and dirtily.

We didn't see anything in particular being dumped from her after-deck, but Pellegrino, out fishing from his opulent motor-cruiser, must have, because, watching him closely through the glasses, we saw Langlois, masked, flippered and bottled, slip over the stern and disappear just as the last rays of the short tropical twilight drew in, and I was about to call it off until next morning.

He was down about ten minutes, then we saw him reappear some little distance from the boat, and hand something up to Ahrlberg, who began hauling in. And that was absolutely the last thing we were able to make out with certainty.

'How the bloody hell do we know that he'll be coming to this lousy island anyhow?' the Gaffer asked querulously.

'We don't,' I said. 'This was their HQ during their trial runs, so I'm assuming they'll stick to their pattern.'

'He might take it straight to the schooner,' Charles mused. 'It's moored at the Long Pier at the moment.'

Probably because this had been bothering me also I answered him shortly and blasphemously—and then, with heart-stopping relief, we heard the beat of the cruiser's motor, as Pellegrino ghosted her in.

It stopped a few yards off-shore and we heard the splash of her anchor going over the side, then more splashes as people waded in to the beach.

'Five of them, sahib,' Safaraz whispered. 'They walk through the water.'

'Anybody left on the boat?' I asked.

'Nobody, sahib. The first man reaches the beach now—he

carries something heavy—another comes forward to help him —now all are on the sand——'

'Let there be light, Charles,' I said, and he pressed the switch on the big portable flood we had set up on the rim of the saucer. Five white faces gawped up at us in dead silence.

'We don't want any shooting, do we?' the Gaffer inquired in tones of sweet reason. 'No, of course we don't,' he answered himself. 'But by Christ, there'll be an Imperial packet of it if anybody is silly. Sit down, the lot of you, just where you're standing at the moment.'

They sat reluctantly. Pellegrino was weeping. Safaraz and I went down and patted them over, but nobody was armed. We herded them into a neat group and switched off the big light and just held them in the glow of a torch.

The Smiling One said, 'I don't know what this is all about, gentlemen. I was invited out fishing by Mr Pellegrino and we were just landing here because we've had a spot of engine trouble. That's so, boys, isn't it?'

There was a mumble of assent and Pellegrino said, 'I just lenda my boat—I don't know nothing.'

'I can explain everything,' Ahrlberg said, and the Smiling One smiled even wider. 'Sure you can,' he said. 'We all can— but we're not. Not until we've got a good lawyer flown in, eh? So belt up, Swede—just belt up, there's a good boy—or pappa's going to get very angry. Very angry indeed.'

And then the police launches arrived.

So that was it. Only Pellegrino was tried in the tiny court-house on Mahé. The sentence wasn't tiny though. He got seven years and a ten thousand pound fine—for criminal con-spiracy and the attempted smuggling of eleven and a half kilos of base morphine—and since prison facilities in the Seychelles are not ideal for long terms, he is doing it, sadly, in Maidstone. The two Langlois brothers and the pitiful old Major made a deal. They got three-year suspended sentences in return for their co-operation in perpetrating a little joke on a safari contractor and a gaggle of minibus tourists in Kenya, Libya, Algeria and points north. It was the Gaffer's idea. My only sorrow is that I had no means of seeing the faces of the Marseilles heroin barons when it finally dawned on them that the twenty-six pounds of white powder they had paid some millions of francs into a Swiss account for, was more suited to cleaning silver than making junkies happy, the real stuff having been burned in the Seychelles General Hospital furnace.

Horton? He was given to Messrs Bayliss and Thorlby on a bail-jumping rap of long ago, as a consolation prize.

Which leaves only the Smiling One and Ahrlberg. Mukherjee flew over with an extradition warrant for the former and a material witness subpoena for the latter, who had seen the light and told all.

'Very quick,' Mukherjee told me with pride the day I got back to Calcutta. 'He hangs next Thursday morning at eight o'clock. Here is the ticket I promised you. Please be at Alipore Jail no later than seven, because they close gates in case of demonstrations by anti-capital-punishment factions.'

'Who's he being done for?' I asked.

'We had a choice of seven, but we thought it would be a nice gesture if we tried him for the murder of a minor European female on Grand Trunk Road—and keep other six up sleeve in case of non sequitur, which is French, I think, for failure to make it stick.'

'Welsh actually,' I told him solemnly, and he thanked me and made a note of it.

But I didn't go on Thursday, because my passport came through the day before and I was so pleased about it that I clean forgot, but I'm told that he stopped smiling at the end —and died whimpering.